Story:
YUU KAMIYA
TSUBAKI HIMANA

Illustrations:
SINO

CLOCKWORK PLANET

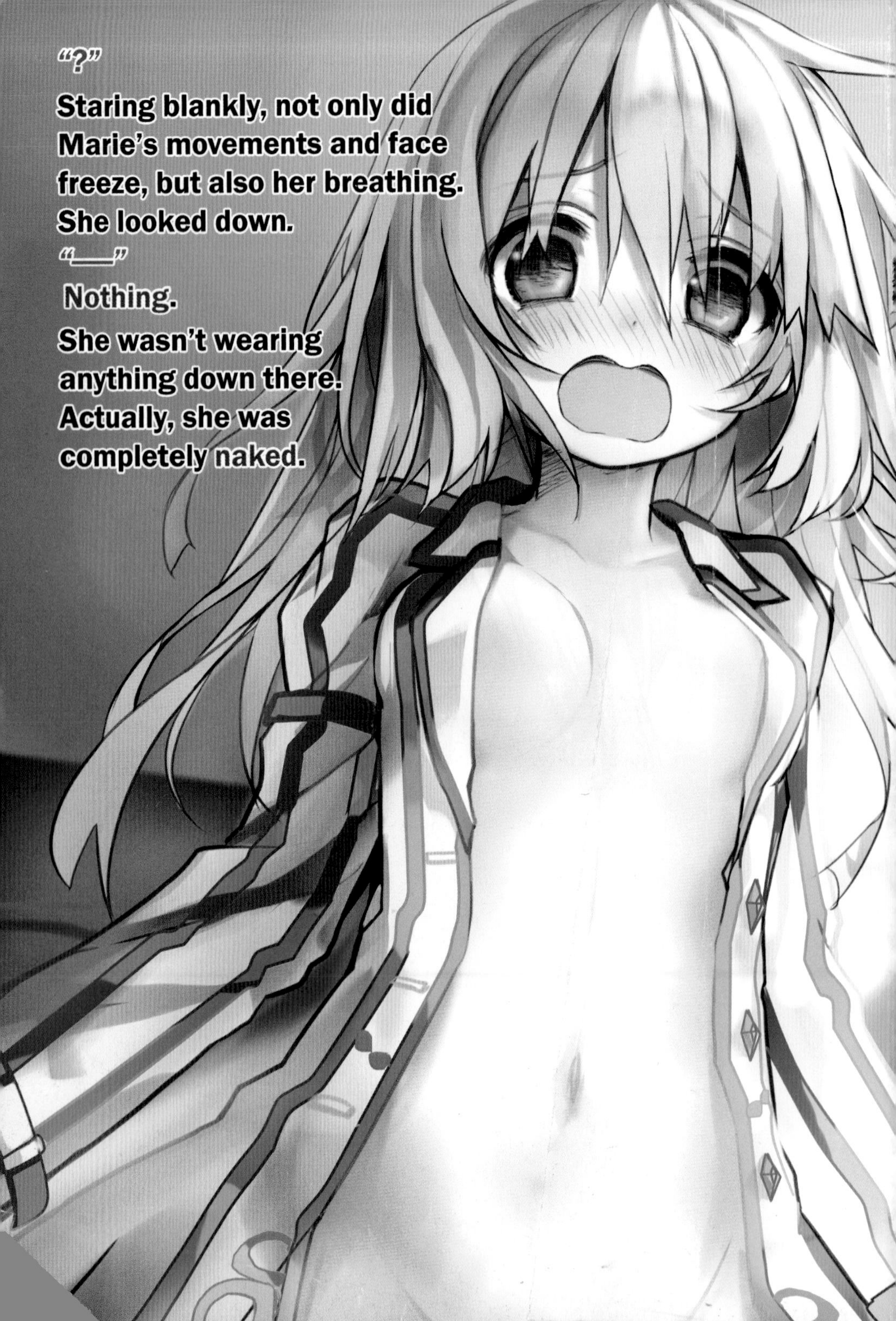
“?”
Staring blankly, not only did Marie’s movements and face freeze, but also her breathing. She looked down.
“——”
Nothing.
She wasn’t wearing anything down there. Actually, she was completely naked.

"I got it already, so at least
put on some underwear."

"'"The Relative Maneuver, Mute Scream'—"
At that instant, in Naoto's consciousness, everything had come to an end.

Vainney Halter
"Jeez, I'd gotten tired of waiting. I'm good to go whenever."
"Want me to beat you to death?"
Marie Bell Breguet

RyuZU
"Master Naoto, you are a pervert."
Naoto Miura
"I'm glad you were here, RyuZU."

contents

Clockwork Planet

Presented by
YUU KAMIYA *and*
TSUBAKI HIMANA

Illustrated by
SINO

CLOCKWORK PLANET, VOLUME 1

Cover illustration by Sino

First published in Japan in 2013 by Kodansha Ltd., Tokyo.
Publication rights for this English edition arranged through Kodansha Ltd., Tokyo.

Translation: fofi
J-Novel Editor: DUNCAN
Book Layout: Karis Page
Cover Design: Nicky Lim
Copy Editor: Julia Kinsman
Proofreader: J.P. Sullivan
Light Novel Editor: Jenn Grunigen
Production Assistant: CK Russell
Production Manager: Lissa Pattillo
Editor-in-Chief: Adam Arnold
Publisher: Jason DeAngelis

ISBN: 978-1-626927-55-1
Printed in Canada
First Printing: January 2018
10 9 8 7 6 5 4 3 2 1

Click, clack, click, clack.

The gears turned and turned.

Systematically, mechanically, inexorably.

They marked the march of time, effortlessly, just by fulfilling their function.

Even if a clock were to stop ticking, it wouldn't matter.

Even if the cogs of time became broken or twisted, they would surely simply continue to turn.

Systematically, mechanically, inexorably.

Click, clack, click, clack—

Clockwork Planet

● Prologue / --:-- / Reconstruct

I know this is sudden, but—

The world already collapsed, long ago.

Whether it be a meteor strike, an alien invasion, a mysterious pandemic, or a nuclear war—

Since time immemorial, people everywhere have imagined various scenarios for the end of the world. Every time a new doomsday scenario was proposed, hysteria would manifest from people's delusions, and spread rampantly—but in the end, nothing would happen. The fact that nothing happened would cause people to worry that the true calamity was simply yet to come, and so the cycle would repeat. The whole thing was like a dog chasing its own tail.

However, reality was not as dramatic as fiction.

No giant meteor came and shattered Earth.

No aliens came from the ends of the Milky Way to conquer it, either.

All diseases, no matter how obstinate or peculiar, could only accept their eventual defeat when faced with human medicine.

And finally, humanity wasn't foolish enough to destroy itself with nuclear missiles.

The actual "End of the World" did not require fantasy, catharsis, or romance. There was absolutely no space for such things to exist in this reality; and reality, though mundane, remained indisputable.

In conclusion,

One day, the Earth suddenly died.

Thus it was announced, without a single anomaly, deviation, or foreshadowing. The scientists had simply concluded that such was the Earth's lifespan. It was once estimated that the Earth had five billion years left. As it turned out, their calculations were a little off—by just five billion years. Can you believe it?

What a farce *that* was.

Everyone was left flabbergasted at the scientists' hopeless incompetence, but there was nothing anyone could do. After all, regardless of whether their calculations were on point or not, the Earth's lifespan couldn't be extended, no more than the hands of time could be reversed.

Earth, being a planet and not a star, didn't enjoy a magnificent finale in the form of a supernova explosion. Its finale wasn't a spectacle of widespread panic at a great disaster caused by colliding tectonic plates, either. The reason was simply that the stored energy in the Earth's core had dissipated over time, causing its activities to grind to a halt. And so the planet quietly died, over a span of about a hundred years.

During that process, nothing changed. As mundane reality hopelessly carried on, human history on Earth came to an end.

Now, then, let's talk about what happened afterward.

An industrious bunch who had given up on Earth created a giant fleet of spaceships and left the solar system, in search of a new world. Like a science fiction movie from times past, they began their space opera, wandering through the dark universe in search of another planet like Earth.

They didn't even know where they were heading, nor were there guarantees that they would safely arrive anywhere. To begin with, one could hardly call humanity's spacefaring technology perfect. Becoming spacedust was far more likely.

No one knows what happened to those who set off on that dangerous journey. In the end, were they able to successfully chart a new chapter of human history?

Bon Voyage.

On the other side of things, apart from those who set off into space, the vast majority of humans stayed on Earth. There were researchers who struggled on boldly, as was customary of humanity, but all their efforts were for naught. Just as the dead can't be resurrected, the planet couldn't be resuscitated.

There were a hundred years left before the Earth would die. Humanity resigned itself and made peace with its fate, atop a planet that was dying a drawn-out death.

The time left was too short for humanity to take counter-measures, and too long to maintain a sense of urgency. The depletion of Earth's resources and energy forbade humanity from even having one last war.

Even at this late stage, reality still didn't become as dramatic as fiction.

...However, thirty years after the Earth had died...

The stage of history, which had become hopelessly dull, made room for a certain man.

He was not a scientist. Nor was he a politician, nor a prophet. Naturally, he wasn't a magician who conjured up a convenient miracle, either.

Did people lend their ears to the words of that man, about whom they knew absolutely nothing, because they were tired of despair? Or was it because they had given up hope?

Regardless, the words that came out of his mouth were so absurd that they managed to shock humanity, long resigned to its fate.

"I've created a blueprint outlining how to carry on all of this planet's functions with only gears."

He was a clocksmith. The man, who called himself "Y," held such a colossal amount of data in his hand as to be inscrutable. He declared to the world:

"Just watch. I'll recreate everything in the world, with gears alone."

On that day, for the first time, reality really did become stranger than fiction.

The man christened his blueprint of innumerable gears thus:

The Clockwork Planet.

A thousand years passed...

•••●●●••

Before he knew it, he'd come back to his senses.

Hey, are you crazy? Do you really, truly understand what you're attempting to do? Okay, calm down and rethink this. You can still turn back . Something this foolish shouldn't be attempted just because you got caught up in the heat of the moment. For starters, what's in it for you?

(What's in it for me...?)

In other words, a return. What Naoto Miura lusts for matches the risk he's taking.

On the roof of a high-rise building, Naoto crouched down amidst its water towers and air conditioning units and tried to conceal his breath. He restrained his pounding heartbeat, and steadied his exhalations.

(Do you even have to ask?)

It's obvious. I'm doing this for her sake.

It's because I want that super-cute girl. Well, actually, I don't know what she looks like, but she's definitely cute, so that's not a problem.

I'll definitely nab you. I'll squeeze you tight. I'll put you on my knees and pet your head, and I'll rub you all over and play with you mercilessly.

All right, steel your heart. Don't be afraid. Use your head. Be cool. Don't hold back. If someone gets in your way, tear them apart, even if they're the president.

Naoto slapped his cheeks and fired himself up.

He confirmed the situation.

Right now, it was nighttime, approaching midnight. The illumination that filled the streets flooded over the edges of the rooftop and surfaced against the night sky, a torrent of light washing away the darkness.

The Light Gears shined brilliantly as they turned, converting gravity into light. Blotted out by that illumination, the stars couldn't be seen in the night sky. Only the gray moon and the "Equatorial Coil" that revolved around it due to its gravitational pull were visible.

"Now then..." Naoto made sure to keep his back firmly against his cover as he looked down from the shadows to the main street below.

The sight that spread out beneath his eyes was "the District of Clocks," Akihabara.

This district, which had flourished as a hub for electronic merchandise in the distant past, was still bustling along at the forefront of entertainment as the capital of hobbies. It was filled with anime, manga, and games, as well as gears, mechanical parts, and automata components. Stores ranging from large retailers to tiny shops were strung together in this district of entertainment.

Naoto recalled that he used to dream of splurging on a "sacred pilgrimage" here someday, but the thought of that didn't do much for him now. After all, he had gotten his hands on something much better—and he'd continue acquiring much better things from now on as well.

"All righty, it's about time now," Naoto muttered as he pulled back.

He picked up a cable left sprawling on the ground and connected it to the fluorescent-green headphones he wore on his head. The cable connected to an amp, and from there to a mixer, an effector, and a noise controller. In addition, countless microphones were also attached to the setup.

Naoto flipped the on switch and then sat down, crossing his legs. After letting out a low groan, the equipment began to work. Naoto's blood boiled with excitement; his heart thumped in his chest.

He focused on his hearing. Then, he then called on her.

"Marie, are you ready?"

"Of course. Who do you think I am?" What answered him was the elegant voice of a young girl. Her tone was haughty and arrogant, yet somehow not unpleasant. Her voice, which sounded typical of someone of high status, struck Naoto's ears.

"I'm counting on you, Meister."

"That's also a given. Make sure you finish your job as well."

"Understood." Naoto nodded.

He then switched the voice line by manipulating the controllers. "Halter, how are things on your end?"

"...Jeez, I'd gotten tired of waiting. I'm good to go whenever," the low, thick voice of a man answered Naoto hoarsely. "More importantly, how are things on your end? How are you feeling? You're the key to all this, you know. We're counting on you to keep it together."

"I'm fine. No problems here."

"Let's get this over and done with already, then. When you get back, this old man will treat you to a meal, 'kay?" Halter added a whistle to his chipper joking, making Naoto crack a faint, wry smile. Naoto was thankful to Halter for trying to ease his nerves.

Finally, Naoto switched the voice line again, this time to the last member of the team. "RyuZU, are you ready?"

"Master Naoto, allow me to advise you that asking the obvious is what idiots do. Your brain's capabilities are regrettable to begin with, so I believe it would be best if you at least *pretended* not to be an idiot."

Naoto was answered by a sharp and wicked tongue. The words, enough to snap a listener's heart in two, came from the voice of a young girl. Her voice was high and clear, like the sound of a music box.

Naoto smiled gently and closed his eyes. "Y'know, RyuZU..."

"Yes, what is it?"

"I love you."

"...I think it would be better if you died, you pig."

"Squeeee!"

Naoto's shoulders quivered as he laughed. The sweet abuse was exquisite. *Bam bam bam*. Naoto smashed the console with his fist like he just couldn't get enough of it. Then, he stood up.

"Okay. Now, then. I guess I'll sing a bit."

Naoto faced the microphones lined up at his feet.

"I'm starting the countdown. Three, two, one—"

As he counted down, he raised both his hands into the air. Surveying the sight of Akihabara before him, he swung his right arm down to the rhythm. His ears perked up, like a conductor leading an orchestra through a symphony.

With a smile on his face, Naoto declared, "Start!"

•••●•••

Immediately after...

A severe earthquake struck, with a thirty-kilometer radius centered on the Akihabara Grid. All lines of communication were cut off, and the internal "Resonant Gears" began to operate outside of regulations. The group of gears in the Core Tower that regulated the city's functions demonstrated unprecedented behavior.

It wasn't just a normal failure, nor was it a malfunction due to the machinery degrading over time. Even though the entire system was running normally, for some reason it wasn't responding to input from its superintendent.

Then, five minutes after the situation began, the previously suspended lines of communication suddenly resumed operation.

Everyone simply watched the situation unfold before them, unable to do anything, when they were assaulted by an excessively enthusiastic "proclamation of criminal responsibility."

"Ladieees aaannnd gentlemen!! Along with the foolish and banal ordinary citizens who are neither gentlemanly nor ladylike, good evening! Pardon me for disturbing you while you're enjoying your weekend night!"

What was transmitted was an altered voice of ambiguous age and gender, and it stopped those who heard it in their tracks.

"As for who I am—it's embarrassing, so I'm excluding, omitting, and cutting it out! I'm gonna blush, dammit! Try asking me again after you've earned more of my favor! Frankly, it's way past my bedtime, so I want to drink my bedtime cocoa, take a crap, and go to bed, but I can't, 'cuz check this out!"

The boy behind the voice left his listeners behind as he rattled on and on in a one-way conversation, like a drunken disk jockey.

"Ah-ah, did you know? For a thousand years, we've been reproducing the meteorological phenomena, gravity, geothermal heat, and everything else on Earth with gears. Nooow then! If what's inside your heads isn't dog crap, you've probably considered a certain possibility once, or haven't you?!"

It can't be.

A few relatively sharp individuals among all those who had stopped to think quietly gulped as they apprehended his meaning. A terrifying thought, simply too hard to believe, came to their minds.

No way, no way, no way—could something so preposterous really happen?!

As if to betray their desperate hope for denial, the voice continued on, even more enthusiastically than before.

"Yaaaaaaaaay! Those of you who thought, 'No way!' Ding ding ding! You're absolutely right! The final answer is preciiisely that impossibility!"

Impossible.

But it was also true that if that *was* the case, then everything about this abnormal situation made sense.

All lines of communication had ceased functioning at the same time. The resonant gears continued to broadcast this live proclamation of criminal responsibility. The city's functions had become disconnected from the superintendent's control. These facts led to only one conclusion.

The person behind the voice affirmed their suspicions in a pompous and delighted tone.

"Today! Presently! As of right now! I've seized control of all the gears that make up the Akihabara Grid! Yay!"

At that moment, the planet's environment was being replicated by gears.

The system operated with the earth's gravity, harvesting energy from the moon's gravitational pull. It was composed of as many gears as there are stars in the universe. What kept the gears chugging along was a design so unbelievably intricate as to approach the sublime.

However, now that the original blueprint had been lost, there was no one who understood its overall structure. It had taken several hundred clocksmiths working directly with the gears just for humanity to finally reach its present state—simply being able to maintain the system.

However...

The system's designer—the man known as "Y"—undoubtedly understood the system's entire structure.

"Y" was the ultimate, supreme genius in all of human history. But at the same time, he was definitely human. The man was neither a god nor a demon, and certainly not a convenient magician. Therefore, it should have theoretically been possible for someone else to accomplish what he had.

If one seized control of the gears, they could manipulate the planet's environment by using the gears' enormous energy output however they saw fit. Such a power would be almighty on a planet fueled by gears.

It would be equivalent to the *authority of God.*

"Now then! To super-celebrate this incredible feat, I've prepared a lovely gift for everyone today. Don't wet yourself from the excitement, 'kay?!"

Those words made the blood of those who understood the situation freeze from fear, and even those who didn't understand grew uneasy with a sense of foreboding.

Please, please let nothing happen.

Paying no heed to their wishes, the voice continued on delightedly.

"Umm, right now it's February eighth, 00:12 a.m. The temperature is thirty-two degrees Celsius. But did you all know? Originally, the average temperature in this region was about five degrees Celsius around this time of year. A defect that popped up in reproducing the environment is what's causing everyone to suffer these sleepless, sultry nights. And so!"

The jesting voice sang brightly, but the words conveyed by that voice were a lethal blow to all, bar none. "Let's balance the account for how hot it was up to now. In short, I'll be lowering the temperature around Akihabara Grid to a measly negative 150 degrees over the next seventy-two hours."

Everyone was left speechless.

What did the idiot behind this voice just say? Balance the account? Negative 150 degrees? There was no debate necessary; such a temperature would be far too low for humans to survive.

This declaration wasn't simply on the level of causing people to figuratively petrify with fear. Akihabara itself would literally freeze over.

"Ahh, now now, you don't need to thank me. No need to bow down in gratitude, either. After all, I consider hearing your cries as you freeze to death the ultimate reward."

Insane: The voice that happily chirped away could no longer be described as anything else.

The authority to freely manipulate the temperature had fallen into the hands of this maniacal scoundrel. None could help but shudder at this terrifying truth.

"Oh crap! I forgot! I have to clearly and thoroughly prove that this isn't some kind of bluff or prank!"

With an easygoing air, as if they had merely forgotten to turn off the television, the mad voice continued on like a tour bus guide.

"Now then, everyone, pleeease take a look at Tokyo Tower through a nearby wiiindow."

Everyone rushed to a nearby window and looked up.

Tokyo Tower.

It was a former radio tower made of steel, painted red and white. Since humans abandoned electricity, it had become a useless landmark. It was the symbol of Tokyo, so it had basically been treated as a historical ruin, preserved for over a thousand years.

And now...

The transformation lasted only an instant.

As everyone watched on, the red steel tower, shimmering in the dark night, froze and turned pure white for an instant. It happened as quickly as soaking a rose in liquid nitrogen and was just as ludicrous.

"Ahh—!!"

The next moment, the tower was crushed by its own weight, breaking into countless fragments. It crumbled away, leaving nothing behind.

Everyone was left speechless as they looked up in a daze at the fragments of Tokyo Tower, dancing downwards like falling leaves. Was what they just saw truly reality? They saw it clearly before their very eyes, yet they still couldn't wrap their heads around it. It was something that shouldn't have been possible, a sight that was simply unreal.

...But reality lay right in front of them. The steel tower that had stood for over a thousand years was no longer there. In just a few seconds, it had disappeared like a dream.

"Did you enjoy that? That's the end of tonight's show! Everyone, please keep warm so you don't catch a cold. Have a good night! Thank you for your kind attention! See you again! Adios, amigos!!"

Immediately after that broadcast of criminal proclamation, which had only lasted ten minutes, ended...

Tokyo's metropolitan area, which held a population of forty million people, turned into a crucible of hysteria. In less than a few minutes, the city's functions became completely paralyzed.

Atop the high-rise, Naoto let out a large sigh, feeling the fatigue from his high-energy talk. A voice called out to him from behind.

"Yo, good work."

Naoto turned around. It was Halter.

He was a big man with a buzz cut. He could be described as burly, stalwart. The sight of him approaching with a jovial smile reminded Naoto of a large, carnivorous wildcat.

"With this, you're now a splendid, superstar terrorist on the Interpol Watch List. Your name will be printed in high school textbooks. How do you feel?"

"Not bad," Naoto replied to Halter's banter, with a faint smile.

Naoto felt neither enthusiasm for having committed a peerless crime nor fear at having turned the whole world into his enemy. The only thing he felt was a sense of liberation at having completed one part of his job.

Just then, a dazzling light suddenly pierced his eyes.

"Target confirmed. All units, begin descent. Your mission is to capture the target."

Tracing the light to its source, Naoto saw three helicopters.

The armed helicopters were like black raptors, hovering silently in the air as their searchlights and autocannons focused on the two on the rooftop. Next, from each of the three helicopters, six bodies jumped down—eighteen silhouettes in total. The figures, the image of upright gorillas with their bulging arms and thick chests, landed onto the concrete surface of the rooftop one after another.

Halter groaned as he ran his hand along his buzz cut. "Assault-type automata in addition to three stealth helicopters. As expected of a superstar. Your fans are crowding forward to meet you after the show."

"If they want my signature, they're gonna have to line up nice and proper."

One of the helicopter's speakers blared over their banter

"This is a warning! Raise your hands above your heads and lie face-down where you are! If you resist, we'll shoot!"

As if to reinforce those words, the eighteen automata pointed their guns at the two in perfect synchrony.

The silent tension made sweat break on Halter's forehead as he said, "Well, what are we gonna do now? This is embarrassing, but I didn't take into account that the response would be this quick."

"What are we gonna do, you ask... It's already over. Ain't that right?"

Naoto didn't become flustered or try to stand up. He continued sitting cross-legged, as if his butt was too heavy to move. He merely let out a shallow sigh. As for why—that was because the situation had already reached checkmate. There was nothing more they could or should do. Naoto understood that.

"Right, RyuZU?"

"Yes. The situation is already over."

Immediately after...

The air creaked as the main rotors of the three armed helicopters were blown off. Caught in a tailspin, they crashed downwards, tracing a spiral in their path.

At the same time, the eighteen automata stopped moving. Their necks were torn off, their arms felled, and their legs severed—the automata, minced into pieces, clattered as they collapsed and exploded right where they stood, faster than the blink of an eye.

As he shielded his face from the incoming shockwave and debris, Naoto saw her.

Since when had...?

A beautiful young girl wearing an old-fashioned black dress was standing right before him. Her hair fluttered in the stormy wind as she performed a curtsy, holding out her full, puffy skirt.

Her skin was so pale that it stood out against the dark night sky; her moist lips were a crimson red, and her eyes, made of golden gemstones, glittered as they reflected Naoto's image.

As the shockwave subsided, she elegantly bowed to Naoto and said, "I apologize for having made you wait, Master Naoto. ...By the way, you still haven't praised me. I believe it is a master's duty to promptly do so before being asked—am I wrong?"

Naoto smiled gently and nodded. "Thanks, you were a big help."

"Is that all?"

"I'm glad you were here, RyuZU. You're the best automaton for sure, RyuZU. If you weren't here, I wouldn't know what to do at all. As expected, Ms. RyuZU is seriously RyuZU-like."

"...I see that your vocabulary is severely lacking. Such exceedingly base words carry not even a hint of good sense. They expose Master Naoto's poor caliber and upbringing—but nothing can be done. I shall accept them begrudgingly."

"So you do have a hidden soft side."

The next moment, Naoto sank to the concrete ground. RyuZU had struck him.

While looking on, Halter asked, "By the way, miss. I believe that according to the plan, you were supposed to retrieve our princess. Where is she?"

"I left her behind."

"You left her...?"

"Because the enemy raid came two minutes and thirty-seven seconds earlier than predicted, I advanced the plan forward a stage and prioritized Master Naoto's safety. It would have been troublesome to save him if he were captured, after all."

"I appreciate that, but what about the princess?"

"There is no problem," RyuZU answered, then took a step back. Simultaneously, heavy gunshots sounded, and bullets pierced the spot where she had been just a moment before.

As for who the shooter was—a young Caucasian girl stood by the rooftop's emergency staircase.

She was Marie Bell Breguet.

"...That's dangerous, princess."

"Halter," the girl called out to the man, who had broken out in a cold sweat as she quickly closed in on him.

At first glance, she appeared to be smiling sweetly. If she were walking down the street, many a man's eyes would surely light up when they caught sight of her. Her face was dainty, her nose tall and pointed, and her softly swaying blond hair balanced out her haughty aura just right.

But her emerald-green eyes were burning with rage.

"Please restrain that piece of junk. Today's the day I'll dismantle her and fix that rotten personality for good."

Halter shrugged his shoulders and sighed. "Don't ask for the impossible, princess. Just what do you expect me to do?"

"When do you plan to capitalize on your career experience if not now? Please use the Marine Corps' uhh, hand-to-hand combat techniques to seize that piece of junk. I don't mind if you break her in the process, okay?"

"I was in the Army, not the Marine Corps. What's this commotion all about?"

Without answering him, Marie swung the pistol-sized mechanical bayonet—a Coil Spear—that she held in her right hand, causing it to transform into its blade mode.

"This crappy piece of junk deserted me and ran away by herself! Despite the fact that I was surrounded by security automata!" she yelled out gruffly, right before she slashed at RyuZU.

The swing was sharp and carried the momentum of Marie's upper body; however, RyuZU evaded it with just a light step.

"Oh my, the plating is peeling off, you know."

"Shut it!"

"Mistress Marie, you are always calling yourself a multi-faceted prodigy, so there is no way you would have any difficulty with a small threat like ten or twenty generic security automata, right?"

"How could that possibly be true?! I thought I was going to die!"

"What—" RyuZU opened her eyes wide in astonishment. "...I apologize. I thought my opinion of you was already as low as could be, but to think that you are such a complete wimp... You have my sincerest apologies."

"...I'm gonna destroy you! I'm definitely, seriously gonna destroy you...!"

"Be quiet—" Naoto muttered, cutting off Marie, who was trying to transform her Coil Spear even further to extend its blade. He was kneeling with his head against the concrete ground.

When he spoke, the three ended their farce abruptly and turned their eyes towards Naoto in silence.

He continued, pressing one ear snug against the ground. "As expected, they're heading towards the 'Actuator.'"

Naoto strained his ears with all he had. Far in the distance... underground footsteps sounded, 5,387 meters away.

He heard all of them, without missing a single one.

"There are 3,021 automata and 1,765 soldiers on foot."

"...It should be safe to assume that that's practically all of the garrisoned forces that could immediately be mobilized."

While rubbing his head, Halter laughed, as if to say, *What an opportunity*.

Marie retracted her Coil Spear. "They should know where we are, too."

"There are seven sources of sound heading straight toward us—they're not stealth helicopters, this time. They aren't loaded with automata, even. They're authentic assault helicopters."

"Out of the heavily armed helicopters that Japan owns, the ones that could be mobilized right now... They're PTK-A74s." Marie deduced.

To which RyuZU inquired, "How much of a threat are they?"

"They're heavily armed, unpiloted, autonomous fighters. They're equipped with two resonance cannons... Well, with seven of them, they can scorch this entire grid without needing to resupply."

"All right, let's get the hell outta here. Hey Naoto, how much time do we have?" Halter asked. Naoto quickly got up.

"About 372 seconds until they arrive—it should be something like that."

"Well then, let us withdraw before we come into contact with them. I shall carry the luggage." RyuZU piled up the pieces of Naoto's equipment and lifted them up easily.

Naoto Miura, age sixteen, male, Japanese.

He was just another high schooler—however, this boy, who had now magnificently become the most heinous terrorist in all of history, had a special power.

Naoto unplugged the unnecessary wires from his favorite pair of headphones, then put them back on his head. After that, he turned on the noise-canceling function.

...Ahh. He let out a large sigh. *It's finally quiet.*

Seeing Naoto like that, Marie asked quietly, "Hey Naoto, are you okay?"

"...Well, yeah, somehow."

"That ability is a burden on your body after all, isn't it..."

"Nah, that's not it. I messed up... Sorry," Naoto replied as he turned around and stuck his thumb up with a snap.

"You see, it seems there's a sex parlor in that building over there."

"...Hah?"

"With the beds creaking and the people moaning constantly, they couldn't be more of a clueless nuisance if they tri—"

Before Naoto could finish, Marie uppercut his chin, her face flushed.

A special power.

This was "Extraordinary Hearing."

Whether it be the things happening in a different building, a battalion of automata and soldiers marching underground five kilometers away, or even trillions of nanogears clicking against each other, he could clearly hear and differentiate all of them.

In this world, where everything was made of clockwork, that was simply too—

Halter called out to Marie, who was stomping on the back of Naoto's head in silent anger. "Oi, cut it out, princess. That brain shoulders the future of the world."

"The world must have gone mad, then."

"...Aren't you being completely unreasonable...?" Naoto groaned underneath Marie's feet.

Halter let out a sigh, "Hurry up, now. It isn't the time to put on a comedy skit."

"...R-rest assured, Halter—" Naoto uttered as he stood up while teeter-tottering. He adjusted his headphones, which had slipped off his ears, and brushed off the dust that had gotten stuck to his clothes. "If we're all together, something as minor as a metropolis of forty million people is so much putty in our palms."

"...Hopefully, you're right," Halter said, rubbing his head. Contrary to the impression people got from his buff physique, he was a worrywart of a middle-aged man.

The four of them ran down the building's emergency staircase and stepped outside. Passing the three helicopters that had crashed and were now in flames, they headed towards the roundabout in front of the station.

A giant display that hung on the outside of the station building was playing an emergency news broadcast, reporting in-depth on this unprecedented act of terrorism.

A high school failure, Naoto Miura.

The prodigy clocksmith, Marie Bell Breguet.

Her ex-soldier bodyguard, Vainney Halter.

And lastly—the mysterious automaton, RyuZU.

They differed in nationality. They differed in age as well. One of them wasn't even human.

How did this group—whose members had almost nothing in common—cross paths with each other? Why did they end up becoming the most heinous terrorists in all of history?

Their secret motives.

A wild ideal and a noble lust.

The hidden mystery of the world that kept the gears turning perpetually.

That's right, the beginning of all this goes back one month ago...

Clockwork Planet

● Chapter One / 00 : 30 / Coincidence

Naoto Miura was only interested in machines.

He was a hardcore machine maniac—no, a machine nerd—er, a machine junkie. He'd liked gears, cylinders, screws, springs, and wires since childhood. He loved the luster of metal and the feel of ceramics as well. *Tick tock, tick tock*—whenever he heard the sound of a clock marking the passage of time, it calmed him down. Whenever he watched the pins of a music box pluck the metal comb, his heart trembled with excitement. That didn't change even as he advanced into middle school.

On the contrary: One could say it got worse.

Naoto didn't pay any attention to manga, anime, or games. Even while his classmates clamored over photos of pinup girls, he'd continue intently fiddling with machinery. Instead of squabbling over whether huge or tiny breasts were better, he was interested in the different methods of powering an automobile. Instead of the swimsuit-clad figures of the girls in his class, he was interested in the contours of machines used for manufacturing. Rather than the adult videos that his classmates lent out and borrowed from each other, he was interested in a documentary on the development of a new model of springs.

Even Naoto was able to notice how out of sync he was from the rest of his peers.

I see, it seems that I'm "abnormal" somehow.

He wouldn't have had such a hard time if he could change his character just by becoming aware of it.

As the saying goes, "The child is father of the man," and so Naoto Miura grew up as himself. By that point, his love for machines had become immeasurable and warped his personality so much that it could no longer be corrected through any amount of effort.

It was already too late for Naoto Miura.

•••●•••

35° N, 135° E.

Underground Floor 1, Kyoto Grid, Japan.

Once called the Thousand-Year Capital, Kyoto was one of the few great metropolises of Japan. Surrounded by a completely mechanized cityscape, somewhat out-of-place wooden buildings—once deemed a World Heritage Site—lined the streets of the district Naoto Miura called home.

In the corner of one end of this great city, in a borderland that could just barely be considered within the metropolitan area, there stood a slightly slanted, dilapidated apartment building. On the seventh floor of this building, which practically screamed "haunted house..."

There was Naoto's home.

"Ahhhh! It was a good day again today!" Naoto yelled, as he ran up stairs that might well collapse any day now.

The small-statured lad wore a black school uniform. The tag by his chest pocket indicated that he was a first-year student. He also wore a pair of cheap, fluorescent-green headphones in an attempt to tame his ruffled hair. His face had no particular features worth mentioning save one: his light-gray eyes, and even those were ruined by his gaze, the deadness of which seemed like a manifestation of his twisted personality.

"Being cornered and extorted for money, forced to be a gofer, having a bucket of water dumped on me, and having my desk graffitied, all while being sniggered and chortled at! Gee, I wonder what else I need to do to unlock the 'Complete Set of Bullying' achievement! Haha!" Naoto laughed drily, bereft.

It had already been a few years since he'd realized what he had sown.

Naoto didn't reconsider himself even after realizing that he was abnormal. If anything, he became bolder. He proclaimed his preferences, displaying his character fully. For some reason, a beautiful upperclassman girl confessed her love to him, but as she wasn't equipped with even a single moving part, Naoto politely declined. Because of all that, he had ended up in his current situation. Even after humanity had begun living atop a foundation of gears, bullying at schools continued on.

He was simply reaping what he had sown for lacking sociability. He understood this, but it wasn't like knowing that made his wet uniform feel any less gross.

"Haah... My goodness. I'm hooome..."

He opened the door, its paint peeling off here and there, and entered his apartment. No one came to greet him.

Naoto lived alone.

His parents had died one after the other a few years back, and he didn't have any siblings or relatives, either. The only things that had been left to Naoto were this home in what might as well have been an abandoned building—and the work tools of his parents, who had been third-rate clocksmiths.

He tossed his bag into his bedroom, then passed through the living room from the hallway, heading towards the back of the apartment. That's where the workshop was.

A stack of odds and ends lay by the entrance, machine tools used to shave parts into the right dimensions were hung along the wall, and an air purifier installed to absorb the dust was operating quietly on the ceiling. In the center of this dimly-lit room was an operating table—rather, a workbench.

Lying on top of it was an automaton.

Her model type was East-Asian. Her figure was that of a young girl around the age of fourteen. Her darkened, glass-bead eyes gazed into the air above her lifelessly. Wires and springs protruded outward from open hatches all throughout her body.

"I'm hooome..." Naoto said to the broken girl.

She was an automaton that Naoto had made by mish-mashing various parts together from discarded machinery. In this era, where the entire planet had been running on only gears for a long time now, it wasn't so hard to recreate the human body using only gears as well.

Naoto frequently found time between school and his part-time job to visit a dump where he diligently gathered gears and screws, one by one. Then, using the machinery and instructional readers his parents had left behind, he'd finally been able to reproduce an automaton to this extent through trial and error. This thing, which had finally taken form, was his precious treasure.

"Nooow then, I guess I'll take a shower to refresh myself, then continue working." Naoto pumped himself up and turned on his heels.

He took off and tossed everything he was wearing (aside from his headphones) all over the place, as he leisurely headed towards the bathroom.

•••●•••

Clonk. Naoto's foot hit the side of the narrow tub.

"Ooooooooh—!!" Naoto let out a strange sound as he sat in the water.

Taking care not to get his magazine wet, he turned a page of the newest issue of Automata Fan.

"Karasawa Heavy Industries' mechanical legs look so smart! Whaaah?! What's up with the architecture of this Double Gear? It's absolutely stunning! Does God run Murakami Industries?!"

What Naoto was intensely reading was a monthly trade magazine for automata enthusiasts. It was an esoteric publication for diehards that explained the industry's newest technologies in detail.

For Naoto, it was his supreme treasure; he read it with love.

"Well, Kaiyodo has the best molding technology, as expected. In terms of overall price performance, Nosain isn't bad either. Mm-hm, mm-hm... For springs, Damase's rotaries are..." Just then, Naoto, who had been cheerily flipping through the pages, suddenly stopped his hand.

What he saw was a feature page on springs for automata. Products ranging from now-outdated masterpieces of the past to the latest parts for military use were compared based on price and performance.

Upon seeing the price for a secondhand copy of the oldest part listed, Naoto sighed, then scratched his head violently.

"Getting a spring is the problem, after all. That's the one thing that I'll never find in a dump."

The generator gear of automata springs used gravity to churn out energy simply by existing. When disposing of a spring, a person was required by law to deliver it to a dedicated facility. As such, unlike other parts, one wouldn't find any of them lying around in garbage dumps.

"...It's not like I have the money to actually buy one, either..."

It had taken him a year to scrape together these parts from all over. After that, it had taken him another two years to form the body by cobbling the parts together after repeated, countless failures. He had invested so much time into making an automaton, and now he was at a dead end.

The problem wasn't just that he couldn't acquire a spring, but also Naoto himself. Despite being such machine maniac that he sometimes forgot to eat and sleep, his technical skills were limited.

Ah, you're well informed for an amateur. Your fingers are nimble, too. Your intuition is decent as well.

But that was all.

It would be another story if he had simply bought and assembled standard parts, but Naoto had neither the knowledge nor the technical skills to recreate an automaton from broken pieces.

Although he studied his parents' used readers, there was only so much an amateur could learn about the immense world of clocksmithing through self-study. He didn't have the money to attend a clock-engineering school, either.

Naoto didn't really know whether the cobble-work body would really move. After all, he had never been able to run a movement test, as the body had no source of power.

Probably, presumably, maybe it'll move, he thought.

That's where he was.

"...Well, it's not like money will come raining down if I grumble." Naoto sighed as he turned his eyes back down toward the magazine.

That was when...

Through his headphones, Naoto's ears picked up a sound he wasn't used to hearing. He spontaneously turned his face upward. Naturally, the ceiling was there, and he couldn't see anything past it.

But he could definitely hear it. Something cut through the wind in the sky far above. That something wasn't an airplane, and it was approaching his location dreadfully fast.

Babooooooooooooooom!

A thunderous roar, loud enough to blow someone unconscious, pierced Naoto's ears.

The bathroom—rather, the building itself jolted vertically, as if the ground had thrust it upwards. Naoto inadvertently dropped his magazine into the bathwater—in the blink of an eye, the ink blurred and the page muddled into a mosaic.

"Gghhwaaaaaaah?! I haven't finished readi—no, that isn't important right now! What the heck was that?!" After a momentary escape from reality, Naoto rushed out of the bathtub in a panic.

The thunderous roar and impact that had suddenly assaulted the building carried a shock as powerful as a direct hit from a bomb or a wrecking ball, or if neither of those, then maybe—

"A meteorite...? No, that's ridiculous!"

As he muttered, Naoto rushed out of the bathroom with just a towel wrapped around him. Just what had happened? For now, he just wanted to make sure that the workshop and the automaton were unharmed.

"Haaaaaaaaaasshhigiggifurkamjahgrp?!" He let out a scream that failed to form words.

At the end of the hallway, the living room, which also served as the dining area, was completely destroyed. The ceiling had completely fallen out. Debris and fine particles filled every inch of the room.

"Wh, What... How could this be...?!" Naoto slumped onto his knees on the spot as he cried and yelled, heartbroken. "What?! What's this supposed to be?! Just what have I done to deserve this?!"

It was like he couldn't comprehend the sight before him.

I was simply enjoying my time reading my treasured magazine when a meteorite fell and destroyed my home. I, I don't expect you to understand what I'm saying, me, but—

"Th-that's right—something happened!" As Naoto felt he was about to faint, he whipped himself back up.

It's not like it really could have been a meteor, could it?

Fortunately, it seemed that only the living room had taken a direct hit. The workshop, which was in the back, might have still been fine.

"Ahh, God...crap, crap! Goddamn it!"

As Naoto screamed, he charged through the scene of destruction, whose air was still filled with fine particles.

"God...why did this have to happen?!"

With tears clinging to his eyes and snot dangling from his nose, Naoto moved the pieces of rubble blocking his way one by one.

"Haah, haah... Ow!" Blood was seeping out of the palm of his hand. Something must have cut it by chance.

While he was pushing aside the rubble, the floor continued to creak. Looking up, he saw a chain of large holes opened up in the floors all the way from his own ceiling to the rooftop.

The floor of this room is still holding up for now, but who knows how long it'll last... It seems like there's no doubt that something fell from high in the sky, but—

"Was it seriously a meteorite...? What kinda crazy development is this... Don't mess with me... Just what did I do to deserve this?!"

As Naoto yelled, he wiped his forehead with his blood-stained hand.

Resuming his task, he thought, *Just what could have caused this?*

If the disaster was man-made, he would demand apologies and compensation from those responsible until they cried.

If it really was a meteorite... No, wait. I've heard that meteorites fetch a good price. If that's the case, there's a silver lining amidst this disaster after all. I might even be able to buy a new home and springs—

Something appeared underneath the rubble, causing Naoto to stay his hands.

"...What's this?"

Naoto stared at the object, studying it.

A giant black box was buried in the rubble—it was a storage unit.

Based on the material it was made of, and how it had been built, one could tell at a glance that it was no ordinary steel case. Only the military or perhaps some research facility somewhere would use something like this. Whatever the case, the contents must have been fairly important.

"Well, it's not a meteorite, but it should be something valuable... I think?"

When he looked closer, Naoto saw that the container's frame was warped a great deal. As one would expect, it must have been unable to fully withstand the shock of the impact after falling from such a high altitude.

Naoto thought silently to himself for a short while before quickly reaching a conclusion.

"...All right. I don't know what's inside, but if it's valuable, I'll be taking it as a consolation settlement, so whoever's responsible, you'd best prepare yourself."

He squeezed himself through the crevice of the warped container and went inside. As he stepped onto the soft, cushioning material, Naoto continued to grumble.

"If it isn't a real treasure, you *really* better prepare yourself. No matter what it takes, I'll find out where this box came from and demand an apology and compensation. To that end, I'll do whatever's necessary, whether it's going to court, or anything else—"

However...

As soon as Naoto saw the container's contents, he stopped talking.

No, he didn't just stop talking; he stopped breathing altogether. Even his heart might have stopped. It was that much of a shock.

The box was a coffin. At least, Naoto thought it was. An intricate glass coffin reminiscent of the moving parts of mechanical clocks, made with incredible finesse.

Inside the coffin was a sleeping girl.

Screws, cylinders, wires, springs, gears—The girl was sleeping silently while covered by these mechanical burial flowers.

Looking to be in her mid-teens, she had smoothly flowing silver hair and a cherubic face. Her skin was coquettishly pale and her lips were red and dewy. One could easily tell, even from above, that beneath her black, old-fashioned dress were long and slender limbs like those of a fleeting fairy.

Naoto was at a loss for words. It wasn't just him; it was unlikely that any critic would have been able to open his mouth in front of her.

There was something "ultimate" here that instantly captured the heart of any who beheld it. The exceedingly simple beauty and loveliness were such that one could hardly believe its artistry was something of this world.

...That's right, its artistry. This was a clockwork doll, an automaton! Not just any, either, but the "ultimate" one...!

The moment he realized this, Naoto lost himself in ecstasy.

It was a "port."

Underneath the deep-black sky, many enormous beams of steel were lined up. Together, they formed a "pier."

Spreading out in the shape of a fan, the 3,500-meter runway was synchronized with the main gear of Osaka Grid, rotating in the opposite direction at exactly the same speed.

Kansai International Airport.

It was an illustrious international airport that had first opened its doors before the planet was covered by gears.

Though it easily boasted a history of more than a thousand years, the architecture itself was new; it had undergone a remodeling just a few years back. The sound of the gears cranking had a firm, clear quality to it as well.

In a corner of the airport that floated in the sky lay what was called Corridor Seven—a runway closed to the public. There was a large transport aircraft parked there.

Work robots entered the opened hatch by the belly of the plane empty-handed, and came out one after another carrying containers labeled with serial numbers, while a large number of ground workers supervised them.

The containers were carried across the runway into the warehouse of Terminal Seven. There, they were transferred onto a truck and shuttled to the scene of the malfunction.

Or so they were supposed to be, but...

"It fell, you say?"

In the reception room of Terminal Seven a young girl wearing a deep-blue shirt underneath a beige summer coat looked back over her shoulder, her head tilted to the side. A man who had been incessantly wiping sweat from his face felt his shoulders tremble.

"Umm, you see...there was a problem, and..."

"I can see that just from looking at your face."

The girl's tone was cold. As she brushed the blond hair by her nape aside, she stared at the man with cutting eyes, urging him to go on. The man, on the other hand, was looking down and was avoiding the girl's stare.

His hunched posture sullied the dignity of both the title of chief of transport—which was how he had identified himself—and the well-tailored suit he was wearing.

"You mentioned just now that one of the containers fell, but I'm having a little trouble understanding what the problem is."

Was it a work robot malfunction, or a human error? Whatever the case, it didn't change the fact that the airport was responsible for the blunder. However, the containers were made to carry precision machines to begin with; thus, even if it fell while being unloaded, there shouldn't have been a problem.

"Or are you saying that a worker was caught in the accident?"

"N-No, there's no problem with the unloading. The rest of the containers should all be processed within an hour."

Marie became increasingly confused.

"Then just *what* is the problem?"

The chief of transport put away his sweat-soaked handkerchief and looked at the young girl with a mortified expression. "The accident in question didn't occur after landing, but during flight."

The girl continued staring at the chief of transport silently, not responding. He might have felt intimidated by her demeanor, for he displayed a frightened look towards the petite girl, more than two decades his junior, as he painfully vomited out words. "Um, p-perhaps because the request was so sudden, um, an error was made in the loading, causing one of the containers to slip off the rails...?"

"It was dropped from the plane during flight?"

"I-I'm terribly sorry... This is the first time that something like this has happened since the airport was founded, so, um, it took time to confirm the situation, causing the report to come in late."

"Which container was lost?" the girl questioned, her voice cold and sharp as a blade.

As if struggling to breathe, the chief answered, "...Container Y D-01."

"..."

"I-I'm truly, terribly sorry for this!"

He bowed his head deeply, but the girl couldn't be bothered to care.

"...In other words, this is what you're saying, right?" The girl's voice sounded like it was coming up from the depths of Hell. "So you're saying that for some reason, during the emergency flight of a jumbo-sized transport aircraft loaded with precious personnel and materials, the hatch opened by itself while one of the 3,558 containers was carelessly left unlocked, and of all things, it just happened to be 'that' most precious and irreplaceable container?"

"Yes..."

"If this is the Japanese's idea of a joke, it isn't funny at all."

"I-I'm sor...!"

Unable to even apologize properly anymore, the man looked at the girl to gauge her current mood. She stared at him with a stiff expression fixed on her face. For some time, the chief of transport felt like a death-row inmate before the gallows.

In reality, that wasn't too far from the truth. This was far past the level of mistake that could be settled with an apology and reparations. It'd be fortunate if things ended with just his dismissal. Depending on the girl's mood, the company itself could be dissolved—but...

The girl smiled. Sweetly and as brightly as a flower. The man's figure was reflected in her gentle-looking green eyes, and her light-pink lips were warped in what appeared to be a smile.

With a spin...

The girl swung her suitcase sharply and smashed it into the man's face. His nose broke, spraying blood everywhere. As the man writhed in agony, screaming like a pig, the eyes of the girl looking down at him were ablaze with flames.

As if she were spitting out something nasty, she said, "Incompetent in his job, feeble excuses, terrible jokes—I heard that Japanese were diligent and capable, but that must be a thing of the past. I get it now—Halter!"

In response, a man with a buzz cut, previously waiting in the corner of the room, began to walk towards her. He was a large man, with a muscular body easily exceeding two meters in height, dressed in a dark-gray suit. No matter how one looked at him, he had the appearance of someone from the underworld, perhaps a hitman or a terrorist.

The man said in a calm voice, "Dr. Marie—I find it questionable for a lady to raise her voice like that. Violence is no good, either."

The girl called "Dr. Marie" snorted and said, "Halter, who was it that hired this incompetent hack?"

The man being questioned—Halter—looked pitifully at the chief of transport sobbing away on the floor. "Wellllll, his career is a praiseworthy one, and I recall that those who handled the loading are veteran workers. Wasn't the schedule rather tight, after all?"

"So what? Dropping luggage from a cutting-edge transport aircraft—such a blunder is absolutely unheard of, and the excuse is that 'we were busy'?"

From her breast pocket, Dr. Marie took out a "chrono-compass"—

an intricate timepiece with nine clockfaces of varying sizes, the proof of being a Meister. She looked at it and sighed.

"...However, it's true that we don't have any time. Ahh, sugar, sugar..."

She fetched a colorful lollipop from her pocket, unwrapped it, then stuck it in her mouth. As she took a lick, she grumpily hurled out instructions.

"Please assemble a recovery team. I don't know about the container, but the contents are definitely safe. She is invaluable. Use any means necessary to secure her."

"As you wish."

After Halter took a butler-like bow, he began tapping away on the telegraph installed in the reception room. Confirming this with a sidelong glance, Dr. Marie exited the reception room and headed towards the lobby.

"...It's true that there wasn't any leeway, time-wise."

In the present world, cities were built on top of gears.

Since the gears were constantly turning, the methods of moving things were limited even between adjacent cities. The only options were the "cylinder train" and air transportation.

However, the structure of the cylinder train didn't allow for sudden changes to its schedule, and in addition, there was a considerable distance to travel this time, so transport by air was chosen out of necessity, but—

102 clocksmiths,

500 automata,

and 3,558 containers.

They'd been ordered to transport such a large load from Canada to

Japan, and in just one day at that. The girl thought it was unreasonable as well, no matter how she looked at it.

However...

"Even so, there's a limit to acceptable blunders...!"

Upon arriving at the entrance lobby, Dr. Marie saw that her staff members had already collected their baggage and were gathered together. These first-rate clocksmiths varied by gender, age, and race—and as soon as the girl showed herself in front of them, they closed their mouths and straightened their backs.

They all focused their eyes on her as they stood at attention, yet she wasn't intimidated in the slightest as she coolly questioned them.

"Are you all ready?"

"Of course, Dr. Marie."

"Good."

Addressing an elderly man who had come forward as their representative—the chief mechanic—the girl continued. "I was told the unloading will be done within an hour. Please finish unpacking the necessary containers for our job out of those transferred to Kyoto's Core Tower by the end of the day."

"Please leave it to us."

"Right after I finish the paperwork for the job at the administration bureau, I'll be joining you all at the scene. We're scheduled to begin work tomorrow morning, at 06:00 local time. Make sure to wind the automata's springs beforehand. I'll be leaving organization of the workflow to each team leader. Are we good?"

"Understood." All the staff saluted as they answered the girl after she gave out her concise instructions.

Standing in the center of the lobby, seeing off her staff as they started to move, Dr. Marie caught her breath. She couldn't help but think that the job this time was full of ill omens. How short the preparation time was, and the accident mid-transport: These were unprecedented affairs.

"...I have a bad feeling. Hopefully my concern turns out to be unfounded." She muttered the last part inside her mouth.

Just then...

"Excuse me. I take it that you're Doctor Marie Bell Breguet from the Meister Guild?"

When she heard the voice behind her, Marie turned around. Standing there was a group of about ten men. All of them wore black suits that looked like funeral wear, with collars neatly tightened by drab neckties.

Repulsed by the homogenous fake smiles they all had on, Marie opened her mouth, feeling uneasy. "I don't like being called by my full name."

"My apologies, Dr. Breguet. We're honored to meet you." The men continued with the eerie smiles pasted on their faces. "We're from the 'military.' On behalf of Kyoto Grid, we welcome you."

"We're sorry. As things happened so quickly, we weren't able to prepare accommodations for your team in time on our end. However, we've booked a room for you, doctor, at Central Hotel, so if you'd like, we can take you—"

"I'm fine." Marie interrupted the man speaking. "I'm thankful for your consideration, but I have to go inspect the scene and set up a repair plan right after I'm done with business at the administration bureau."

"Right...but where will you stay then, doctor?"

"My staff sleep huddled together under a single blanket at the scene when they're not working. Naturally, I'll be doing the same."

"You, the daughter of the Breguet family...?"

"We didn't come here to sightsee." As if to declare the conversation over, Marie turned her back on the men and walked towards the entrance. The men chased after her in a hurry.

"Please wait, Dr. Breguet. In that case, please stay at the hotel just for tonight. We've already completed preparations for a dinner meeting as well, so..."

"I don't have time for that." Marie continued to walk without giving them even an inch.

Behind her, one of the men rubbed his hands together as he clung on. "Dr. Breguet, I don't think you need to rush so much."

"That's right. There are always four thousand clocksmiths and over ten thousand automata conducting maintenance on the gears in Kyoto. The safety measures are exhaustive."

"Of course, for the duration of this job, we'll give orders for them to follow your commands as well—"

"That's unnecessary." Marie turned her head back and informed the men indifferently, "The work will be done by my staff only. To that end, one of my subordinates will go to receive the measurement data in my place later on."

"Right, that's fine...but I don't think there's anyone who grasps the city's functions as well as we do; Kyoto is under the jurisdiction of the 'military,' after all."

"Tuning a city is delicate group work. If our coworkers aren't fellow master clocksmiths, we won't be able to cooperate smoothly."

"Dr. Breguet, with all due respect, they are the top engineers of our entire country..."

"This country's jokes really are the worst. No one understands unless you put it bluntly." Marie brought a kind smile to her face and said, "Amateurs should get out of the way—that's what I'm saying."

"What...?"

Marie pierced the men, all flabbergasted by her too-abrasive words, with a chilling gaze. She sneered. "Why don't you say what you really think? 'This is the 'military's' turf. Don't act by yourself, let us get involved too.'"

"N-no, by no means are we thinking such things..."

"If you spill a drop of wine on mud, it's still just mud; but if even just a little bit of mud mixes with wine, the wine becomes undrinkable."

"..."

"I only demand one thing from you all. Wait obediently in the corner with your mouths closed. Of course, you *can* do that much, right?" Leaving them behind without bothering to check their reactions, Marie turned on her heels and passed through the entrance gate.

Halter had gone ahead. He waited for her with a luxury car reminiscent of a black jewel at the roundabout in front of the airport's entrance gate. Handing her heavy luggage over to Halter, she got in. After he finished loading the luggage into the trunk, Halter got into the driver's seat and tightened his seatbelt.

"Start the car, please."

"Roger."

•••●●●•••

"Things are proceeding just as planned, aren't they?" one of the men in black suits uttered as they saw the luxury car fading into the distance. Strangely, there was neither anger nor frustration on his face from being told off by a little girl. If anything, he looked like he felt relieved; he even had a small smile on his face.

They exchanged words ridiculing the girl as base smiles came to their faces.

Another one of them grinned from ear-to-ear as he agreed. "Thankfully, she's a haughty little girl, just as the rumors say. She'll be truly easy to manipulate."

"Now then, we just have to let her work hard for us."

There was no one else around to hear their conversation.

"Ah...I'm tired."

Inside the running car...

Whoosh. Marie deflated like a balloon and laid her face onto the adjacent seat.

Watching her through the rearview mirror, Halter smiled bitterly. "Thanks for your hard work."

Marie answered him in a childish tone as she flung off her summer coat and kicked her boots off. "Thanks doesn't cut it. Having to deal with hyenas wherever I go—you've seriously gotta be kidding me."

She took out a chocolate bar from the pocket of her bag and began chewing on it.

"Both the 'guild' and the Japanese government weren't any help at all in making the necessary arrangements for the job. Why should I

even have to negotiate with local organizations when it's not my job as a clocksmith?" The noble princess who had ordered an adult man around with her chin was nowhere to be seen as the girl grumbled, curled up in a fetal position on the rear seats. She just looked like a wanton, cheeky girl in her early teens.

Grinding his teeth to keep from laughing at the gap between her two personalities, Halter chided her. "Hey now, princess. Please don't forget to act befitting of a lady just because you're in a car."

"Leave me alone."

"It's my job, so I can't. Ahh, see, the bottom of your shirt is all rolled up."

"So? What, do you want to see?"

"I ain't interested in kids, but don't tempt me like that in another ten years."

"Die."

Wham. Marie kicked the back of the driver's seat forcefully. Halter's face hit the edge of the steering wheel, but he laughed it off.

"If the brats at the academy saw you like this, they'd faint."

"Like I care. Do you know who I am?"

"Well, of course," began Halter, with a devilish smile.

Ahem. He cleared his throat before answering more fully. "You graduated top of your class from several famous universities. You became the youngest student ever when you enrolled at age thirteen, and you were able to reach the top ranks of all two hundred million clocksmiths in the world—a Meister. You're the great Dr. Breguet, the young and beautiful genius. That I'm given the privilege to be your secretary is more than I could ever ask for my humble self."

"You're making me sick, stop!" Marie screamed like a woman

in distress while Halter paused, grinning. With a gentle gaze, he continued chiding the girl, who puffed her cheeks up.

"However, princess, try not to make unnecessary enemies."

"What, are you lecturing me?"

"I'm giving you advice. I understand that you feel fed up. However, their faults aside, the transport company and its employees are still an undeniable part of the gears of society. There's nothing to be gained from earning their resentment, only things to be lost."

"I think I was plenty kind, though. If it was 'Elder Sister,' the entire company would have been erased from this Earth."

"You can't compare yourself to such an atypical case..."

"What could those imbeciles possibly do to me in the first place?"

"...Indeed, they can't do anything. Nothing at all."

That was what was scary about them. The young girl still didn't realize that. That she was still so green, despite standing at the pinnacle of ability throughout the entire world, caused Halter to furrow his eyebrows in concern.

"...Well, it really is strange, though." As Marie leaned back against the seat, chewing on her chocolate bar, she tilted her head to one side. "Those military men were annoying, so I drove them away. Still, why did we have to come in such a big hurry when there's a military base nearby?"

"Hmm...? Now that you mention it, what *was* the reason we were dispatched this time?"

"A common gravitational irregularity. An error occurred in the Core Tower and the gravitational force won't return to its normal value. In terms of numbers, it's one percent stronger than normal right now."

"That is strange, indeed. It seems like the regular maintenance should be enough to take care of something like that."

"No kidding. It isn't nearly enough of a problem to summon us from Canada in a rush. 'The safety measures are exhaustive,' my ass. If that's the case, then don't call us."

"Wellllll, their numbers may be one thing, but the military's engineer corps can't compare to us in terms of technical prowess. From the Japanese government's standpoint, they're probably afraid that if they don't send a request in to the Meister Guild just in case, they'll be made to take responsibility if something goes wrong."

"It's always politics, politics, politics... Having my vacation canceled for the sake of stinky geezers keeping up appearances is simply insufferable. Ahh, how I yearn for the absinthe in Paris."

"That's not something a pretty young girl should drink."

"Shut it."

"Sure, sure—so, I take it you want me to head to the administration bureau first?"

Marie nodded in response as she broke the chocolate bar into pieces with several snaps. "Ahhh... Yeah. Please do. After I finish the paperwork there and write up an operation plan for the job, I'm going to sleep for today, but if *she* is found, wake me up at any time."

"Roger that."

Visible through the car window, the center of the metropolis—the Core Tower that would be their workplace for a brief period starting tomorrow—towered high into the sky, and the Equatorial Spring, as if to divide that same sky, was turning today as usual.

This world that was composed of countless gears, more than there are stars in the universe, drew the entirety of its energy from the gravitational force of the moon. The Equatorial Spring was what converted that potential energy to mechanical energy by turning, freeing up that enormous amount of energy for use.

The Clockwork Planet.

A mechanical world where everything was governed by gears, whether it be the wind, the temperature, the weather, or even gravity. Both the dried-up oceans and the lifeless landmasses had been entirely shaved off, including the earth's crust that they sat upon, and replaced with gears.

Nowadays, there was nothing left. It was a clockwork void floating somewhere in the cosmos. That was the current state of the Earth, a culmination of what had starteda thousand years ago.

But even for this world, reminiscent of an incredibly intricate, mechanical timepiece, it was imperative that regular maintenance ensure its proper functions. As long as it was mechanical, it couldn't tick away forever. Someday, it would break, grow old, rot, and in the end, come to a stop.

Before it came to that point, someone had to use their hands to conduct maintenance on the mechanisms of the planet.

That was her—Marie Bell Breguet's—job.

"Seriously... I want to drink absinthe."

Basking in a decadent mood, Marie gazed vacantly out the window at the scenery passing by.

•••●•••

Naoto slowly approached the "coffin" in front of him.

"The floor might collapse at any time, so I have to hurry and move her…"

The floor creaked from even his slightest movement, making him break into a cold sweat.

He groped about the "coffin," smearing his hands all over it to try and find a lock, but he couldn't find an opening. It appeared that the coffin didn't have a standard lock. On the other hand, there were lots of movable parts, like a puzzle…

"Like this… Is it here? No, this isn't it. How about this? Grrr, don't be such a pain—"

Click!

Something meshed together where his hands were, and a heavy spring popped out inside the coffin. Naoto heard the sound of gears turning as white steam vented from the aperture.

"All right, it's opennn!"

Naoto pushed open the lid, not waiting for it to slowly open by itself. He unfastened the belt that had locked the automaton in place. He then yanked out a bunch of cables attached to her—their purpose was unclear—in one go, before dragging the automaton girl out from the coffin.

She's light. That was the first thing that came to his mind.

She weighed as much as one would expect of a real girl her size. For a full-sized automaton, though, she was too light. It'd be possible for a sex doll automaton, but there was no way that one as high-quality as this was a simple toy.

Then again, what's with the softness of her skin? What maker is this skin material from?

"Wait, this is no time to be thinking. If I don't hurry…"

He quickly threw her arms back over his shoulders, straining to pull her out of the storage unit this time.

From the living room that had endured a forceful makeover, creating a new, open-air atrium, the silhouette of the Equatorial Spring that powered the planet could be seen against a sky full of stars.

For an apartment on the level of an abandoned building, the impact of the container was probably equal to a meteorite crashing.

...If I keep twiddling my thumbs here, I think it'll collapse for real...

As Naoto looked around restlessly, wondering what he should do, he happened to notice that there was a seal engraved onto the nape of the girl's neck.:

Y. [RyuZU]

"...RyuZU? Is this your name?"

Of course, no response came, but there was no mistaking it.

Naoto wondered what he should do with the "Ultimate Automaton," or rather "RyuZU"—for the time being, he decided that he should collect the tools he would need.

Brushing aside the rubble, he headed to the workshop where, luckily, there didn't seem to be any damage. When Naoto pushed the door open and entered, he saw that his stack of odds and ends had collapsed and were scattered all over the floor, along with his tools. Taking care not to step on them with his bare feet, he advanced to the workbench at the center of the room.

He looked down at the half-complete automaton for a moment...

Making up his mind before long, Naoto moved it to the hangar and laid RyuZU down on the workbench in its place. During that time, the building continued to creak, swaying, as if to warn him.

Naoto touched RyuZU's neck and focused on his hearing.

"...Her spring is moving, but nothing else is running. Is she broken?"

If that was the case, he had no choice but to fix her here. Not all the tools he needed could be brought outside, and furthermore, when it came to the miniscule gears used for automata, a single speck of dust could cause an error. This cleanroom was absolutely necessary for working on them.

Naoto's stomach tightened with resolve.

I'll finish repairing her and escape before the building collapses.

"—All right!!" He slapped both his cheeks and fired himself up.

Naoto put on his work clothes, wrapped a hip pack from his wall around his waist, and positioned the room's surgical lamp over the workbench before turning it on.

Preparations were complete.

Naoto lifted the girl into a sitting position, then pulled down the zipper on her back. He took off her dress as if peeling away the wrapping paper on a present, exposing her pale, dainty shoulders and delicate back.

With the apartment no different from an abandoned building, it continued to creak as it trembled. Naoto got to work. He turned RyuZU onto her back and felt around between her shoulder blades with his fingers. Underneath the soft skin, there seemed to be a lump of some sort. He pressed down on it lightly. The metal *click* of a pin being disconnected could be heard, and RyuZU's back opened up in pieces like petals from a line in its center.

It's like a flower blooming.

"...Wow." Underneath her exposed skin was an operation mechanism made with such transcendent finesse that it was like an entire universe was crammed inside it.

Naoto gulped.

If the situation were different, he would have scrutinized her so hard that his gaze would have bored a hole in her, but—Naoto shook his head before he carefully inserted a tiny tool into RyuZU's back.

If someone—for example, a Meister—were to see this, they might have let out a scream.

Compared to RyuZU's exceedingly sophisticated makeup, Naoto's hands were simply too clumsy.

He worked hesitantly, racking his brain, and wavering with uncertainty. Even so, he was able to hit the right place somehow—or at least, that's what he thought. He kept choosing the wrong tools again and again, so he had to keep starting over. First and foremost, he didn't have the blueprint to refer to, and furthermore, he wasn't even using any measuring instruments.

An automaton, which reproduced the human body using only gears, was an aggregate of fine parts that numbered in the trillions. If one were to try to mend the operation of these microgears without the blueprint, just to locate the parts that were out of order would require expensive equipment.

Yet Naoto continued working by feel, simply straining his ears from time to time.

Despite all that, there was no mistake in his work. It was as if he could tell where the broken part was without even examining her...

"Is this it?"

That's right, of course Naoto could tell where the broken part was. If he listened carefully, he could hear it.

In the grand orchestral performance to which even a Viennese symphonic orchestra would raise a white flag, there was a sound like a kindergartner playing the melodica mixed in. A single smudge surrounded by otherwise perfect art. There was no way one could catch that sound and let it be.

Despite being perfectly designed and perfectly made, it's running defectively right now. To put it bluntly, yeah—I'm super-annoyed.

But the problem was...

"More importantly, what part was it again...?"

Naoto's knowledge and technical skill didn't match his special talent at all.

He didn't have even the slightest idea of what the part's function was, or why it was broken.

In the end, the only thing that Naoto could do was work by feel slowly and cautiously, like testing a keyhole with countless keys, straining his ears all the while.

If his hand accidentally slipped, he might end up cutting the pseudo-nerves, which were thinner than spider silk. The microgears might get bent. If the Main Cylinder were to be damaged, there'd be no salvaging the situation. If one began to count the risks, there would be no end. It was a tightrope walk.

...It took Naoto three full hours to complete his precarious repair work.

• • ● ● ● • •

"...Phewww...!"

It had only been three hours.

However, it was a terrifying three hours that shaved entire chunks off his soul more so than it drained his physical stamina.

Naoto had expended all of his willpower, and his breathing was ragged as well.

"I-It should be fixed now... right?" Though he had confidence, he still felt anxious. His ears told him that there was no mistake. Even so, it wasn't like he was able to actually verify the structure.

Though it was too late now, feelings of regret welled up within him regardless. Had it really been okay for an amateur like him to have tampered with this supreme machine? If he screwed up somewhere, wouldn't he have done something irreversible?

Such thoughts assaulted him with terror, making his entire body tremble, but—Naoto shook his head.

"...No, all that's left is to rewind the spring and she should...restart."

Naoto's hands trembled as he extended them towards the girl's nape—her silver hair hid the screw of her spring underneath it—and began to silently turn the screw.

However, the state of the apartment was really getting precarious. Not only was it shaking, but thin fragments were now peeling and falling off the ceiling as it cracked.

"...Haah... Haah..."

He turned the screw around and around, building up the elastic energy needed for startup. However—no matter how much he wound the spring, there was no response. Gut-wrenching regret strangled Naoto.

No, no way, no way no way! Did I really screw up somewhere?

"God damn it...you've gotta be kidding me!"

Crack—

He heard a forboding sound, but he didn't see it, and frankly, he didn't want to learn where it had come from. Even so, Naoto's ears assertively declared through his headphones...

That the building would collapse.

"Ah, crap..." He turned his gaze upwards.

The ceiling began to collapse just then, pouring down onto Naoto—and RyuZU as well.

At that moment, however, his hands felt a faint reaction. In a flash—without any forewarning—RyuZU sprung up from the workbench.

All of a sudden, she was in full operation.

With movements unbelievably fluid for having just started up, the girl pulled Naoto into her embrace. While carrying Naoto in her arms, the actuators in her legs ran full-throttle, causing her Accelerator Gears to turn with raging force, and RyuZU broke through the glass window at the speed of an artillery shell.

All this happened in the fraction of a second before the ceiling collapsed.

"Oh, cra—"

They were falling down. Inertia seized their bodies.

The fall from the seventh floor of the apartment building should have been about twenty meters. ...However, the automaton girl who held Naoto in her arms smiled with an air of refinement—and nonchalance.

Naoto was mesmerized by her profile.

The time that passed didn't even amount to a few seconds but felt many tenfolds longer.

As they approached the ground, she adjusted their headlong position by swinging her legs grandly, turning the two of them upright.

She landed.

"...!!"

Boom. The sound of a heavy collision. And yet, Naoto didn't feel the shock of landing at all.

Just how advanced is the Shock Remover packed inside her? Did that break the mechanisms in her leg just now? Ahh, I hope the glass didn't damage her artificial skin—

"......"

RyuZU loosened her hold without a word, allowing Naoto to quietly step onto the ground. Unable to stand, he sank down on the spot.

Unable to think with his mind practically blank, Naoto looked up at the girl, dumbfounded.

"Ah—"

Her topaz eyes, which glittered blazingly and bewitchingly, looked down upon Naoto. She blinked repeatedly.

A breath leaked out from between her narrowly parted lips, stirring the air.

"Y—ou—" A voice muddied with dissonance spilled out as her vocal apparatus vibrated.

It was a malfunction. Was it because she hadn't been turned on in a long time? The girl placed one hand on her throat and tuned her vocal apparatus while staring up at space.

She eventually lowered her hand gracefully and nodded, looking satisfied. After that, upon adjusting her posture and tidying up her disheveled clothes...

She stood there looking perfectly ready, as if she had already been waiting in that perfect state for many hundreds of years.

After leisurely turning her eyes to survey her surroundings, the girl looked down by her feet.

"Are you the one who kindly repaired me?" She had a high, clear voice, like that of a music box's metal comb.

She was a delicate, lovely maiden with skin the color of liquid silver, wrapped in a dress so black it seemed like it had been tailored from the darkness of the night. Her topaz eyes glittered with gold as they gazed fixedly upon Naoto, who remained at a complete loss for words.

"My, for me to be forced to hibernate for 1,804,926 hours because of such a trivial failure—has human intelligence still yet to exceed the level of a flea, even now? Or are you, from whom I cannot detect any sense of intellect or refinement, somehow the first graduate who ought to be commemorated?"

If Naoto strained his ears, he could faintly hear the inorganic pumping sound of her Main Cylinder. Yet, its rhythm overlapped somewhere with the beating heart that was ringing in his chest.

"...My goodness, the stupidity of humanity is the one thing that truly knows no bounds. If possible, I would prefer my master to be a lifeform superior to an insect, but..."

While spewing venom from her sharp tongue, the girl extended her hand towards Naoto with a graceful gesture. In contrast to her scathing words, her gaze was sweet, and her mouth formed a gentle smile.

Naoto gently smiled back in response, extending his hand forward and sticking his thumb up.

The next instant—Naoto lost consciousness.

Clockwork Planet

● Chapter Two / 03 : 18 / Complication

It was 03:18:24 a.m.

Marie Bell Breguet woke up. Kicking off her blanket, she sprung up violently.

In the center of a small, dark room that was originally used for file storage, Marie concealed her breath and honed her senses.

...What was that just now?

She felt anxious for some reason. Even though she should have been sound asleep from the fatigue caused by all the travel, she had abruptly awoken.

Marie slowly got up, stepping onto the ground from her makeshift bed.

Silence—her surroundings were dead quiet.

There were still a few hours until dawn. Her staff were also resting right now in preparation for the quagmire ahead. The only ones awake at the moment should have been the observation squad's night-shift staff. Marie was tempted to wrap herself back up in her blanket as well...

However, she didn't do so. She couldn't afford to discard this mysterious feeling and leave it as it was.

Marie was not only a genius, but a Meister as well. Having worked out in the field almost daily since her youth, she had sensed countless irregularities and dangers throughout her career. Her ability and experience were warning her. That was the kind of feeling she, the great Marie Bell Breguet, was getting in this current situation.

Something *had* to be amiss.

"Is anyone here?!" Marie stood up as she shouted. She put on a coat and dragged her cumbersome body to the door, pushing it open.

She entered the dark hallway. Right next to the door, something started moving sluggishly. That something was a middle-aged man with a buzz cut who, despite having a giant body like a bear's, exuded so little presence that it was unsettling.

Halter—the man who had been wrapped in a blanket on the floor—lifted his head up.

"...What's wrong, princess? Did you have a bad dream or something?"

"Want me to beat you to death?" Marie glared at Halter with a threatening face. "Get up already, you fat oaf. Go bring me the measurement data starting around 120 seconds ago at once."

"All right. I'll be back immediately. ...Ah, and also—"

"What? Get going. On the double!" Marie's expression was severe.

In an effort to pacify her, Halter replied, "I get it already, so at least put on some underwear."

"Ehh?" Not only did Marie's movements and face freeze as she stared blankly, but also her breathing.

She looked down.

"..."

Nothing.

She wasn't wearing anything down there. Actually, she was completely naked.

Here was a girl genius haughtily throwing out her chest with her hands on her waist while fully exposed.

"...Uuugh!"

Looking back up, she saw that Halter was already gone.

Marie had reflexively raised the palm of her hand up, but upon losing her target, she hastily rushed back inside her room as her face flushed bright red.

As Marie had demanded, Halter returned quickly.

Just as she finished picking up and putting on the clothes she had flung off, there was a knock on the door.

"By all means, please come in," Marie said stiffly. Halter entered with a heap of documents in his hand. Marie had been lying in wait to kick Halter's shin as he entered, but gave up the idea when she saw the observation squad following him inside.

A brawny thug was one thing, but there was no way she could show herself being immodest in front of Meister Guild's outstanding staff members.

Biting down to stifle her tongue click, she hurled a sharp glance at Halter.

I wish you'd just die, you small-time punk.

It was unclear whether Halter noticed Marie's glare as he leaned forward and lay the heap of papers on the desk in the room. The squad leader, Hannes, picked out a single document from the giant stack and presented it to Marie.

"Dr. Marie, about the results of the observation just now—"

"The gravity was fluctuating intermittently, right?" Marie beat him to the punch.

Having had his words taken from him, Hannes's eyes widened. "My, I'm impressed. So you were aware."

"Just a conjecture. I had a feeling that was probably the case."

"Indeed, it's just as you say, doctor. In the past hour, the reference value intermittently fluctuated between 0.92 and 1.04, three times."

Halter interjected with half-baked politeness. "...A fluctuation of about 0.1g? No, the difference is actually even smaller. I'm surprised you noticed. It shouldn't have been strong enough to wake someone up though, right?"

"You're a cyborg, so the tourbillion mechanism implanted inside you ends up negating fluctuations in gravity within the margin of error," Marie answered, as she glanced at the biggest man in the room.

Halter, who served as both Marie's bodyguard and secretary, was originally from the army; he later rose up to become a clocksmith. His body had been mechanized when he was young, so though he had enough power to break combat-use automata with his fists, in exchange, his artificial body wasn't as sensitive as a body of flesh.

"Even if you say that, it's still only on the level of the force felt when riding an elevator, no?"

"That's more than enough. Besides, that isn't where the problem lies." Marie shrugged her shoulders.

Hannes continued in agreement, "It's true that the range of fluctuation itself is within the margin of error, but the problem is the number of times it happened. The frequency graph is also reading an unprecedented pattern even when compared against all the data from the last thirty years. It's currently stabilized at 1.03g, but..."

"From what one can tell from reading this observational data, another one's about to come."

Groan. Marie suddenly felt the weight of her body increase, causing her to pause. It wasn't enough to make her collapse to the ground, but it wasn't something one could ignore, either.

Analyzing the extra weight pressing down on her entire body, Marie muttered, "—It's 1.34g now."

"Dr. Marie, this has to be..."

"Indeed, this problem doesn't seem like one that can be dealt with as simply a common gravitational irregularity anymore. If it continues worsening at this pace, it'll eventually affect everyone above the gears as well."

As for what this implied...

"In the worst-case scenario—the metropolitan mechanism might collapse."

"......"

Hearing Marie say such things in a matter-of-fact tone caused a nervous chill to run down the backs of all present.

If this was as much as the gravity fluctuated, at most it would only make one nauseous. But what if an even stronger gravity started weighing down? Or if it dropped down to zero gravity? One might suddenly be squashed under one's own weight, or thrown up into the air, for that matter.

Or rather, the mechanism would probably just malfunction once the fluctuations went beyond the extent that the escapement could adjust for.

It'd be one thing if it were the mechanism of an automobile or a home appliance, but if the twelve clock towers that governed the metropolitan environment and the core tower that pierced all the way up to the stratosphere from the center of the city were to break—reconstruction would simply be impossible at that point.

This city—Kyoto—would end up being lost forever.

Even after a thousand years, the Clockwork Planet that reconstructed the world using gears still remained a black box that no one could reproduce. Even the Meisters, of whom there were only 6,305 in the entire world, couldn't do it.

"Everyone, please listen." Marie spoke up.

She looked out over all her present staff members, then continued in a firm voice.

"Though I'm sure you're all already aware, the situation has taken a turn for the dire. Whether it be the urgent dispatch order or the innocuous malfunction report that didn't match that urgency, the job was suspicious from the start, but—"

Marie paused for a moment.

She opened her feet up to her shoulders' width, placed her hands on her waist, and hoisted her right hand up with composure.

With the small body of a young girl yet the majesty of a queen, Marie asserted, "We're all widely acknowledged, first-rate clocksmiths here. It's true that we probably can't match up to 'Y,' who created this world; however, you and I are all rare talents gathered together from the entire world. There's no one better than us, nor is there a malfunction we can't resolve. Before we move on, please recall that fact first."

Upon hearing those words, ones that could even be called arrogant, the expressions on the faces of the staff changed.

She was right. There wasn't a single person among the Meisters dispatched here that was incompetent.

Each one of them was a self-made, expert technician who had started out as a Lehrling, then became a Geselle after going through rough jobs out in the field, and finally a Meister after acquiring both expertise and experience.

From its director, Marie, all the way down to the lower-ranking staff that made up the observation squad, the Meister Guild had nothing but talent, forming a technical vanguard that would be welcomed with open arms by private enterprises and militaries anywhere in the world.

"That's right. We are the Meister Guild."

The Meister Guild.

An international organization whose goal was to maintain and preserve the planet's mechanisms. Boasting more than half of all Meisters as its members and armed with the best technology and equipment, it was a troop of clocksmiths who faced off against malfunctions in cities all over the world. It was a non-governmental organization whose activities were unconstrained by any political or ideological consideration.

That was the "Meister Guild."

"It seems that there's a fitting reason that HQ made us come here from the other side of the world in such a rush to forcefully intervene, after all. I also sense something suspicious from the military's attitude... Well, we're used to being hated by that lot, aren't we?"

The bitter laughs that spread throughout the staff spoke to their experience.

"This one's going to be a handful. Let's enjoy it as much as we can." The springy way Marie said that made it sound as though she really meant it. "I don't know what's going to come up yet, but I've concluded that whatever it is, it'll be a pressing matter."

Then, putting her thick layer of resolve into words, "Observation squad, please pinpoint which floor of the Core Tower contains the source of the fluctuations. The masses of mediocre technicians out there couldn't finish a job like this even if they spent a year on it—but we're going to finish it in two weeks!"

They answered in unison: "Understood!!"

Marie's demand was so unreasonable as to be ludicrous, yet all of her attending staff answered her with charged voices.

Having given detailed instructions to the observation squad, Marie saw them off as they returned to work, after which she flopped onto her makeshift bed.

"Ah... It's so tiresome."

"You did good work. That was a pretty rousing speech." Halter held out a cup with steam rising off the top to Marie, who was groaning at the ceiling. It was a well-blended hot cocoa made with ample amounts of milk and sugar.

Marie abruptly rose up to receive the cup, then curled her lips in irony. "Man, I'm really glad. To think they would be fooled by a speech from a little girl like me."

"They knew better, but let themselves be fooled because they're adults."

"I wonder if that's the case."

"It is. There's no way an idiot who seriously acts complacent in front of a mechanical malfunction of a metropolis could ever become a Meister. Even though I'm a clocksmith who's stuck at Geselle rank, I can at least tell that much."

"......"

Halter picked up a metal folding chair and brought it next to the makeshift bed before sitting down in front of Marie, who remained silent. "It's gotta be scary. It's gotta be unbearable. If you screw up somewhere, people will die. Cities will be blown away. Even so, everyone here is a wicked gambler who sticks his neck into the fire of his own free will—look, in the same way, there's also a little girl here desperately putting on a tough facade even as she's on the verge of wetting herself."

"...Well, it is comical, isn't it."

"Well, yeah. You can't do anything but laugh." Grinning broadly, Halter continued. "Laugh, fool yourself, and likewise, act tough. There's no other choice. As an adult, it'd be too embarrassing to cower in fear like a wuss while a cute little girl is tackling the problem head-on."

"For being so lowly, you sure can talk." Marie put her lips to the edge of the cup as she let a smile escape. The sugar mixed into the cocoa sent a pleasant buzz to Marie's tired brain. "In that case, shall I treat you as an adult and work you to the bone now?"

"Your wish is my command, princess."

"Investigate the military. I want to find out what they know about the situation."

"Hmm? I thought they were openly disclosing the information they have."

"It's true that there wasn't anything suspicious in the measurement data they disclosed. But, I can't think that they spat out all of the information too obediently. I want both evidence of the cover-up and the information being covered up."

"In other words, do you mean to say..." Halter lowered his voice as he muttered, looking serious, "...That the military is intentionally concealing a fatal malfunction?"

"At the very least, the possibility exists."

"...Is the situation that bad?"

"Probably. The fact that Meister Guild dispatched us here all the way from the other side of the world without any explanation bothers me."

"You think the information was leaked? But if headquarters got ahold of information that's being concealed by the military and the Japanese government, wouldn't they say something about it to us?"

"It might be that they have no proof. Also, even Meister Guild isn't free from entanglements with the outside world, you know? After all, it can't ignore the will of its sponsors, the five great corporations—and there are those who want to eliminate me as well."

"...Hey now, that sure sounds menacing."

Marie showed him a broad grin. "Isn't that what you're here for?

Marie Bell Breguet. The youngest person in history to ever become a Meister, as well as the daughter of the president of the Breguet Corporation, one of the five great corporations.

Though she hadn't ever been publicly criticized, given her ability and status—she was nonetheless used to having looks of jealousy and hatred thrown at her. Given the opportunity, people who would sabotage her were a dime a dozen. When such characters resorted directly to violence, it was Halter's job to protect her.

"If it ends up just being me overthinking things, then no harm done. But I want to be sure, just in case."

"Roger. I'll try sounding things out for now."

As Halter stood up, someone knocked at the door.

"Hmn? Please, come in."

"Excuse me." The one who entered after receiving Marie's permission was a member of the observation squad that had just left earlier.

"What's the matter? Did something unexpected occur while you were working?"

"Not quite. Actually, I have a report on the Y D-01 container."

"Gah! Was RyuZU found?!"

Seeing Marie straighten her back and lean forward seemed to have made the staff member awkward, as he reported in a faltering voice, "No, well, you see... By reverse-calculating the air route, we somehow managed to pinpoint the location where it fell, but..."

"And?" Annoyed by the staff member's equivocal manner of speech, Marie tightened her fist.

"There happened to be an apartment building right below the location where it fell."

"...An apartment building?"

"Yes. You see, I was told that the impact of the fall, well...caused the entire building to collapse."

"...Huhhh?" Her voice inadvertently escaped from her mouth. At the same time, the cup fell out of her hand. Hot cocoa scalded her skin as it spilled all over her knees, causing Marie's body to reflexively jump up, jittering.

"Are you all right, Dr. Marie?!"

"I'm f... Th-there's no proble..." Marie answered, swallowing her urge to scream. Abruptly snatching the towel that Halter handed her from her side, she looked up at the staff member, tears welling up in the corners of her eyes. "C-co-llapsed...you say?"

"Right, well...how should I put this, it seems like the building had been considerably deteriorated to begin with..."

"What? Hey now, don't tell me there were casualties?!" Halter cried out.

The reporting staff member denied it in a hurry. "No, the silver lining was that there were no casualties. For all of its size, it had relatively few residents. That, combined with the fact that there appears to have been a rather large margin of time before it fully collapsed, seems to have allowed all of the residents to escape in time."

"I-I see. I'm glad to hear that..." Marie said in relief as she wiped the cocoa off her legs.

The staff member continued, "Ah—about that...things aren't looking so good, actually."

"Hm? Is there something else?"

"You see, what I'm saying is, the apartment building collapsed."

"What? You told me that already." Marie said in confusion as she knitted her eyebrows.

The staff member, seeming to have become impatient, exclaimed, "As I keep saying, it *collapsed!* The Y D-01 container fell below the local grid along with the building!"

As if a flare had suddenly flashed in front of her, Marie's pupils constricted into dots. It had been a while since she last experienced this sensation.

She reflexively asked again, "What did you just say?"

"The Y D-01 storage unit fell below the local grid. Fortunately, the rubble from the collapse stopped at a shallow floor of the city's mechanism; however, the report mentioned that we didn't prepare any machinery used for civil engineering, so recovering the container would be extremely difficult."

"C'mon..." Halter groaned as he put his hand on his forehand.

The situation was such that even he didn't have the composure to joke about it, but upon seeing his mistress petrified in dumb amazement, he managed to just barely remember himself. He suggested in a low voice, "...At any rate, let's contact headquarters. For this accident, we need to have them send the supervisor of the legal department as well as machinery for excavation over there. There was an asset even the Breguet Corporation can't simply disregard in that storage unit, so they'll manage things for us if we explain what happened."

"R, Right... It's as you say. In that case, I'm sorry to trouble you, but could you handle that process?"

"Understood." Halter nodded, then left the room together with the staff member.

As the door closed, Marie, left alone in the room, curled her lips in irony. "...Looks like it'll be a fun job this time, seriously."

•••●●●•••

At the same time—03:17:46 a.m.

Naoto Miura woke up.

He was in a park, an athletic park with both a spacious sports field and children's playground equipment. Underneath a roofed rest area set up in a corner, Naoto ground his teeth as he covered his ears.

"...Shut up."

Dissonance sounded. He was used to hearing abnormal sounds from the municipal mechanism, but it was especially hard to bear right now.

Truly unpleasant sounds were coming from the gears on the twenty-fourth floor of the Core Tower, which was around 70,620 meters underground. That was what woke him up. Normally, the noise-canceling function on his beloved headphones would erase such noises, but—well, his headphones were missing...

But before that...

"Why...was I sleeping here?" Naoto muttered, as he tilted his head. Perhaps because he had slept on a hard surface, his whole body felt as heavy as lead, like he hadn't slept at all.

"I see that you have woken up, Master Naoto."

Naoto had yet to fully awaken when a cool, beautiful voice reached his ears from behind. Turning around, he saw the face of an angel just before his eyes, causing him to inadvertently throw his head back in surprise.

The gemstone eyes, which glittered gold, gazed intently at him. They were beautiful enough to make one lose one's breath—but at the same time, one couldn't read the thoughts behind those artificial eyes.

...If I remember right, this girl...

Naoto gasped and tried to stand up, but ended up staggering.

Groan. A heavy pressure pushed down on his entire body. His hands, which had been propping him up, slipped, and Naoto rolled off the bench. The rebound from hitting the ground made his head hit the edge of the wooden bench forcefully.

"Gahhhhhh, my head feels like it's going to crack open!"

As Naoto held his head, kicking about in agony, a sweet voice fell upon him from above. "What a novel calisthenic exercise. Master's refined taste reaches far beyond the current times."

"That's not what I'm doing! More importantly, what was that just now?!"

"It seems to be a fluctuation in gravity. The cause is probably a slight error in the municipal mechanism."

"Damn government buffoons. At least maintain the mechanism properly, dammit!" While grumbling, Naoto stood up. As he brushed off the dirt that had gotten onto his clothes, he turned to face the owner of that sweet voice once again.

The girl looked dainty as she sat on her heels while kneeling on top of the bench. Realizing that she had apparently been providing him with a lap pillow until he had woken up, Naoto became internally flustered.

"Umm, your name is RyuZU...right?"

"Yes. My humble name is RyuZU, and I am the First of the Initial-Y Series."

Seeing RyuZU's elegant smile as she answered him finally lit up the pivotal memories in Naoto's mind, causing him to rapidly reconstruct his memories of last night.

As he thought back on those freshly reconstructed memories, Naoto laughed in exasperation. "...That was a crazy night, huh?"

Everything had been normal up until he got home from school.

But after he'd returned home and took a bath, a meteorite came crashing down. The "meteorite" turned out to be a mysterious storage unit, and within was an automaton that looked like an angel—and to top it all off, things ended with a do-or-die repair job in a building that felt like it was going to collapse at any moment.

"Ah—that's right! What ended up happening to my apartment?"

"If you are referring to your place of residence, Master..." RyuZU answered his words by turning her gaze. In the direction she was looking, red smoke could be seen climbing up to dissolve into the dark of night.

"That smoke... Could that be coming from the apartment I lived in?"

"Yes. As the collapse of the building caused a fire and a cave-in, I evacuated to this park with you."

If Naoto strained his ears, he could hear the siren of a fire truck mixed within the noises of the city.

It seemed like this was a park several blocks away from the apartment building. As he composed himself and confirmed his surroundings, he realized that he had seen this scenery before.

"...Heheh, goodbye, dear home... At last, I've become homeless as well." Naoto thought back nostalgically upon his apartment which had gone from near-ruins to actual ruins at long last.

"And it's not like I have any money, either. What should I do from now on...?"

"Regarding that," RyuZU addressed Naoto in a serene voice. "Before your residence completely collapsed, I retrieved some clothes and a few valuables, Master."

"Whatcha say?!"

When he heard that, Naoto looked and found various belongings of his on the table of the rest area.

"Ooh, my wallet and passbook and seal! And my headphones!" He put his beloved headphones back on straight away.

In addition, his school uniform, school satchel, sneakers, and his portable tools were also neatly lined up. Seeing the paltry fortune that he thought had been lost along with the apartment building, Naoto let out a cheer.

"Also, pardon me, but I took the liberty of looking at your passbook—Master's name is *Naoto Miura*—is this correct?"

"Huh?" When she asked that, Naoto realized he hadn't told her his name. "Ahh... yeah. That's right."

"Then," RyuZU bowed her head reverently while still sitting on her heels. "Let me begin by deeply thanking you for repairing me. Furthermore, although it occurred while I was unconscious, I deeply apologize for having destroyed your residence, Master Naoto. The one responsible for this should surely bury their head into the ground in apology, but for the time being, I will—"

Naoto lost himself in wonder as he listened to RyuZU's apology, which was refined and old-fashioned, but also had a poisonous tinge to it.

Her specs, which had been demonstrated the moment he finished repairing her, were tremendous.

Her judgment that allowed her to grasp the situation around her immediately upon starting up. Her mobility that allowed her to escape with Naoto in an instant before the building collapsed. Furthermore, the consideration to retrieve what belongings she could from the building right before it collapsed entirely while Naoto had been unconscious.

And on top of all that—this fluent apology of hers.

"There's nothing to apologize about." Naoto shook his head. "Rather, I've gone past merely being shocked at your abilities to even being deeply moved by them, RyuZU."

"Hearing that pleases me above all else. In that case, may I have permission to formally register you as my Master and accompany you as your servant, Master Naoto?" RyuZU extended her hand towards him.

Master Confirmation. The contract binding master and servant.

"Eh...?" Feeling an abrupt sense of mysterious discomfort, Naoto hesitated. "No, that's a bit..."

RyuZU tilted her head slightly to one side, looking perplexed.

"Let me see, could becoming my Master possibly inconvenience you in some way? Considering how perfect and overly capable I am, would it hurt your tiny, mitochondria-sized pride if I were to serve you?"

Naoto had wondered about RyuZU's tone of voice since she'd started up.

She has a wicked tongue that knows no restraint—so why doesn't it irritate me?

Shaking his head to dispel these tangential thoughts, Naoto answered, "No, that's not it. RyuZU, you're an amaaazing automaton, you know?"

"Yes, I know. And?"

"To have such a large number of parts crammed into such a small size, you're a work of art in terms of both form and function."

"Yes, I am relieved to see that Master Naoto has more of an

aesthetic eye than empty sockets."

"Even among the latest models, there's no automaton more charming and perfect than you, RyuZU!"

"Yes, naturally. I do not know what caliber the latest automata are, but if humanity could create ones that even reached my feet, I would not have slept for as long as 206 years." RyuZU replied immediately, brimming with confidence.

Her words shocked Naoto, causing him to shout, "Two hundred and six years?! Just when were you created then, RyuZU?!"

"About a thousand years ago. Is there something strange about that?"

"A thou—?!"

About a thousand years ago. In other words—an automaton manufactured when the Earth was converted into gears.

...Could it be?

What was this perfect automaton, which seemed like the very embodiment of the word "ultimate?"

Really, why didn't I find it strange to begin with?

What *was* she, that even the latest automaton models couldn't compare with her?

"RyuZU...just what are you?"

"What do you mean?"

"Well, I mean, come on! One, you fell from the sky! Two, you're super cute! You clearly give off the vibe that you're technology from the future!"

"What about it?"

"Well, it's just... Anyway, I'm just a high school student, you know?"

"Is that so? Given that you were able to repair me, Master Naoto,

I believe that you should be the human with the most outstanding technical ability on this Earth. Am I wrong?"

"Nononono! There's no way that's true! I'm just a high school student. If anything, I'm a loser in life. If you had to, you could say I'm a non-normie."

"In that case, why did you start me up?" RyuZU inquired, looking perplexed.

"That's because..."

All of a sudden, Naoto realized.

...Why?

It was just as RyuZU said. What had he intended to do by fixing this automaton?

Naoto turned to face RyuZU anew.

An antique doll, supposedly made a thousand years ago.

I see. This doll is so adorable, pretty, and perfect that one would hesitate to touch her. ...Really, isn't she too *perfect?*

The functions she'd shown immediately upon start-up exceeded those of a military model, and both her speech and expression just now were astoundingly natural. Though even current automata could pull off everyday conversation and emotional expression, they would always leave behind a sense of artificiality, no matter how advanced they were.

In contrast, RyuZU felt so human that she even gave off the illusion that she really was alive.

Even if one ignored the fact that she had been made a thousand years ago, there was no way an automaton with such high specs could have been made by a private individual, and for a commercial-use, maid-type model made by an enterprise...her functionalities were too advanced.

"Then, was it the military?"

She didn't look like a mass-produced product, so was she a secret prototype of a new, weapon-grade model?

...No, no, there's no way.

Even if she were a new model of military-use automaton, there was neither meaning nor an explanation for her form being that of a teenage girl.

It might not be technically impossible, but if the developer were to announce such a beautiful girl as the new weapon, their necks would undoubtedly fly off before they could even finish. The more Naoto thought about it, the more lost he became.

Who manufactured this automaton? Where did he come from, and for just what purpose had he done so?

Wasn't she made with an extraordinary purpose in mind?

Isn't there something preposterous right behind my back?

Considering those points, no matter what a transcendentally cute automaton with flawless finesse she was, to casually bind her in a contract of master and servant from the heat of the moment would be—wrong.

"...Is that so..." Perhaps RyuZU guessed Naoto's thoughts from his expression, for she quietly lowered her extended hand. Her elegant, composed, and gently smiling expression hid a tinge—really, just a tinge—of emotion. That made her feelings all the more apparent.

"I see that I am...unnecessary." Her words were those of sorrowful lament, springing from the gloom and loneliness she felt upon realizing no one needed her.

In that instant—a gigantic balance scale popped up inside Naoto's head.

On one side sat this supreme automaton, and on the other, the yet-unknown dangers that would surely assail him.

Is my mind telling me to weigh these two things against each other?

...Fine, why not.

In his mind, Naoto laughed daringly as he first placed RyuZU on the left plate.

As soon as he placed her onto the plate, the scale broke, splitting with a twang as the plate with RyuZU on it continued downward, cracking the table right open and digging a crater into the floor, before exploding, smashing Naoto's reason and hesitation and various other important parts of his consciousness into smithereens.

"I'm so sorryyyyy! I *super* want youuuu!!!" Naoto prostrated himself impetuously at something approaching the speed of light.

Curling his body into a half-circle as he threw his four limbs and his head onto the ground, he spit out his true thoughts. "I was acting tough! At this point, I don't have even the slightest intention of letting you go! I don't care what happens anymore, so please take care of me forever!"

As he yelled, fully prostrated, he thrust both his fists into the air with astonishing force while keeping his elbows on the ground.

Right, these are my true thoughts, my true feelings. Who can blame me? What kind of idiot would pass up such a delicious treasure? Manufacturer? Original owner? Her true identity? As if I care about any of that! Regardless of whether what's behind her is the military or an enterprise—if I can get hold of RyuZU, then that's the be-all, end-all. That's an absolute fact!

"In that case, allow me to borrow your right hand. Also, if possible, could I have you stand up?"

Naoto sprung up like a spring, and promptly extended his right hand forward.

RyuZU wrapped his palm with both of hers, upon which she said, "Well then, excuse me—*nom*."

She took his ring finger from its tip to its base snugly into her mouth. Naoto felt a chill run down his spine as he inadvertently let out a moan.

RyuZU's hot and tender tongue was vivaciously twirling about inside her mouth. As if trying to explore Naoto's ring finger, her wet tongue assiduously licked and licked it, twining around and kneading it. The lubricant excreted from the soft and supple material sloshed around, making foaming sounds.

My finger is going to dissolve.

Naoto experienced the false impression that, at the rate things were going, his ring finger would be completely sucked into nothingness from its tip by RyuZU. He felt a murky sense of guilt and indescribable pleasure at this immoral situation of making the girl, who was as beautiful as an angel, put his finger into her mouth.

Just as Naoto was about to lose his marbles from the sensation that burned his brain...

...He heard the sound of an immeasurable amount of gears turning in unison from within RyuZU.

"Ngh—ahh..."

It seemed like that was the proof that the confirmation was complete. RyuZU discreetly separated her mouth from Naoto's finger.

With his mind burned white, Naoto felt RyuZU's cheek with the

palm of his emancipated hand. What pushed back against his hand felt warm and soft.

With glistening eyes, RyuZU nestled her cheek against his hand as she sighed passionately before swearing, "The First of the Initial-Y Series—RyuZU, Your Slave, swears to accompany Master Naoto, devoting absolute submission and loyalty to him as his servant until the very moment her gears break down and cease to turn."

RyuZU had put into words a proclamation that, far from just a simple Master Confirmation, carried sacredness akin to that of a wedding vow.

•••●•••

"Wai—I'm already... Eeek, eeek..."

Beneath the invigorating morning sun piercing through a clear, dazzling-blue sky...

Naoto clung onto the guardrails of Kamo-oohashi Bridge as he gasped excruciatingly, his breath in complete disorder.

"I, I can't... Miss, RyuZU, I really can't... Help me."

"Master Naoto, to breathe so hard from such trivial exercise, I am surprised that you have been able to survive up to now, with that feeble body of yours."

"...After such a thing happened yesterday, *hahh,* without nearly any sleep or a proper meal, *eek...!* Making me...run to school... To call me feeble...well said..."

"I am honored to receive your compliment." RyuZU briskly turned aside Naoto's sarcasm born from his desperation.

About an hour away on foot from where Naoto's apartment

was, if one traced the Kamogawa River upstream, there was a school building in the back of the "Kamogawa Delta," the confluence of the Takanogawa and Kamogawa Rivers.

That was Tadasunomori High School, the public school Naoto attended, run by the local ward.

"Though I may look like this, I'm actually a recipient of the perfect attendance award, you know." When Naoto told RyuZU that, he ended up being forced to run, practically being dragged all the way there.

However, looking at his watch, it was still only 7:12—There was still plenty of time before class started.

His eyes becoming teary in light of this fact, Naoto addressed RyuZU. "To begin with, I literally lost my home, you know... Shouldn't I be more concerned with things like where I'm going to sleep and how I'm going to eat today than going to school?"

"Master Naoto, please rest assured: Regarding that matter, I will make the proper arrangements while you are attending school. Whatever reason there may be, I would not have any face left to save if you were to fail to receive the perfect attendance award because of me."

Naoto looked up at RyuZU with an eye half-closed.

"What about the matter regarding your master dying from sleep deprivation and overwork as the result of that?"

"I would be unable to take responsibility for that, as that would be due to Master Naoto's infirmity and feebleness, a result born of your neglect of your own health that took place before I came to serve you."

"Yeah, well, that may be true, but..."

"Frankly, it would be none of my concern."

"That really is frank!" Her words, which were all too abusive, made

Naoto burst into laughter.

RyuZU couldn't help but spew venom every time she opened her mouth, but it wasn't really unpleasant. Naoto couldn't feel any malicious intent in her words.

In no way does this mean I've awakened to a new fetish, Naoto told himself.

"...Master Naoto?"

"Ahh, sorry, sorry. By the way, you said you'd make arrangements, but what exactly do you plan to do? I only have enough for this month's food expenses in my bank account..."

"I was not depending on your resourcefulness to begin with, so worry not. If it is simply provisional lodgings and living expenses, I can procure those on my own," RyuZU answered with an unconcerned look.

Naoto made a dissatisfied-looking face at those words. "By that, do you mean that you're going to get a part-time job, RyuZU? I don't know about that..."

"You say the strangest things, Master Naoto. Please use common sense. Money is not something one gains by working."

"...That's the first time I've ever heard of such an outlandish common sense."

"In the first place, I belong to Master Naoto. Even if only temporarily, for me to be used by some bastard scum who knows not even his own father would be both logically and physically impossible."

"..."

...Could this be a so-called "*tsundere*"?

Catching himself inadvertently slackening his mouth, Naoto returned to the topic at hand in a fluster.

"In the end, what do you plan to do then...?"

"Master Naoto, please stop worrying about every conceivable piece of trivia. Even if you are hopelessly ruined in the moment, those who are elite should always maintain composure."

"I don't remember becoming anything like an elite... But well, fine." Naoto sighed before continuing, "Well, it's true that the three hours it took me to repair you yesterday used up all of my willpower and stamina and left me completely exhausted... If you're willing to take care of things for me, that couldn't be more welco—hey, is something wrong?"

Naoto lifted his face upward, upon which he saw RyuZU making a stiff face with her eyes wide open.

She spent a full five seconds like that, after which she said, "... Excuse me. Just a moment ago, I checked over twenty million times whether I had misheard Master Naoto's words."

"Uh, did I say something strange?"

"You said that you repaired me in three hours."

"Yeah, I did. What about it?"

"...May I ask you a question?"

"Oh, sure. Ask me anything," Naoto answered with a smile.

With an elegant gesture, RyuZU placed one hand on her chest. "Question: How many gears am I composed of altogether?"

"Ummm... 4,207,600,008,643 gears, I think?"

"...Please state the regular frequency marked by my main cylinder."

"That's the biggest one in your spine, right? If so, 6,254,941,395 hertz."

"...How many artificial nerve pathways are linked to my spring?"

"Of the ones directly linked, 15,045,549,846 pathways. Including the ones linked by resonance, 62,945,634,574,578 pathways in total."

"...Master Naoto. To confirm, have you seen my blueprint?"

"No? I mean, something like that exists?"

"It does not. It should not. That is why I am inquiring. Why does Master Naoto know my makeup down to such fine details?"

"Why, you ask?"

"With an instrument of measurement an individual could own—no, even with the measurement machine of a specialized institution, a feat like analyzing my full makeup in three hours should be impossible. As such, I can only conclude that you knew my blueprint beforehand."

His expression blank, Naoto tilted his head at RyuZU, who was pressing him for an answer.

"I mean, the actual article was right in front of me, you know? Even if I don't examine you with a machine, if I just listen to the sounds, that much is immediately obvious. Isn't that common sense?"

RyuZU stared at Naoto with eyes filled to the brim with suspicion. "Now *that* is the first time *I* have *ever* heard of such an outlandish common sense—the sounds, you say?"

"Well, I suppose it's something like a unique little trick of mine? My ears have always been sharper than others'. If it's just the makeup of a machine, I can tell that much by listening carefully, even if I'm not looking directly at it."

"Does that apply to me as well?"

"Yes, if I listen to the sounds. Your body is very pretty, RyuZU. Everything is in harmony, without even so much as a single fingertip's worth of superfluous elements. So to that same extent, it was readily apparent where the malfunction lay. There was a noise mixed in with all the pleasant sounds, so I lost my cool and just started repairing you without thinking. I'm not sorry for what I did."

"........."

"Hmm? Is something wrong, RyuZU?"

"Master Naoto."

"Yeah?"

"Master Naoto, you are a pervert."

"Yeah. ...Huh? What does that have to do with what we were just talking about?" Looking puzzled, Naoto raised himself up. "Now then, I guess I'll get going."

While Naoto and RyuZU were resting, more and more students in the vicinity could be seen on their way to school. As the students crossed the bridge, their gazes surrounded the two of them as they exchanged whispers from a distance.

RyuZU watched the students' behavior, puzzled. "...Strangely, it seems we are gathering a lot of attention. What could be the reason for this?"

"Ah, well, that's understandable. It's because someone like me is with you, isn't it?"

RyuZU nodded as if satisfactorily convinced of Naoto's answer. "It is a self-evident truth that the peasants' envy, base to the point of making one nauseous, would gather upon me, who possesses beauty akin to that of an angel that has descended down from the heavens. What a foolish question that was; do excuse me."

"Yeah. You're not wrong, but in this case, I'm also present."

"In other words, Master Naoto, the one who stands at the peak of the inferior lifeforms known as humanity, and I, the most prized treasure of the realm above the clouds—being together doubles the awesomeness those peasants behold, right?"

"That's totally wrong. What those glances mean is, 'Why is that unremarkable bastard together with such a transcendentally cute girl?'"

"Master Naoto. While it is true that you are so lowly that I cannot bear to even look at you, there is no just reason for you to be disparaged by base humans that are beneath even the level of worms crawling on the ground."

"Even I'm gonna cry soon, you know."

While almost breaking down on the spot, Naoto shook his head. "Well, it's whatever. I'm merely reaping what I've sown. Besides, this is nothing unusual for me."

However, RyuZU shook her head in restrained anger. "No, this is not fine."

"Why?"

"Because it is absolutely baffling. I cannot comprehend the basis on which this group of people can define you as someone to be despised."

Naoto raised his eyebrows, as if perplexed. "Rather, let me ask you instead. On just what basis are you rating me so highly, RyuZU?"

"The only one in all of humanity who could repair me while I was broken was you, Master Naoto."

"But that's only your perspective, right, RyuZU? Most people won't think that."

"Is that not because those people are a useless bunch beyond feeble-mindedness and cannot comprehend even that much?"

"But society is made up of them, RyuZU. And those who no one understands are the same as nonexistent—that's the rule of this society."

...After a long pause, RyuZU opened her mouth reluctantly.

"While admitting to being refuted by Master Naoto is exceedingly disagreeable, I will admit that you have a point."

"I see that you get it now. Are we all good, then?"

Naoto stood up and was about to get going when RyuZU seemed to think of something and stopped him.

"I apologize. May I ask just one more thing?"

"Mm, what?"

She asked, as if trying to sound something out, "I have heard that the creatures known as humans exhibit a mysterious acquired trait in which they classify being favored by an unspecified large number of the opposite sex as having high social status."

"I'd like to hear in detail where you caught wind of such a thing, but yeah. What of it?"

"Is that an easily understandable 'good point' that raises the reputation for a member of the group of people that Master Naoto belongs to?"

"Huh? I don't see where you're going with this..." Naoto said as he tilted his head. "Well, of course popular people are automatically highly rated. After all, that basically means that they have allies."

"Understood."

"I don't really get what you're saying, but I'm gonna get going now, okay?"

"Yes. Well then, Master Naoto, I shall see you again in a bit."

While finding RyuZU's gaze curious as she saw him off, Naoto headed towards the school building.

Passing through the side entrance shoe lockers without stopping, Naoto headed to the foyer behind the main entrance. His own slippers had been stolen long ago, so he borrowed a pair of guest slippers instead. Then, he hurried to the classroom as his slippers made sticky sounds.

The hallway near his homeroom was filled with noise and activity; however, no one greeted Naoto upon seeing him. The only thing different was that in place of the usual snickers, whispers were being exchanged instead.

Entering the classroom, Naoto placed his satchel on top of his desk and sat down. It was covered in graffiti that he'd even become somewhat attached to, at this point. Spending the rest of the time until homeroom pretending to be asleep was Naoto's go-to plan.

Covering the desk with his face on top of his arms, RyuZU's words inadvertently ran through his mind.

"Reputation, huh...?"

To be honest, he wasn't interested after all.

The eccentricities of a talented person might be passed off as a fly in the ointment, but a useless oddball would only be treated as a black sheep.

Furthermore, Naoto had no intention of concealing anything, whether it be his uselessness or his abnormalness.

That's why the current situation was just him reaping what he had sown. It was annoying, but there was nothing he could do.

As he lay face-down on the table thinking about such things, he genuinely became sleepy.

...Well, so many things happened after all. Can't be helped, can't be helped...

Usually he would get up when his homeroom teacher came, but Naoto decided that he would just go to sleep like this for today.

And so, he fell into a deep sleep.

•••●•••

"Nghh...?"

Naoto woke up from the unusual commotion in the classroom.

Suspecting that it had become lunchtime already, Naoto looked at the clock, but the time was only 10:46.

It was still only just time for third period to begin. He had only slept for about two hours.

Naoto lifted his head, wondering just what the commotion was all about, at which time he heard:

"Ah... I know this is sudden, but I'll be introducing a transfer student to our class."

Upon the classroom podium stood the teacher in charge of third period's lecture, and a single girl.

She was a beautiful girl, so much so that it looked like she were sparkling. She captivated the eyes of those who beheld her just by standing there. Her pure-silver hair swayed sleekly, and she had pale, almost transparent skin. Her lips were a light, peachy pink color, her cheeks radiated rosiness, and her eyes were glittering gold, like a crown.

The students in the class were left flabbergasted in unison at such beautiful features; they were hardly believable for a human.

"...Whatcha doin'?"

Naoto inadvertently spoke out in his local dialect.

Perhaps the girl at the podium heard him, for she took a step forward and waved at Naoto gently.

The gazes in the classroom that had been thoroughly taken by the otherworldly beauty refocused all at once onto the unremarkable loner in the class.

"My humble name is RyuZU Your Slave. Though I will be studying with everyone starting today, I do not have any interest in getting to know all you honorably banal and base people, so I shall be just fine without your care, thank you."

The sight of the silver-haired girl bowing as she smiled like a blooming flower caused Naoto's face to fall onto his desk once again.

• • ● ● ● • •

"I judge that with this, a 'good point' that the masses can readily understand has been created."

"Uh-huh... Well, yeah. You're right. It's just that, there's an expression in this world that having too much is just as bad as having too little, you know?"

Naoto pointed that out as the piercing gazes from those around him made him draw his shoulders inward.

Jealousy, hatred, disgust, enmity... If those gazes had physical power, Naoto would surely have been killed several times over by now.

"If my companion is a beauty like you, now they'll be like 'Why is a bastard like him...'"

"...To state my impressions frankly, I have come to feel that it is easier by far to teach a cow how to walk on two legs than to expect rationality from humans."

"Well, I won't deny that."

From third period onwards, the rest of the day was like a storm for Naoto.

RyuZU, who had forcibly snatched a seat next to Naoto, stuck to him tightly for the whole lesson. When it came time for lunch, she sat down on Naoto's lap and fed him his lunch, urging him to open his mouth now and then by saying "Ahhh" in a monotonous tone. Afterwards, she took him to the courtyard and sat down on the grass, then grasped Naoto's head and coercively laid it above her knees.

Naoto wasn't one to mind the public eye (if he had been, he could never have proclaimed his abnormality), but neither was he cheeky enough to be able to enjoy RyuZU's lap pillow while feeling the immense pressure from others who would love nothing more than to tear him limb from limb.

Probably because they flirted so incredibly brazenly and overbearingly, their classmates only looked on from afar, not conducting the typical question time for transfer students until school ended, when a few fearless souls finally stepped up to the plate.

However…

"Uh, umm, could I have a bit of your time?"

"Yes? Do you have some business with me?"

"Ah, r-right. Well I'm sure that as a transfer student, there's a lot—"

"I see. However, I do not have any particular business with you, so I shall be excusing myself."

"—of things you don't know yet, so—er, huh?"

…

"Hey, heyy heyy! You're so pretty, RyuZU-chan."

"Yes. I am aware of that. What of it?"

"Aware?… Uh, errr. RyuZU-chan, you're kinda—"

"Could I have you not call me by name with that honorable brain of yours, from which I cannot perceive even a glimpse of intelligence? Furthermore, to append the –chan suffix to my name…! Come again after you have discerned your own place. Actually, you need not bother. After all, it would just be a waste of time."

......

"Ah—I'm a second year. My name is—"

"You must really detest me, to wear a face like that, which could spoil my mood all the way from a floor above. However, I am sorry to say that I lack the faculty required to hold an interest in ants, so I request that you kindly take your leave."

"Er, huh, no umm—I'm actually quite pop—"

"Sir, I told you to disappear. Or—is it that human language is too difficult for you?"

....

"Ah—"

"Before you speak the words in your mouth, please first carefully consider whether it is worth wasting the Earth's oxygen, the many lives that were sacrificed to provide you with the calories you would expend, and above all, my precious time—if so, then please, do continue."

....

Heaps of corpses lay everywhere.

When she talked to Naoto, she had the smile of an angel; but, when she addressed others, she skewered them through. Her verbal abuse was that of a demon, with a frozen expression and a merciless tone of voice.

As a result, during the time that Naoto and RyuZU walked from the classroom to the school gates, boys and girls numbering in the double-digits ended up suffering deep wounds.

•••●•••

Exiting through the school gates, Naoto and RyuZU walked along Kamogawa River.

While passing by an old man doing his best at running and a college student practicing her instrument, the two of them walked from Demachiyanagi towards Shijou Street.

"Master Naoto, you seem to be awfully tired," said RyuZU, looking back at Naoto, whose footsteps were heavy.

"Right, well... That would be thanks to you. Today's situation must be what the phrase 'bed of nails' is used to describe."

"To mind the gazes of the riff-raff to such an extent, Master Naoto really is a coward—not that this is particularly surprising, or anything."

"Please stop, I think I'm going to discover a new horizon anytime now."

After wriggling his body in seeming agony for a while, Naoto continued.

"By the way, I have a question. How did you transfer to my school, RyuZU?"

"I submitted a notification of transfer, of course," answered RyuZU, looking calm and composed.

"I mean, even if you give me such a reflexive answer... Can you really start attending on the same day that you submit your notification?"

"I simply had a little 'talk' with the principal."

"...'Talk'?"

"It is something that Master Naoto need not know about."

"No, wait. I'm starting to feel really anxious, now."

"It really was not anything worth mentioning. I simply made a tiny amount of small talk regarding the hair-shaped accessory on top of the principal's head."

"You threatened him! You do know that that's a threat, right?!"

"But it wasn't really a threat? I simply made a trivial request after the small talk."

"...Umm, Miss RyuZU? I believe you said that you'd handle our housing and money, but you weren't planning to do it through crime... right?"

"Master Naoto."

RyuZU looked at Naoto with a smile that seemed like it would make those who beheld it fall in love.

"'Crime only becomes crime if it comes to light.' This is timeless common knowledge, you know."

"...Allll right, I heard nothing just now. More importantly, you said that you found a place for us to sleep tonight, but where did you decide on, in the end?"

"You can see it already. It's the hotel behind that high-rise building called 'The Oh, Yes.'"

"...Miss RyuZU?" Naoto froze to a standstill right on the spot. "If my memory isn't failing me, wasn't that a love hotel?"

At Naoto's question, RyuZU widened her eyes.

"It is just as you say. Honestly, it surprises me that you know it, Master Naoto. Could you have stayed there before?"

"You know that that's not possible. I simply knew that the normies in my class go there often—hey, who cares about that! Like we can stay in a love hotel—what are you thinking?!"

"However, that love hotel, 'The Oh, Yes,' is the cheapest accommodation in Kyoto Grid right now, not to mention it has full amenities."

"That's not the problem! In the first place, if we were to be seen leaving a love hotel together, we'd be expelled instantly, you know?!"

"...I remain unconvinced. In that case, please let me hear Master Naoto's great alternative plan." Offended, RyuZU slightly puckered her face up as she spilled out her sarcastic words. In response, Naoto thought as fast as he could, before concluding,

"...F-for now, let's stay at a manga café tonight!"

Naoto took RyuZU's hand and began walking.

Perhaps they had wasted too much time by the love hotel, for the crowd of people walking through the shopping district grew as the surroundings slowly darkened.

By the time they finally found a manga café lying around the corner, the sun had completely set.

"Well, I guess this is fine. If we wait a little longer now, we can stay for cheap tonight with the overnight deal." Naoto spoke as he turned around, upon which his expression immediately turned severe.

Before he realized it, three men had surrounded RyuZU from both sides.

They were about the age of college students. Each and every one of them had a dirty face, slovenly clothes, and was jingling glittery bling with their hands.

Of the three of them, Punk A accosted RyuZU in an obnoxiously familiar tone.

"Hey hey heyy! You're a reaaal babe, aren'tcha?"

"Yes. What of it?"

"Ahahahaha, 'what of it,' she says! But she seriously is a fine jewel, isn't she!"

"Say, say. Won't you come play with us? We'll treat you to dinner, y'know?"

Naoto grasped the situation immediately.

Lured by the ultimate prize that was RyuZU, Punks A, B, and C had gathered around her. They were a type that Naoto would normally have no point of interaction with. They normally wouldn't even register in each other's field of vision, after all. If he somehow did end up getting involved with them, he could get by by laughing sycophantically like a fool, but—

"..."

Naoto's entire body flared red-hot.

Abiding by his impulse, he grabbed RyuZU's hand.

"RyuZU, we're going."

"Yes."

RyuZU nodded and tried to leave with Naoto, but the group of three men didn't permit that.

They quickly routed in front of them, blocking their path.

"Hey now, little boy... What's thiiis about, all of a sudden?"

"This girl is about to go on a date with us, y'know? Kids should get the hell outta here."

Punks A and B threatened Naoto as they displayed smirks bordering on the obscene.

The remaining Punk C looked Naoto up and down with bloodshot eyes.

"Who're you supposed to be anyway? Don't tell me you're her boyfriend—?"

"Nice joke, Taku-chan! I'm telling you, no man, there's no way!"

As the three of them exploded in laughter together, the one who first accosted RyuZU, Punk A, reached his hand towards her.

As soon as Naoto noticed that, he immediately struck the punk's hand down with all his might.

"That hurt... What's with this kid, eh?"

The smirks disappeared from their faces, replaced by the signs of swelling fury.

Even so, Naoto continued to yell at them, driven by his own fury.

"Shut up, already—She's not someone that's okay for a sorry lot like you to touch. Can't you even tell that much, you self-proclaimed homo sapiens?! Keep your shamelessness limited to your ugly faces, you walking garbage!"

Uh, what the hell am I saying? warned the relatively calm portion of his brain.

Even though his opponents were punks that didn't look too fit, they were still a group of three young men, whereas he was only a sixteen-year-old boy, and a small and frail one, at that.

If it came down to a fistfight, no matter how much he struggled, there would be no future for him but to become a punching bag.

Even though they might have been able to escape peacefully if he had conducted himself more wisely—for some reason, Naoto's heart harbored no regret.

If he had had the chance to start over, he definitely would have done the same thi—no, he would have thrown in a kick as well, next time.

That's right. If they're gonna make a move on RyuZU, I'll protect her at any cost.

The three punks, whose faces grew even uglier as they were distorted by fury, came grappling towards Naoto.

Naoto glared at the three of them as he pressed his lips tightly together.

Immediately after, he heard a refreshingly cool voice.

"Thank you. Allow me to revise my perception of you up a notch, Master Naoto."

"Whah?" Naoto asked back spontaneously.

Right after that, RyuZU's skirt began to flutter slightly.

That was as much as Naoto could tell with his eyes, at least.

However, wind and sound, along with—something else—flew past the three punks, as if brushing by. A strange sound of things unfolding rang out.

Everything, from the punks' shirts, pants, accessories, to their shoes, underwear, and hair, was torn asunder, falling down while fluttering in the air.

"I apologize."

RyuZU pinched the hem of her skirt and made a curtsy to the punks who had sunk to the floor, naked.

"I was already in a bad mood as things were, from the attitude the riff-raff at school displayed towards Master Naoto, so when you all pushed me over the edge, I inadvertently ended up doing *this,* in a flare of anger. I do not particularly regret anything, either."

"Ah, ahhh, holy..."

"On another note, I offer my gratitude to all of you, as I am truly glad that you stopped before striking Master Naoto. No matter how much of a pervert you are, even you would feel queasy seeing a freshly severed head, right, Master Naoto?"

RyuZU revealed a thin smile.

However, the temperature of her gaze was absolute zero, as if she were looking at flies swarming rotting flesh.

Even the dumbest blockhead on the block would surely know what her gaze was implying.

The three naked punks scrambled off like stray dogs. Their screams caused a commotion, and the angry roar of what was probably a policeman could be heard from afar.

"...L-Let's enter the manga café already. It's too dangerous for you to walk around at night, RyuZU!"

Naoto pushed RyuZU's back, entering the store hastily.

This manga café was one that Naoto knew well.

The store was wide and bright inside, and every nook and corner of it was thoroughly cleaned. None of its facilities were damaged either, and the refreshment bar had many choices for drinks.

RyuZU stopped and surveyed the interior of the store. "...It is so-so, I guess." She pouted, looking unsatisfied. "However, I believe that 'The Oh, Yes' is a better place to stay in after all. Do you prefer a narrow and suffocating room over a broad and comfortable one, Master Naoto?"

"Yeah, whatever, let's just say I do. Okay?"

As the two of them approached the counter, a young male employee came out from the back. He opened his mouth blankly for a moment upon seeing RyuZU, but he immediately pulled himself back together and managed a smile.

"W-welcome. Do you have a membership card?"

"I want the overnight deal," said Naoto, presenting his card.

"If you start now, you'll be charged the standard rate for one hour. Is that fine?"

"Yes. I'm fine with that, at this point."

"Thank you. What seat would you like?"

Naoto hesitated.

He fretted over the map of the store's interior that the employee presented. Cafeteria seat, box seat, business seat, reclining seat... There were many kinds of different seats, but as far as ones that were suitable for two people to stay in...

As Naoto wavered, RyuZU stepped forward from the side.

"We'll take a couple's seat."

"Eh...?"

"Certainly. Your seat will be box number four."

Ignoring Naoto, who was stiffening up, RyuZU promptly finished the process, taking the receipt and Naoto's membership card back from the employee.

"Wha, RyuZU?! A couple's seat?"

"Was that not your intention? Rather than a wide bedroom, you would prefer to glue yourself to me in a confined seat. Are you impressed that my keen eyes were able to grasp your perverse desire?"

"No, that's not it! I didn't even think of that!"

"If I think about it that way, then there would be a rational explanation for why you obstinately rejected the love hotel, but..."

"That's because I'm underage!"

"Please rest assured, Master Naoto. No matter what kind of peculiar lusts you harbor in your chest that would be condemned by society, I intend to accept them in full."

"I'm saying—no, never mind. If I think about it, it's safer this way."

"True. It seems that the public order is not excellent around here after all. As long as I am here, there is no problem at all, but it is still important to avoid unnecessary danger."

"Right, yeah... Danger–not for us, but for those who would harass us," Naoto muttered in a small voice.

If by any chance, an idiot shows up and makes a pass at RyuZU, a murder might end up happening in the store...!

Upon entering the designated cubicle, Naoto collapsed onto the two-person sofa, completely exhausted.

"...Today was long, too long..."

Fatigue that felt as heavy as lead weighed down on his entire body.

He wanted to sleep like a log, just like this, but he couldn't. Naoto sighed deeply, straining his body as he stood up sluggishly.

"Master Naoto, where are you going?"

"I'm going to borrow the shower here. I sweat a bunch in the morning, after all, so it'd feel gross to sleep like this."

"I see. Understood."

Passing by RyuZU, who bowed lightly at him, Naoto walked towards the shower area.

However, after advancing for a short while, he stopped and turned around.

"Say, why are you following me?" asked Naoto. RyuZU made a puzzled face, her eyes slightly widened.

"...? Was that not an order for me to wash your back?"

"I didn't say anything like that at all!"

"Yes. However, Master Naoto, you do not appear comfortable being candid with your desires, so I tried to make a read on the true intentions hidden behind your remarks."

"Don't bother!"

"...Really? Are you sure? You mean to say that you do not wish for a special act of servitude involving body lotion and sponges after we have both stripped in a narrow, locked room?"

"............"

"Master Naoto?"

"...No, I'm fine. I'll be showering by myself."

"Is that so. In that case, I shall return to our seat and wait for you."

"...Yeah. See you later, then."

RyuZU returned to their seat after bowing once.

After her figure had fully disappeared, Naoto spontaneously collapsed onto his knees.

Sniff. Naoto wiped the tears that had formed at the corners of his eyes, muttering,

"...Seriously, what the hell am I doing..."

"Whoa! What's this?"

When Naoto returned, refreshed from his shower, the couple's seat had become buried in magazines and manga of various genres. RyuZU was reading them at a startling pace as she sat modestly on the far side of the sofa.

She stopped her hand temporarily and faced him.

"Welcome back, Master Naoto."

"Ah, yeah, I'm back... What's up with all this?"

"I am gathering intelligence; these are a part of that. I have been asleep for as long as 206 years, so I thought I should fill in my knowledge of the modern world as much as possible."

"...This manga is a part of that too?"

"Mass entertainment is an important reference."

"I-Is that so… You do that, then; meanwhile, I'll be sleeping, because unsurprisingly, I'm pooped."

"I see. Please have a good night," said RyuZU, turning towards Naoto and sitting on her heels.

As he sat down beside her on the sofa, Naoto asked, "What about you, RyuZU? I guess automata don't sleep. What about your spring?"

"Do not worry, it is self-winding."

"Ahh, I see… Huh? The winding is completely automatic? For turning over four trillion gears?"

"Yes. What about it?"

Naoto took a breath, then nodded.

"Oh, nothing. Rather, it'd be weird if you couldn't do that much, huh."

Even a state-of-the-art automaton seems to need to have their spring wound about once a week, you know…

Naoto realized once again just how high-end RyuZU was.

Compared to the capabilities she's shown me up to now, I guess having a self-winding spring isn't anything special at this point… Naoto convinced himself like so as he made his arms into a pillow for his head before closing his eyes.

Immediately after, RyuZU whispered in a cold voice, "Could you be ignoring me?"

"Huh?"

Naoto reflexively opened his eyes, upon which he saw RyuZU's unsatisfied-looking face right next to his, making him swallow his breath.

"Are you ignoring my lap pillow?" RyuZU asked as she tapped her thighs. *Pat-pat.*

Naoto darted his eyes about before asking back, "...Can I?"

"You have already done so, both this morning and during lunch. Not to mention, Master Naoto is my master now. Would it somehow be inconvenient for you to do so?"

"No siree, not at all." Naoto replied immediately as he placed his head on RyuZU's lap.

As the soft, warm, almost melting sensation made him sigh, he wriggled in his seat slightly before closing his eyes and immediately beginning to drift off.

"Master Naoto."

"Yeah?"

"I watched you for the whole day today."

"Yeah."

"To be perfectly honest, Master Naoto is completely inexplicable."

"Is that so? Well, I guess I can't deny that."

"Yes. In addition, Master Naoto is self-deprecating to the extreme."

"You're right," Naoto groaned as if regretful. "Sorry... for being an uncool Master."

"It is important to be humble, yes... But even so—"

Naoto waited for her to continue, but—

"...No, it is nothing important. Good night."

"...Yeah."

He fell asleep immediately.

As RyuZU combed Naoto's hair gently with her hand, she let out a whisper, "...Master Naoto, what do you think of me?"

There was no answer. RyuZU didn't really wish for one, either. After observing him the entire day, she understood that Naoto wasn't interested in anything but machines.

In that case, the reason he had desired her, an automaton, was that she was an excellent machine. But if that was all there was to it, then why did he treat her like a human girl?

"Really, how incomprehensible."

RyuZU slipped out a chuckle as she cast her eyes downward. She thought back to the trouble they had gotten caught up in just a little while back.

Whether it had been because he saw her as his possession or as a girl remained unclear. But whatever the case, Naoto had tried to protect her.

...I am treasured.

She had been able to ascertain that fact—then, wasn't that enough?

Revealing a smile without even a hint of poison, RyuZU continued combing Naoto's hair.

It'd been twenty-six hours since the entire staff began analyzing the phenomenon together.

The work was proceeding smoothly.

Of the twenty-seven floors the core tower possessed, they'd already finished confirming the first two.

Unfortunately, they hadn't discovered a point of malfunction yet. Still, if they continued at this pace, they had estimated that it should be possible to verify all the floors within two weeks.

However, in spite of that—they couldn't genuinely rejoice.

"...The work is proceeding too smoothly."

Indeed—that was the biggest irregularity of all.

The reason why the work was proceeding smoothly—that was solely because there were no nuisances in the way.

Nuisances, or namely, the military.

Of course, as long as the treaty was in place, the military couldn't openly obstruct the Meister Guild. The most they could do is to offer "assistance" politely. While the Meister Guild expressed gratitude towards that offer, it gently declined, so as to be able to work smoothly. Nevertheless, the military took pride in maintaining the day-to-day municipal mechanisms and were surely displeased to have outsiders intruding and taking charge. There was also the issue of appearances in front of the city's residents.

As a result, the military was quick to cut in citing excuses like "preventing leakage of classified information" and "bearing responsibility"; the Meister Guild advanced its work as it evaded that interference.

From the military's perspective, the Meister Guild was a vulture who snatched away their work and the credit that went along with it.

From Meister Guild's perspective, the military was nothing more than a group of incompetents who were all talk.

That was something Marie and her staff were confronted with regularly; however—

"To think that I would only spot a few clocksmiths from the military's Technical Force the whole day today..."

She wasn't entirely indifferent.

After all, she had been offered "assistance" when she had arrived, and even now there was an auditor belonging to Technical Force silently monitoring them from the corner of the meeting room.

However, that was the extent of the military's presence.

After she had refused the first offer of assistance, the military had readily drawn back. The core tower, as the heart of the city, was usually crammed with over a thousand staff members, but those staff also accepted their dismissal from the case without a fuss.

If anything, for them to be understanding to this extent made Marie feel suspicious instead.

The impenetrable orders from the Meister Guild.

The sudden fluctuations in gravity before dawn.

The suspicious response from the military.

Even if they were small abnormalities, when lined up one-by-one, they made Marie envision the worst-case scenario.

"There's a chance that this really is the possibility I've considered."

"Dr. Marie..."

A young member of the staff addressed her in a small voice.

Sensing what he wanted to say from his expression, Marie nodded.

"I know. Don't worry, I've already prepared for that."

"Then, as expected, did they...?"

"I can't say anything for sure. However, I think I can find out soon enough."

Perhaps the staff member sensed an unsettling tinge to Marie's countenance, for he returned to his station after clearing his throat meekly.

"Now then."

Marie headed towards the elevator shaft with a leisurely stride.

The auditor from Technical Force followed after her without a word.

He probably served as the lead clocksmith here when things were normal. He had a broad chest as one would expect from a soldier, and next to his breast pocket was a badge proving that he was a Geselle.

While waiting for the elevator to come, Marie addressed the man.

"I'm just going out to breathe in some fresh air. Do you mind?"

"Do as you wish." The voice that answered was surly.

However, Marie showed no signs of caring. After awhile, the elevator arrived, and she entered it and pressed the button for the surface level.

Right now, Marie and her staff were working 8,200 meters below the city grid—the third floor of the core tower. Even this elevator, which moved at a speed of 1,000 meters per second, took eight minutes to travel one-way between the surface and the third floor.

For a while, Marie gazed at the depth meter above the elevator doors. But, eventually, she seemed unable to bear the silence any longer, and she turned around, saying, "That gun is a BR-19, isn't it?"

Marie spoke to the man in a bright voice. Her sight was turned towards the gun holstered on the man's waist. He didn't answer, simply maintaining his posture of standing at attention; however, without paying any mind to that, Marie continued, "That gun shoots a bullet not by the gears turning against each other, but by them turning in the same direction at high speed, thus compressing and subsequently releasing air—though its recoil is stronger than a conventional gun, one can use that recoil to amplify the compression of the next shot. In order to take advantage of that, its stopping power is also outstanding by necessity. Its loading capacity is typically seven bullets. I see that there are barbed wires surrounding the grip to prevent the gun from being seized. Its caliber is—my, a .45? If the priority is placed on sheer power though, wouldn't the BR-sp33, a short assault gun, be better?

The man made a half-exasperated face at Marie, who had fluently explained standardized military pistols.

"You seem to be quite informed, I see."

"Yes. They're guns manufactured by my father's corporation."

"Oh, that's right. You're the daughter of the president of the Breguet Corporation.

"Did you know? Those born into the Breguet family have the details of all the products designed and sold by the company drilled into them. We're talking about one of the Five Great Enterprises here—so the entire catalog ranges from cribs for babies to jumbo-sized transport planes. I think you can imagine what a task it would be to memorize all of it."

"That must have been very hard on you."

"Indeed, my childhood was full of drudgery."

"However, frankly speaking, I cannot understand what the point was in you learning all that. If you were an employee, it'd be another story, but was that kind of education really necessary for the family princess?" The man's voice had a scornful-sounding ring to it.

However, Marie smiled as if to say, *That's just how I feel as well.* "You think so too, do you?"

"Yes, I think it really was a waste of time. If you had the time to learn that kind of stuff, there were surely plenty of other things you should have learned instead."

"It's just as you say. Perhaps something like this, for example?"

"Hah? Gah—?!"

As soon as he opened his mouth, the man ended up laid out on the floor.

"Er, ergh, oooof...?!"

He couldn't understand what had happened.

Even though he was technically an engineer, as a part of the military he had received combat training as well. Even if he wasn't part of an infantry unit, he had trained enough to be able to deal with two or three punks easily.

Yet, to be knocked down in an instant without even being able to resist, have his weapon taken from him, be trampled on by a girl who was merely sixteen years old, and to top it all off, have a gun up against the back of his head—just *what* was going on?

"I told you, didn't I? That I've had the 'details' of all the products drilled into me. That includes the 'usage instructions,' you know? By the way, could I have you be quiet for the time being?"

"Y-y-you bitch, what is the meaning of t—oof?!"

Marie abused him in a vulgar tone. "Hey, I told you to be quiet, didn't I? *Damn dog.*"

It was an exceedingly relaxed tone of voice containing neither excitement nor nervousness. The man's will to resist was sucked out of him by those words and the sensation of the muzzle against the back of his head.

The elevator arrived at ground level.

The doors opened along with the sound of the gas turning off. Apparently, someone had been waiting in front of the elevator. That someone was a giant, bear-like man—Halter.

He looked inside the elevator, upon which he slapped his own, bald head with his hand in exasperation.

Sounding sympathetic, he addressed the man being trampled upon by Marie. "It's been a calamity for you too, hasn't it? Well, just consider yourself unlucky and—"

"Save your chit-chat and get in the elevator."

"Yeah, yeah. Well then, excuse me."

Halter got on and pressed the button to descend. The elevator dropped rapidly once again, then came to a manually forced halt after about ten seconds.

Inside that inescapable elevator, Halter tied up the man's hands and feet. The man struggled during the process, but there was no way he could oppose Halter, a cyborg, with his body of flesh. He was simply left restrained on the ground.

Stamping on the man's head, Marie spoke. "Now then, shall I have you bark out a few things?"

"Guh..."

The man struggled, wriggling about, but the foot on his head didn't sway one bit. Seeing him like that, the corners of Marie's mouth stretched upwards. "My, my, what's the matter? Is that supposed to be a form of resistance? Wriggling about like that, it's like you're enjoying this, you degenerate."

"Aren't *you* in a good mood, princess."

"I liked disciplining my dog when I was a kid. He was a large, cheeky one, but by the end he had become a cute doggy-woggy who whined if I pulled his chain, like this."

Marie pulled up on the man's necktie. Having both his head stomped on and his neck strangled, he let out a strained groan as he writhed in agony.

"By the way, Halter, did you bring the toy for me?"

"Yeah, just in case... Are you seriously going to use this?" Halter seemed reluctant as he took out a white syringe. The barrel was filled up with a mysterious silver liquid.

Upon seeing it, the man's face cramped up in terror.

"Wha... H-hey, what is that?! You're planning on injecting me with something?!"

"What, you ask? Truth serum, of course."

"Wha—"

"...It'd be great if that were the case, but unfortunately, I don't have that on hand. After all, we're civilians, remember?"

"As if you bastards could be considered civilians!" the man screeched.

It was a heartfelt assertion that anyone would have agreed with; nonetheless, Marie paid him no mind as she grinned happily, continuing on, "Actually, it's mercury."

"Mer...Mercury?!" The man gasped as his eyes stretched as wide open as could be.

"Yes. The substance used in automata maintenance."

"Y-you bastard, are you insane?! If you inject something like that into me, I'll—"

"Well, I think you'd die, right?" Marie laughed smugly. "So what? It's not a big deal, right?"

"......"

The man's face had turned pallid. His mouth was stiff, and tears welled up in his eyes. His arms and legs trembled all over, his entire body drenched in cold sweat.

"Now then, shall we set the rules? I'm the master, and you're the dog. Obediently answer everything you're asked with a 'woof-woof.' What do you think? Simple, right?"

"Y-you bastards, don't think you'll get away scot-free from t—

ghhff!!"

Marie stamped down on his face forcefully, then said, "Hey, it's 'woof,' right? Why can't you understand such a simple thing? Could it be that you're making light of me?"

"Y-you brat... Gah!"

"Do you want me to stamp on that pathetic brain of yours until everything spills out? You think a measly, half-baked clocksmith like you can defy me? Hey: Know your place, you worthless dog."

"Now, now, princess. You're going too fast right out the gate." Halter interjected, in a seemingly chiding tone.

Seeming to sympathize a great deal with the man whose face was a sloppy mess from tears and a bloody nose, Halter addressed him with a gentle voice. "Say, buddy. The princess has gotta be enjoying herself a great deal, but I genuinely just want to ask a couple questions. If you just answer me honestly, I'll release you. I promise."

"Guh...ugh..."

"I have two things I want to ask, okay? The first is 'Where is the point of malfunction?' The other is 'How much does the military have a grasp on?' Will you do me the favor of an honest answer?"

"N... no. I can't." The man looked frightened, shaking his head as he looked into Halter's eyes.

"C'mon, buddy. Don't make it too troublesome for me, 'kay?"

"If I tell you, I'll be killed!"

"Then, do you plan to play along with the princess's fetish until you die?" Halter asked as he jerked his chin towards Marie. She brandished the syringe in delight.

"Let me warn you ahead of time: the princess is the real deal, you know? She's an extreme sadist. She's a socialite who was born in France, so she seriously thinks of common men as nothing but livestock."

"I-I can't."

"Hey, buddy."

"If I told you bastards, even my family, who escaped the city, would be killed by the military—!!" The man howled as he sobbed. "Damn you, you brats! If you want to kill me, go ahead! I'm not going to say anything, got it?!"

"Hey now, calm down buddy—or should I say, Mr. Ryoji Nijima."

"Wha..." Suddenly being called by his name, the man was startled. "How do you know my name?" he squeezed out as he trembled, upon which Halter smirked and showed something to him.

A small white plastic plate.

It was an ID card.

"?!"

"Wasn't it a mistake to mention that they had escaped from the city? Residents of this city who are currently away from home and named 'Nijima-something...' I could figure out who they are in just fifteen minutes, you know?"

"Halter, we're done with this man, so dispose of him. We're moving on to the next target. Ah, and don't forget to have his family die, *in an 'accident*,'" Marie ordered in a pompous tone.

Halter shrugged his shoulders and thrust the muzzle of his gun against the man's temple.

"Well, that's how it is—sorry."

"Wait! Wait up!! I get it, I'll talk! I'll tell you anything you want to know!"

"You'll *what?*"

"Please let me answer your questions. I beg of you... gh!"

"Very well."

Looking down on the cowering, hyperventilating man, Marie said, "Then, first question: Where is the point of malfunction?"

"Th-...The twenty-fourth floor."

"The twenty-fourth floor... It's awfully deep down. If I recall correctly, that floor has systems for controlling atmospheric pressure and gravity, yes?"

"Th-that's right... the fatal malfunction lies in the nucleus of the atmospheric pressure control system..."

"Good. You've become awfully obedient, haven't you. So, how much does the military have a grasp on?"

"Th-that's..."

"That ain't even worth asking, princess," Halter interjected. "They have a grasp on *everything,* and fully understand the situation. They've abandoned repairing the mechanism. Despite knowing where the point of malfunction lies, they aren't forwarding us that information. That's also why they've taken all their repair staff off the case, right?"

The man remained silent, not answering.

And that silence was the most convincing answer of all.

"Hmm... I see. So in other words, our job is to save this city of twenty million residents that the military has abandoned repairs on," Marie concluded, while nodding.

But the man sneered at her as if he had grown unhinged. "Hah—hahahahahah! If you think you can fix it, then try all you want."

"My, how cheeky. If I treat you with just a little kindness, you *immediately* go overboard. How hopeless. Could it be that you lack the ability to learn, you mongrel?"

"Hah—hahahahahaha!! Like you bastards could repair it!"

"Could you not treat my top-notch staff like they're the same as you imbeciles?"

"Heh... I don't know just what kind of distinguished masters you bastards are, but it's already way past the time you would need to fix it!"

"...What do you mean by that?"

"I mean just that! This city will be 'purged' in just forty-two hours!

Purge.

It was an intentionally executed process—the collapse of a city.

Detaching a city that had had an irreparable malfunction occur before it affected the entire planet's mechanisms—an act of "quarantine," so to speak.

"Don't fabricate such a grandiose lie. There's no way an evacuation advisory wouldn't have been announced already if there's going to be a purge in forty-two hours."

"It was announced...to the military and government officials, long ago."

"..."

Halter grabbed the jeering man by his collar and shouted in his face. "You guys! Do you plan to simply watch the twenty million residents of this city die?!"

"Hah... Acting like you're any better! Are you bastards even conscious of the fact that there's been several cities purged after you guys failed to repair their mechanisms?! Do you bastards not realize that in the end, even the technical skills you boast of were polished by killing people like that?!"

"Shut that filthy mouth of yours, you low-life." Marie glared at the man.

Marie rushed back to the worksite on the third floor, and upon arriving, she shouted out without even stopping for a breath. "Everyone, stop what you're doing and listen up, please!"

The staff looked up from their various tasks, wondering what was going on.

As Marie looked over each of their faces one by one, she declared, "The abnormal area has been identified! There's a malfunction in the atmospheric pressure controls on the twenty-fourth floor!! All staff members are to immediately begin transferring there! Once you arrive, please begin examining the part of the mechanism that you're assigned by your squad leader!"

Though all of the staff's eyes widened slightly, they began to evacuate the floor right away. In the corner of the room that had stirred all at once into a commotion, members from Technical Force goggled at the sight, as if to ask, "Why?"

Before Marie had realized it, Konrad, the service chief, was standing beside her. He told Marie, "You truly are an astonishing person, Dr. Marie. How did you do it?"

"I simply requested the information from them sincerely, with all my heart."

"Hmm, I see—you did something rash."

Chief Konrad smiled bitterly, as if to chide her, but Marie paid his expression no mind.

"More importantly, please hurry—the time limit is forty-two hours."

The observation squad let out a cry to those words. "No way! If there's only forty-two hours left, there's nothing we can do!"

"Even if the abnormal area has been identified, finding the exact point of malfunction and testing possible restoration methods would require one week!"

"Then are you going to tuck your tails between your legs and run?" A green flame blazed in Marie's eyes as she glared at them. "The military has abandoned repairs on the mechanism. It's already been decided that this city will be purged. They plan to just let the residents, who know nothing, die."

"Wha...!"

"That can't be! Are you sure that's not some kind of mista—"

"No, if we're talking about them, then anything's possible! That's the military for you!"

Marie's rage immediately spread throughout the attending staff. Being flooded with gazes of contempt and censure from dozens of people, the members of Technical Force could be seen making off in haste.

Marie clapped both hands together and yelled out, "If it comes down to it, I'll bear the responsibility for the unavoidable evacuation advisory. At any rate, for now, please start moving. From here on out, we can't waste a single second!"

After that, the staff began to move like a squall. Both the large amount of equipment and the documents scattered all around were tidied up in just five minutes.

After the last group of staff had left, Marie turned her head to survey the hall, and sighed forcefully. She leaned her back against the wall and slowly slid down until she hit the floor, then hugged her knees and laid her forehead on them.

Her hand was shaking.

She still felt the sensation of piercing the man with the syringe.

The feeling of the gun in her hand, the tenderness of the human body she had trampled, the man's spiteful vitriol, all of them still remained.

I thought I could do it. If I ordered Halter to, he probably would have done it for me. After all, that used to be his profession. Yet, I didn't do so. I thought that if it were my older sister, she would do it herself, since she probably wouldn't hesitate. So, if it had to be done, I thought that I should at least do it with my own hands and by my own will.

That was her intention when she began the "interrogation," but—

By the latter half, she had grown wanton.

Stabbing the man with the syringe was despicable of her. There had been no reason to do it. It was simply to dispel her frustration. It was nothing but an emotional outburst of violence. It was indignation towards someone who had abandoned his duty and responsibility of rescuing twenty million people.

And also...

"Repair it in forty-two hours? That's *impossible*... How many tens of trillions of parts do you think there are?!"

It was indignation towards herself, for wanting to run away in the same way, rather than bear that same duty and responsibility.

Her lips trembled.

"Oh, God..."

Marie didn't believe in God. At least, she had never believed in any gods named by man. Marie had come this far by putting her faith in human reasoning and intelligence.

Even so. Revelations had descended upon her before—Marie knew of times when she had racked her brain in crucial moments, and the gears in her suddenly and subtly clicked. She believed that beyond a sharpened mind and logic lay an existence unfathomable to humanity.

Marie lifted her face up slowly, after which she stood up.

"I've gotta go... Right now, I can't waste even a single second."

After all, divine favor is only bestowed after one has exerted oneself to the fullest.

Wiping away whatever it was that had formed at the corners of her eyes, Marie began heading towards the twenty-fourth floor.

● Chapter Three / 11 : 45 / Conflict

"Why did things turn out this way..."

The time: lunchtime on a weekend. The place: a burger shop on Shijou Street.

RyuZU asked Naoto, who was lying face-down on the table and looking totally worn out, "Master Naoto, are you aware of the phrase 'fine feathers make fine birds'?"

"Yeah, I know its meaning. It feels spiteful of you to bring it up to me, though," Naoto answered in a groan. He looked completely different than usual.

He was wearing the school uniform, denim shorts, and black shirt that he wore day in and day out, but in place of the cheap, overworn sneakers that he usually wore were black leather boots—which, despite their simple design, were rather tasteful. His voluminous, ruffled hair been turned into a neatly trimmed shorter cut that curled outwards.

At this point, no matter how one looked at it, Naoto had become a "stylish person," a comrade of the normies.

...In appearance, at least.

"I didn't know what to expect when you told me we were heading out in the morning, but… being thrown into a barber shop, then taken all over the place shopping has made me seriously tired…"

"Master Naoto, it wasn't a barber shop, but a beauty salon."

"How are they any different?" Naoto grumbled as he raised his face.

RyuZU, who sat facing him, was attracting all sorts of attention from the crowd in the store.

I guess that's a given.

After all, RyuZU was "inhumanly" beautiful.

She had lustrous silver hair that swayed softly, a face as white as snow, and eyes that glittered gold. On top of that, her ethereal limbs made her appear like an angel even when she was simply sitting.

However, RyuZU paid no heed to those gazes of admiration, saying, "With all due respect, Master Naoto, this much personal grooming is a given. I think your shabby looks would go to waste if you wore only your school uniform every day, forever."

"I have no idea what I'd be wasting if that's the case, but…" Naoto said as he exhaled a small sigh. "Well, it's true that loitering about until nighttime in my school uniform would be a bad idea… but wouldn't a go-to of mine like Uniloq or Shimumara have been fine?—"

"Master Naoto, to look good in Shimumara or Uniloq would require both a suitable flair and face."

"D-don't say face…" Naoto said in a trembling voice, but RyuZU ignored him.

She continued. "Should *inadequates* pick something out half-heartedly, they would have even their financial sense questioned, much less their looks and taste, making their inadequacy all the more apparent. Though admittedly, to be daft enough to deliberately challenge oneself like that despite everything would be sublime, in a way."

"...RyuZU, aren't you awfully well-informed despite having been asleep for two hundred years? Did you look this up in the manga café?"

"Yes, that is a part of it. However, it is also that both brands have existed since a thousand years ago, and it does not seem like they have changed their direction much during my slumber, either."

"Wow... Those brands have had that kind of public image since a thousand years ago?"

RyuZU nodded; however, Naoto suddenly tilted his head.

"By the way, I guess this is late, but how did you find the money to pay so gladly for these boots and my haircut?"

"I raised it," RyuZU answered with a calm face, but Naoto knit his eyebrows.

"More specifically?"

RyuZU smiled sweetly and presented Naoto's passbook to him.

...Now that I think about it, I've left her with my passbook the whole time, haven't I, he remembered.

He had completely forgotten about it. Naoto opened his passbook for the first time in a while.

"..."

He froze.

Looking at the zeroes, there were one, two, three... There were a *lot* of them.

"M-M-M-Miss Ryu, R-R-R-R-R-Ryu, Ryu, R-yu-yu, Ryu...ZU?"

"Master Naoto, no matter how impressed you are by my abilities as the pinnacle of all this world's automata, you need not have expressly sang my name in praise with such awful musical sense."

"That's not it at all! Rather, huh? Like, is this for real? What? How...?" Naoto spurted out in such a fluster that his pronunciation went awry.

RyuZU gazed pityingly upon seeing him in such a state. "Master Naoto, please rest assured, by no means will we end up being chased by the police."

"Umm, that explanation only makes me more uneasy, you know." With an eye half-closed, Naoto asked, "Seriously, what's up with all this money?"

"While it may have been impudent of me, I took the liberty of putting Master Naoto's paltry savings to work."

"By investing...uh, with just that little to start with?"

"A credit-based economy is but the generic term for financial systems in which it is possible to generate wealth out of nothing when taken to the extremes. If one has a thorough knowledge of the structure of the system and the intelligence to navigate it, accumulating this much money is not even a trifle of trouble."

There's no way that's how she got the money.

So Naoto thought, but if he pressed her, he'd probably end up discovering the truth, which he'd rather not know. He kept his mouth shut.

RyuZU smiled with the face of an angel.

"In any case, as you can see, we need not worry anymore as far as finances are concerned. Hereafter, I shall pay for expenses like Master Naoto's food and clothing, so you can lead a life that can at least be considered civilized. As such, please do not worry about the future. Enjoy the life of a kept man—excuse me, I mean a life of luxury."

"...Didn't you say 'kept man' just now?"

"No? Even if I did increase your savings by a more than a hundredfold, the capital did come from Master Naoto's savings, so this wealth is all yours. Even if you were to blow through it like a kept man would, there would not be even a sliver of justification for you to be called a kept man, you kept man."

Naoto collapsed without a word.

...A kept man, huh... I'm a kept man, huh...

...And I'm not even the kept man of a woman I seduced, but an automaton.

RyuZU, who was in top form, kept raining down the salt on him.

"If Master Naoto were not in the poorest segment of society, or more specifically, if you had even a single usable bill in your wallet, I would not have had to do this, you know."

"But I did! If I withdrew some savings, I would have had some!"

"In that situation, I believe you would have exhausted all your savings the moment you entered the beauty salon."

"Spending that much money on a measly haircut is bizarre! It's just gonna grow back in no time!"

"It's a necessary expenditure," RyuZU declared. "Even though Master Naoto is shabby, short, and suffering destitution as a sacrifice to capitalism and democracy, if I do not have you keep up a minimal level of grooming as my master, then as your follower, *my* caliber will be questioned."

"...Ah—" Naoto nodded.

Now that I think about it, it's true that the absurd number of gazes that gather on RyuZU invariably focus on me afterwards.

As if to say, "Why this chump?"

"I see. I get it now. I'll pay more attention from now on, so I don't embarrass either of us."

"Also, it was an expression of gratitude for the other day."

"Gratitude? Did I do something to be thanked for?"

"If it is not in your memory, feel free to forget what I said just now."

After that, they exited the burger shop and began walking through the shopping district, heading towards the station; however, Naoto stopped when they came across a flowery-looking boutique aimed at young women.

Staring fixedly at a set of frilly dresses displayed behind a pane of glass, Naoto called out, "RyuZU, wait up a bit."

"...Master Naoto, if you are interested in cross-dressing, please mention that from the start. A dress wouldn't go well with the clothes I've chosen f—"

"That's not it! Forget that and come with me for a bit."

Naoto pulled the venom-spewing RyuZU by her hand and entered the store.

"Welco—whoa," the clerk who had come out from the back cut herself off, and her eyes widened as soon as she saw RyuZU.

Naoto had already gotten used to that kind of reaction since they got it wherever they went, so he ignored it and approached the mannequin that was being displayed through the window and checked the price tag.

"...Hey, RyuZU, could you wear this for me?"

"Are you telling me to undress myself on the spot? Never mind, it is not a problem. Meeting the needs of my master is also a part of my—"

"Quit intentionally misconstruing me! Use the dressing room! Excuse me, she'd like to try on this set of clothes."

"Huh?! Ah, r-r-right, please wait a moment."

The clerk who had been enchanted by RyuZU came back to her senses and began moving.

After watching her disappear to the back, RyuZU began suspiciously, "...What is the meaning of this?"

"Nothing, really. Look, just try it on."

"Do you mean to say that you are displeased with my usual attire?" RyuZU said as she spread her arms out.

Indeed—though RyuZU was wearing a school uniform now, she also had the set of clothes she had originally worn: a black, classic dress with ample amounts of frills and lace that seemed to have been woven and tailored from the darkness of the night.

That was probably why she hadn't paid any attention to her own clothes, but...

Naoto smiled upon seeing the clerk return with the clothes to try on. "I think your usual dress looks good, too. It's okay, just try this on."

"...Certainly."

RyuZU looked grudging and reluctant as she entered the dressing room with the clothes.

Shortly after—

"Is this fine?"

The curtain was pulled back.

Even the female clerk who snuck a peek gasped in amazement at the sight of RyuZU.

A velvety, lustrous white camisole, a pink skirt made of cloth that had been layered several times over, and a shawl that was the same shade of pink. Every one of them left a gentle, light impression on the viewer, as if one were looking at a carefully wrapped confection.

"Yeah, I was right. It looks really good on you!" Naoto smiled enthusiastically, but RyuZU seemed hesitant.

"...Is that really so? I do not think this is proper wear for a servant, but..."

"That's not true. Miss RyuZU, you really are the best."

"However, if I walk alongside Master Naoto like this, it would be as if, rather than a servant... Never mind. Now then, I would like to receive an explanation anytime now."

"Explain what? Why I had you try this on?"

"As far as other matters that require an explanation, one would be why Master Naoto's critical thinking skills require him to ask."

"Because, I mean, I'm having so much fun. It's like we're on a date," Naoto answered with a serious look, to which RyuZU made a sour face, as if she had just inadvertently chewed on bitter pills by the dozens.

"...Master Naoto, do you call bringing your watch along on a walk 'having a date' with it? Your language interpretation is awfully profound and novel, I see."

"Hmm? You sure say some strange things. It's not like you're a watch, RyuZU."

"In that case, what am I?" RyuZU tilted her head slightly and sharply exhaled. "What am I to Master Naoto?"

"A super cute automaton girl."

RyuZU opened her eyes wide at Naoto, who had answered without a moment's pause. "...Cute, you say?"

"Yeah! I may have no eye for my own clothes, but I do have an eye for automata! I'm confident enough to assert this: The cutest automaton in this universe right now is you, RyuZU!"

"...Without even a point of reference to compare me to, how can you assert that I'm the cutest in the uni—"

"It's a self-evident truth!!" Naoto declared without wavering, then seemed to suddenly realize something as he gushed, "Ahh, but I'd like to play around with your hair a bit as well. You have such beautiful hair, after all."

Naoto reached his hand forward and began playing around with RyuZU's hair. She wriggled her body, her face seeming to say that she felt a bit ticklish. Just then—

"Ah—"

RyuZU was taller than Naoto, and when he extended his hand towards her head, he ended up tripping over the step of the dressing room, whose floor was slightly elevated above the rest of the store.

The curtain that he'd tried to grab on to in a fluster slipped right out of his hands, causing Naoto to dive right into both the dressing room and RyuZU's bosom.

RyuZU, who ended up pushed down with Naoto's face buried in her chest, remarked in a dispassionate tone, "...I see. So you had an advanced calculation like this in mind. Allow me to applaud you, Master Naoto. I am forced to admit that this scheme of sexual harassment surpassed my calculations."

"What? No, that's not it, okay!"

Naoto abruptly popped his head up. RyuZU gazed at him coldly.

"As I suspected, do the organisms known as humans ultimately only exhibit abilities that exceed their own limits when pursuing base and vulgar lust?"

"No, that's... Ahh, ugh, I can't deny that in all cases, but..."

"So what do you plan to do now?"

"Huh? What do you mean?"

"After purposefully pulling the curtain closed as you fell, shoving me down in an isolated room and panting roughly through your nose as you enjoyed my breast components to your fill, surely you do not plan to pass this all off as a coincidence."

"Err, I do, actually. Is that bad?"

"Right, that is bad." RyuZU breathed out a small sigh, then said, "... Well, it is fine, I guess. I cannot help but admire how you wrung that meager intelligence of yours to one-up me through deception. Please state your demand. What is it you desire?"

"Eh? It's okay for me to demand something?"

That very moment, the capability of humans to exceed their own limits that RyuZU had mentioned just before manifested itself in full force as thoughts hopelessly suffused with worldly desires ran amok in Naoto's mind.

All just to pick out the most suitable option from his endless sea of desires.

In all sincerity, men *are* an incorrigible bunch.

"Th-then...how about you start by stripping down?" Naoto pressed RyuZU as he made a fondling gesture with both hands, wiggling his fingers deviously.

"..........."

Right now, the woman was exceedingly troubled.

She worked at a boutique marketed towards teenage girls.

Though her friends told her she looked like a college student, she wasn't an employee of the store. She was its full-fledged owner, and the merchandise on display were all items she had meticulously and proudly selected herself.

The selection at the store was a mass of frills and lace that one might end up dismissing as simply sweet, white, or gothic Lolita, but the clothes here were completely incomparable to the cheap imitations of the fashion used in cosplays. The only Lolita clothes here were ones that measured up to her professional standards.

"For starters, Lolita fashion is a burst of imagination that expresses the fleeting, innocent sweetness of a young maiden..." Once she began talking, she couldn't stop. The store was packed with that passion and taste of hers.

Now then, it was just a short while ago that a couple consisting of a girl who was a drop-dead beauty and a boy who was, eh, cute for the effort he put in, entered the store she was so proud of.

When she'd brought them the set of clothes that the boy had requested, the beautiful girl had kindly unveiled herself wearing the outfit. She was so marvelous that she made the store owner let out an inadvertent sigh of wonder.

Ahh, that's right. It's precisely for this kind of girl that I've gathered all these clothes.

...However...

The couple was acting strange. When the owner had heard a clamor in the dressing room and took a look, she found that the boy had plunged into the beautiful girl's stall, after which he'd simply remained in there without coming out.

Feeling uneasy about all this, the owner approached the dressing room—and she could hear rough panting from inside!

"I cannot strip any more than this."

"No, you still can. See, you still have one more piece left. I'll help you take it off."

"Ah—"

"Wow—so this is what it's like, huh... I guess I can't really say. After all, I'd only seen it for just a few hours in a dark place before. It looks totally different from that time... So amazing..."

"Master... Naoto. Please do not spread it open so mu—"

"Ahh, I see, so you're sensitive here. Then, how about here..."

"Please...do not touch me there."

She was shocked. Bewildered. Baffled.

Uh, what am I supposed to do in this situation?!

It had been three years since she'd opened the store; by this point, she'd become well used to managing it, but this kind of situation was still a first for her.

Nearly all her customers until now had been teenage girls, and though they'd bring a boyfriend along sometimes, there had never been anyone extreme enough to do the deed in the dressing room.

She clasped her newly heated cheeks with both hands, wriggling about anxiously. She recalled the lover that she had broken up with after a fight around the time she graduated from college.

Ahh, I'm not unsatisfied with my current life of working myself to the bone chasing after my dreams, but even so, there are still times when I feel hopelessly lonely—

"Ahhh—"

"All right... I'm in deep now. *Wow*—amazing. I didn't think that it'd be so complicated inside."

The store owner snapped.

I don't care anymore. To begin with, this is my store. It's a store where adorable little Alices wear frilly dresses and show me their sparkling smiles. Just what kind of adult actions do you think you're doing in this wonderland of mine, you lovebird punks? Just blow up, why don't you?!

Pulling back the dressing room's curtain with one swift jerk, she yelled, "Hey, what do you two think you're do...ing?"

Her voice tapered off and vanished.

The scene inside the dressing room was far more confusing than she had imagined.

The girl is half-naked, her clothes are open—that much makes sense, but what's up with her back? The skin is splayed open, and there are gears inside? And this boy's sticking a thin screwdriver into her inner workings, and using a magnifying monocle to peer zealously inside, what's he—

"Ah...ngh!" Upon the boy slightly turning the screwdriver, the beautiful girl—rather, the beautiful automaton girl—let out a coquettish moan, and writhed.

As the owner stared blankly down at the two of them, the boy noticed her and scratched his head. "Umm... Sorry, we're in the middle of maintenance right now. Ah, we'll take these clothes. How much are they?"

She answered with a smile.

"Leave, you perverted brat."

•••⬤•••

...How many times has it been now?

Marie sighed deeply in the provisional meeting room, which used to be a storage area.

Despite the entire staff force pulling continuous all-nighters after moving to the twenty-fourth floor, the problem had yet to be resolved.

Right now, Marie was in the middle of her fifth meeting for reports and devising measures regarding the repair work.

Those gathered here were, including Marie, the chiefs of observation, analytics, service, and communications, plus the heads of material management and transport. None of them could hide their fatigue.

Hannes, the chief of observation, spat out, "The problem is that we can't pinpoint the cause of the malfunction. While there's no mistake that there's something wrong with the regulating mechanism for atmospheric pressure, the quantifiable values themselves are normal. In other words, we can't say that the cause is simply a degradation or breakdown of the system."

The Butterfly Effect.

It is the concept that even a trivially minute alteration can induce a huge change over time.

The Clockwork Planet, recreating the entire planet's mechanisms—its structure was so mysteriously complex that it was impossible to fully grasp, no matter how much one tried.

Even if an abnormality occurred in one system, replacing or repairing just that system usually didn't solve the problem. As for why, it was because the cause of the problem often lay in a completely unrelated section from the system being affected.

It might be nothing more than a loose screw or a small gear becoming deformed.

However, when small irregularities like that piled up, they would sometimes eventually result in a fatal error.

The present situation that Chief Hannes was explaining fit that bill precisely.

"Kyoto's city mechanism systems are separated by floor, so the irregularity on the twenty-fourth floor is definitely the cause of the problem. That's something that all the observation squad can attest to. However..."

Massimo, the chief analytics officer, continued after him, "Based on the observational data, the calculated potential patterns of malfunction reached as many as 563,499,352 possibilities. If we had at least a month... No, even if we only had two weeks, it'd be possible to pinpoint the right one if we worked diligently, but..."

In the current day, where the planet's blueprint had long been lost, finding out the cause of a malfunction was done through brute force. One had to create an overall diagram lacking any repetitions among all possible combinations, then check the portions that seemed like probable causes one by one for whether they had any relevance to the malfunction.

If there was only one cause, then things would still be manageable, but when there were two, three, or four causes, the possible paths leading to the malfunction propagated endlessly.

If one considered that, locating the cause of error in the estimated two weeks that Chief Analytics Officer Massimo gave would be astonishingly fast; however, Marie shook her head with a rueful countenance.

"We don't have that kind of time."

"But Dr. Marie, no matter how you look at it, as things are now, we simply don't have enough time to finish the job," the communication chief said with a pale face.

"Would it not be possible for us using our current analytical data to make a behind-the-scenes political deal to postpone the purge?"

"I'll try to, but it'll probably be difficult. How's the work proceeding overall right now?"

Service Chief Konrad answered, "In order to speed things up, we've narrowed down the likely patterns of the cause to 35,034 possibilities. The service squad and the communications squad are working together testing out those possibilities right now through trial and error."

"What was that selection based on?"

"Just my intuition."

Everyone rolled their eyes, except for the chief analytics officer.

However, Konrad simply shrugged his shoulders, saying, "If I were to embellish what I did a little, I basically discarded patterns that were of the same type and gathered similar cases from our work log up to now, then put them in order by likeliness and ease of verification. Well, put bluntly, it was just my personal biases at work."

Marie inquired, "Do you expect things to go well?"

"Not really, no."

"......"

"However, if we didn't at least do that, it would be impossible to finish verifying all the possibilities. Rather, it's questionable whether we'll even be able to adequately test all of the approximately thirty-five thousand possibilities in the current situation."

"You're sure there are no other means we could take, right?"

"Given our current equipment and method, this is the best we can do." The chief of service nodded, and the head of transport stood up while breaking out in a cold sweat.

"Dr. Marie, if it's almost certain that we can't prevent the collapse of the city, shouldn't we consider how to escape?"

Observation Chief Hannes stood up in anger. "Are you telling us to accept the purge?! Running away would be the same as what the military is doing!"

"Of course, I, too, have the resolve to continue the repair work until the very end! However, to be practical, if we can't expect to succeed, we should consider the next best plan."

Marie asked with a stiff face, "Do you mean to say that we should announce an evacuation advisory to the residents?"

"Yes. If we start now, it shouldn't be impossible! Shouldn't we be prioritizing the residents' safety and publicizing the information we have?"

"We don't have that authority. For starters, how are we supposed to evacuate twenty million people by just ourselves?" said Marie calmly. The head of transport ground his teeth.

Their own city was going to be purged.

True, the resulting chaos when that information was publicized would surely be on an unimaginable scale.

Not everyone could simply evacuate on their own. The transportation facilities would surely be overwhelmed across the board, not to mention that there were also residents who physically couldn't move by themselves.

To begin with, just where were they supposed to evacuate to? And what would happen after that?

The head of transport refused to back down, asserting once again, "True, it will probably be both dangerous and chaotic. But rather than expend our resources on a hopeless repair, shouldn't we consider how best to limit the number of victims?"

"In that case, wouldn't the military potentially expedite the purge to conceal the truth?" Service Chief Konrad muttered as if speaking to himself.

In that moment, a dreadful silence fell upon the meeting room. Each head of staff, including Marie, had an indescribable look on their faces, and the head of transport gasped in a cramped, terrified voice.

"...Surely not, they wouldn't..."

"What reason do they have to hesitate? They forsook the residents long ago. In that case, wouldn't it just be a matter of sooner or later to them?"

"This city has twenty million inhabitants, you know!"

"Like I've been saying, it makes no difference to them." The service chief snorted before continuing. "Listen up. To us, the worst-case scenario would be the city collapsing along with twenty million victims, but that's not the case for them. What would trouble them the most would be the fact of the military forsaking the city going public."

"That can't be—!"

"How naïve of you. The reason the military isn't interfering with us right now is because this is convenient for them."

"What do you mean by that, service chief?" Marie asked.

The service chief stroked his white-flecked beard as he let out a deep sigh.

Out of everyone in the room, Service Chief Konrad was the most senior clocksmith.

He was a great veteran who had reached the point of slowly

transitioning from his prime to old age. Ever since he became a Meister in his youth, he had always worked on the front lines. His experience and technique were acknowledged by everyone. Considering his talent, it wouldn't have been strange for him to be leading this group instead of Marie if he had wanted to, but he hadn't tried to do so. He preferred taking the position one step back, where he could simply give casual advice to his juniors.

Even now, he looked like he was chiding all the young faces present with his gaze as he opened his mouth and said blandly, "Listen up. First, let us assume that it's impossible to repair this city in the ten hours we have left. At the very least, that's what they think, and looking at things objectively, they're exactly right."

"Service chief! But—"

"I know, so just calm down, Hannes. Of course, I haven't the slightest intention of giving up either. But that's not true for the military. They gave up long ago and decided on the purge. The problem is what comes after that. What will happen to them after the city collapses?"

"What will happen? That's..."

"Will they be disparaged? Yeah, they'll be demeaned to all hell, all right. Though it's said that dead men tell no tales, an entire city will have collapsed and been annihilated. There's no way they'll be able to keep everything concealed. The heads of everyone in charge will come flying off. Considering the damage that will have been done, you could even say it'll be quite fortunate for them if things end with just that. Now, that's where we come in."

The service chief turned his head as he surveyed all the faces in the room.

While everyone remained silent, Marie spoke up as their representative. "In other words... 'Even though we called Meister Guild and had them conduct a do-or-die repair on the city, the problem was beyond even them. As such, we were unable to save the precious lives of the city's residents.' Is that the scenario you're talking about?"

The service chief cracked a cheerful smile. "Dr. Marie, you are a kind girl, aren't you?"

"Whaa?" Marie's persona slipped as she inadvertently let out a sound of confusion.

As he shook his head, Service Chief Konrad gazed at Marie as if he found her reaction adorable. "Unfortunately, what people call 'society' is something so filthy that it's irredeemable. Understand? They probably plan to spin things this way..."

Service Chief Konrad paused for a breath before announcing, "They'll say, 'While we were making do-or-die repairs on the city, the Meister Guild forcefully interrupted us and ended up failing, causing an abrupt collapse for which we were unable to prepare an evacuation in time. It's exceedingly regrettable that things have turned out this way.'"

....

Just then, there was a loud noise as the door of the meeting room opened.

It was a bald man in a black suit—Halter.

He raised his hand awkwardly as the rueful glances all focused on him. "Excuse me—I was contacted by Meister Guild headquarters just now, you see."

"What did they say?"

Without answering her, Halter approached Marie and held some documents in front of her eyes.

She took them and quickly ran her eyes over the pages.

In them was—

"Rr...!!"

Krrrnnch. With the look of a demon on her face, Marie crushed the documents in her hand.

•••●•••

"What is the meaning of this?!" Marie shouted, slamming both hands on the table so forcefully her hair flew up in a storm. But the man she shouted at looked completely relaxed, wholly unperturbed as he sipped black tea from his cup.

The man had introduced himself as Limmons.

He was a bespectacled man with delicate features and neatly combed hair. He wore a black-striped suit. He was the liaison sent from headquarters, and it was his order that Marie be summoned to the Central Hotel from the core tower.

...At a time like this, when every minute and second is more precious than anything else!

Thinking that made Marie all the more angry.

"As I've been saying," Limmons said with a composed look on his face, "from the reports you sent us, we've come to understand that the commission this time is a military conspiracy made with the intent of avoiding responsibility—and also that there are no prospects of finishing the repairs as of right now."

"That's—!"

"As such, it wouldn't be in our best interests to remain on the scene—that is the verdict of headquarters."

"...Are you telling us to forsake this city?"

Limmons smiled sweetly at Marie, who was trembling all over, and said, "Please rest assured, Dr. Breguet. Headquarters is aware of the situation as well."

"...Are you saying that you guys will resolve the situation politically for us?"

"Yes, of course. This failure won't end up damaging your reputation."

"Just what are you saying?" Marie said, nearly growling, "Who's talking about my career? I'm talking about the watershed question of whether this city will be purged!"

"It'll be purged," Limmons said coolly.

He stood up and turned his back to Marie, who was at a loss for words. Approaching the window, he looked down on the cityscape beneath him through the spotless glass as he continued, "The City of Kyoto will be purged. That's something that's been decided."

"...Really, what are you *saying*?" Marie asked, left practically gasping from terror, but Limmons didn't respond.

While continuing to look down on the cityscape, he pushed his glasses up with his index finger. "The military won't stop at this point, you know, Dr. Breguet. Given that they've been found out by us, if they abandon the plan now, all that would be left is the fact that they tried to conduct a mass killing of the city's residents."

"That would be just as bad as them going through with it!"

"If they dispose of the residents, they can make any excuse they want. Moreover, headquarters has already approved."

Marie's breath got caught in her throat. "What did you say?"

"If this kind of secret is exposed, it would lead to unrest, as people lose all trust in the military. That wouldn't be a desirable outcome for us, either. In order to prevent that from happening, we have no choice but to take the blame for the time being. This is headquarters' verdict."

"Have you guys gone crazy?!" Marie exploded, but Limmons shrugged her words off like a breeze.

He didn't even turn to face her.

"Dr. Breguet, how about you think about things calmly for a bit? What will remain after we expose the military's conspiracy? We humans number four-and-a-half billion. We have on our hands over twenty thousand core towers and metropolitan areas; adding in the supporting clock towers, there are over six million regions we have to maintain. If this incident were to cause the military to collapse, who would do the maintenance work?"

"That argument is completely irrational! Logically speaking, we should put a stop to their conspiracy precisely so that nothing like this ever happens again."

"Do you expect the military to purify itself? That's impossible," Limmons said as he turned around. "The situation this time was caused by the military's inadequacy. The purge is to conceal this situation that they cannot handle. The people should just rely on the Meister Guild instead, you say? But we can't handle every situation like this, either. Putting ability aside, we definitely lack the numbers necessary."

"...What are you implying?"

"It's a case of give-and-take." Limmons smiled thinly. "Both the military and the Meister Guild would be troubled if the other were lost. Considering that we are guilty of siphoning outstanding talents from the military's localities as well, wouldn't it be fine to take one for the team once in a while?"

"...Are you saying that you don't care if you kill twenty million people for that?"

"They're *sacrifices* who ought be mourned." Limmons nodded. His expression revealed that he didn't really think that one bit.

"Now I thoroughly understand what you're saying!" Slamming the documents onto the table—the ones with the order to withdraw written on them—Marie turned on her heels.

"Oh, my, Dr. Breguet. Where are you headed?"

"I'm heading back to the worksite and continuing the repairs. Regardless of what headquarters says, we won't give up."

"Goodness, I'd be left in a pinch if you were to act at your own discretion like that."

"Like I care. We're leaving."

Calling out to Halter, who had been waiting like a statue in a corner of the room, Marie began to walk towards the door. As she grasped the doorknob, intending to walk right out, Limmons called out to her.

In a voice as cheerful as could be, he said, "In that case, I shall strip you of your authority."

Marie stopped dead in her tracks.

She turned around.

Before Marie's sharp gaze, Limmons took out a scroll fastened by a blue cord. He unfastened it and rolled the scroll down. His rimless glasses turned opaque from the white light reflecting on them.

"You, the honorable Marie Bell Breguet, were appointed Head of the First Division's Second Brigade on the tenth day of April in the one-thousand thirteenth year of the Wheel. However, as it has been confirmed that you have breached direct orders from headquarters, I hereby strip you of your seat and its authority by means of a simplified resolution."

Finishing his recital of the scroll, Limmons extended his hand and showed it to Marie.

"The decree has been written in proper form. Would you like to confirm?"

Marie remained silent as she walked up to Limmons, upon which she snatched the scroll from his hand. She narrowed her eyes into a line as she traced its contents.

From her side, Halter stepped forward and asked, "Excuse me, Mr. Limmons? Sorry for butting in, but pray tell—why do you have such a document so conveniently prepared?"

"Something along the lines of making doubly sure we considered every contingency. As it turns out, it ended up being useful, after all."

As a nauseating, faint smile crossed his face, Limmons continued. "If it were possible, I would have liked to settle things without using it, but I can't simply let you do as you please with a hundred clocksmiths who possess precious technical skills."

Marie rolled the scroll back up neatly before stowing it inside her pocket. Afterwards, she lifted her face and threw a glare at Limmons with dark, bitter eyes.

Limmons raised both hands up and put on a show, jesting, "Now now, please don't consider disposing of me and pretending that you never heard what was just said."

"……"

"I've already sent a copy of the same document to the city's military. Having been stripped of your seat and authority, you are now just an ordinary person without the privileges accorded to a Meister. You won't be allowed to enter the core tower without the military's permission."

The sound of teeth grinding escaped Marie's mouth.

She scowled at Limmons and made a face that said she would gladly strangle him to death any number of times if she could, but—suddenly, her glare wavered and she looked perplexed.

She tilted her head to the side slightly, and took her eyes off Limmons as she stared up into space. Her eyes widened.

I remember now.

Marie said quietly to the faintly smiling man, "You called yourself Limmons, right?"

"Yes, what about it?"

"I remembered just now. I've seen your face at the get-togethers of the five great enterprises in the past. As I recall, you were a dependent of the Vacherons."

Limmons's smile disappeared for a moment, and then he smiled faintly once again.

"Indeed, I'm honored to have you remember me, Ms. Breguet. We were in the same year at the academy as well. Do you remember that, too?"

"No, not at all."

"...Is that so? Well, I wasn't talented in that field, unfortunately. As you can see, I'm working on the administration side of things at headquarters now."

Vacheron.

It was the name of a clan behind another one of the Five Great

Enterprises that rivaled that of the Breguet family Marie belonged to—and also a sponsor of the Meister Guild.

As much as the Meister Guild liked to call itself a nonprofit organization, as long as it was an organization based on the movement of people, things, and money, it couldn't completely exclude the will of its sponsors.

It was a matter of fact that the management of Meister Guild included those related to the Breguets and the Vacherons—in other words, representatives of the five great enterprises. Marie knew that, and had even used it to her convenience before.

However—

"Is this all a painting arranged by the *Vacherons*?" Marie asked in a low voice, as she stared at Limmons.

He had said that there would be no damage done to Marie's reputation, but there was no way that was true. If the purge was enacted, the military would push the blame on Meister Guild, and if Meister Guild accepted that, they would shove the responsibility onto Marie—and in turn, the Breguet family.

There was no way the other four families wouldn't take the chance to chip off some of the Breguet family's influence.

In other words, this is a collusion between the military and Meister Guild. A plot by the Vacheron family to enervate the Breguet family's power!

However, Limmons only shrugged his shoulders at Marie's condemnation.

"I have absolutely no idea what you could be suggesting."

He showed off a sluggish, sludge-like smile. His expression substantiated Marie's conjecture more eloquently than anything else.

"You...bunch of...!" In her anger, her voice had gotten stuck in her throat. Her head was burning white-hot.

She couldn't understand.

If they did something like this, Meister Guild's reputation would take a big hit. The trust and pride their predecessors had built up with their blood and sweat starting a thousand years ago would be irreversibly stained with dishonor—and for something so senseless!

She recalled what she had said to Halter before.

"What could those imbeciles possibly do?"

I feel like I understand the meaning behind those pacifistic smiles now. The dreadful power of those who can't do anything. Understand? No, I could never understand this. Like I would let myself understand this.

What is sacred? The precious legacy left to Meister Guild that must be protected above all else: tenacity, pride, ideals, life, and the purity of the soul!

Yet, for those things to be discarded for something so small, narrow-minded, ugly, filthy, and repulsive that it can't even be dismissed as mere jealousy or envy—and for it to be done so easily.

Marie couldn't understand.

"Marie!!"

Being yelled at unexpectedly, Marie came to her senses.

"Let's go. Staying here would only make you sick," Halter said, his voice firm.

Marie was about to reflexively yell back, but she restrained herself. She tightened her trembling fist and calmed her breathing, then nodded.

"...Right, let's go."

Marie and Halter silently exited the room. Suppressing her impulse to wreck the faint smile on Limmons's face beyond all recognition as he saw them off required an unbelievable amount of self-restraint.

The two remained silent as they advanced through the wide corridors before arriving at the elevator corridor. Halter pressed the call button, and they waited quietly for the elevator to come. Though in reality it only took a little more than two minutes, to Marie it felt like an hour, or even two.

When the elevator arrived, they boarded it and Halter pressed the button for first floor.

Marie reached her limit.

"AAAGHRRRRRAAAAAAAAGHHHHHH!!" she bellowed, kicking the wall of the elevator with all her might, causing it to sway so much that the emergency shutdown was triggered.

"Calm down, Marie."

"Shut up!!"

Marie swung both hands about as she rampaged. Halter was about to lay his hand on Marie's shoulder to try to pacify her when Marie punched his hand in defiance. The fact that that didn't shake his hand in the slightest vexed her so much that it made her rage explode even further.

She cried, yelled, and bashed Halter with her fists. Panting roughly, her light golden hair disheveled, she slammed her foot against Halter's log-like legs and trampled on his feet.

Halter didn't resist. He bore the brunt of the girl's rage that had been unreasonably directed towards him in silence.

Of course, as he had been mechanized, such a feat wasn't difficult at all.

Marie pulled Halter in by his suit and smashed her head against his solid abdomen. *Thud.* The shock spread throughout Halter's body.

"Do you even get it?!" Marie yelled, her head still smooshed against his abdomen. Her voice was hoarse and trembling. "Hey, do you even get it? This city! Twenty million people! For the sake of ruining me—for something as pointless as that, they'll be sacrificed as collateral damage, did you get that?!"

"That's not true," Halter asserted solemnly. "Marie, that's not true. Don't flatter yourself. The military will conduct the purge whether you're here or not. The Meister Guild just threw you in for the ride."

"How could you possibly know that for sure?!" Marie shouted as her rage burst a second time. With her face still buried in his abdomen, she struck Halter's chest with her small fists. "If I weren't here, Meister Guild might have pressured the military! More clocksmiths might have been sent! The purge might have been avoidable!"

"Even so, it's not your fault."

"Shut up!!" Marie shouted again, then punched Halter.

Halter didn't waver. He stood silently as he was shouted and punched at. Suppressing a girl with a body of flesh would be easy, and aside from that, he wasn't so inept that he wouldn't at least embrace and comfort a crying girl, yet he didn't do so.

He knew that's not what Marie Bell Breguet needed.

After a short while, Marie calmed down and become motionless, her face still against Halter's stomach.

Her shoulders eventually began to tremble.

"...Heheh... Heheheh, hahahahahahaha!"

In a burst, her face twisted as she let out a loud laugh. Her eyes were swollen and a little red. Halter sighed as he diligently pretended not to notice the stains that had gotten on his suit.

"...Have you calmed down?"

"Calmed down? What are you saying, Halter? I'm calm, all right. This may be the first time my mind has been so crystal-clear since I was born."

"You really don't look that way, though."

"Ohh! Ohh, sorry about that, Halter! Are you mad at me because I punched you just a wee bit? Yeah, I'm really sorry! But thanks to that, I feel totally refreshed!"

"I'm sure glad to hear that." Halter grumbled, as he relaxed his shoulders and straightened his wrinkled clothes.

He pressed the button for the first floor again, restarting the stopped elevator. Looking on, Marie let out a low growl of a laugh.

"Very well, you feeble-minded political crooks! Pull on others' feet as much as you'd like. Taking away even the last privilege of wretched creatures without recourse would simply be too pitiful, after all!"

"...This is hopeless," sighed Halter. Marie ignored him and furrowed her eyebrows.

"Think, Marie. There should be something. Some way to break out of this crappy situation." She pinched her chin and licked her lips as she mulled the situation over.

The military won't stop. Meister Guild can no longer be counted on, either. It's probably impossible to hope for a political resolution at this point. At this point, evacuating the residents would also be impossible. In that case, there's no option left but to finish the repairs before the city is purged.

Well then, what are the obstacles to that option?

There's no time. Okay. There's nothing I can do about that at this

point.

In that case, let's think it over: Can I finish the repairs to the city in the eight hours left?

Negative. Realistically speaking, it's impossible. Then, what if I change the method? As long as the point of malfunction is located, can the repair work itself be finished within the time limit? Affirmative. However, I need a way to put that into practice—a method to promptly locate the point of malfunction.

"Think, Marie. It should be there. There should be some way!"

...Of course, no matter how much she racked her brain, no such method came to mind.

Even though they were a gathering of the most outstanding staff and equipment in the world, they still weren't magicians.

Some things are impossible. One must acknowledge that...but... however...even so...!

"For something to be 'impossible' just because of those imbeciles' meddling is utterly unacceptable!"

The elevator arrived at the first floor, and the door slowly opened.

Let's continue thinking about this in the car, Marie thought as she lifted her head.

Just then...

She saw a face that she very much recognized before her.

"..."

"Say, RyuZU. Is it really fine for us to stay in a place like this?"

"Master Naoto, that flea-sized modesty of yours may be a virtue, but may I suggest that you act with a little more dignity, and composure that befits my master?"

It was a duo of a short, headphone-wearing boy and a girl with

However, RyuZU is an irreplaceable, precious asset to our family. I firmly request that you return her immediately. The compensation that is properly due to you shall be processed as a priority under my na—"

"No way. I refuse. RyuZU is mine," Naoto cut Marie off and discarded her proposal childishly.

Marie, whose face had crumbled in disbelief, turned her head and looked at Halter.

"Let's kill this guy and bury him. That would solve everything."

However, Halter waved his hand, warning in a low voice, "...Cut it out, princess."

"What? We're in an emergency right now. We don't have time to waste on dealing with an idiot like h—"

"I told you to *knock it off,* Marie!"

Startled by Halter suddenly raising his voice, Marie shut her mouth.

Immediately afterwards, she realized.

"Wha...?!"

Just when had...?

Rising from underneath the table, two black scythes surrounded Marie's neck.

RyuZU, who seemed to have unleashed *those* objects from under her skirt without stirring at all, was reflecting Marie's stiffened face in her eyes, as unreadable as ever.

As someone who had disassembled her body for maintenance before, Marie knew that was the one and only weapon RyuZU was armed with—and also that it possessed the ability to easily sever alloy-armored military tanks, much less a human, in just an instant.

beautiful silver hair.

She had no recollection of the boy. The girl was the problem.

Marie knew the face of that girl well. She had seen that girl's face many times since she was a kid. More specifically, it was the face that had slept in her family's treasure house. Since Marie had become a Meister, she would bring her out to the worksites, and whenever she had spare time, she would challenge herself by trying to fix her and make her move once more.

"A-a-ah..."

"Hm...?"

"Is something the matter, Master Naoto?"

A perplexed face turned toward her.

The stunningly beautiful girl—or rather, automaton, was unmistakably operating.

—YD-01, First Machine of the Initial-Y Series, RyuZU.

Seeing the flabbergasted Marie, the slim hope that could possibly overturn this situation tilted her head, looking puzzled.

The lobby on the first floor of Central Hotel had become something like a mall.

There were shops on either side of the entrance; on the right were fine-dining restaurants, and on the left were boutiques and brand-name shops lined up in a row.

In one of those restaurants, having moved to the café lounge from which the hotel's courtyard could be seen, the first thing out of Marie's mouth was, "I'll have you lend me your hand, RyuZU."

Without reservation towards the automaton sitting opposite her, Marie placed her hands on the table and bent forward boldly. RyuZU looked at Marie with indecipherable golden eyes and a somewhat cold expression.

Naoto, seated beside her, raised his hand and asked, "Er, could I ask something really quick? To begin with, who are you?"

"You don't know who *I* am?"

Naoto shrugged at Marie's suspicion.

"Not one bit. Are you someone in show business? I'm not the kind of person who watches TV and the like, so..."

Halter, who was sitting next to Marie, slapped his bald head and laughed. "Show biz, huh? That's a good one."

"Halter, is this the time to be fooling around?"

"You say that, but that isn't actually incorrect, is it? I forget whether it was for *Automata Fan* or *Technical Weekly*, but you modeled for the front cover of a magazine several times, didn't you?"

"That was only because Elder Sister ditched that project, so I was forced to do it instead."

"*Automata Fan*? If that's the case, then I should have seen your face before..." Naoto muttered as he tilted his head. That was a magazine he had unfailingly and devotedly bought every issue of for as long as he could remember, yet he had no recollection whatsoever of the golden-haired girl in front of him.

Naoto shrugged. "Well, I guess there's no way I could remember all the little details like cover models... So, who are you, then?"

"You keep asking who I am, but who are *you* supposed to be?" Looking displeased, Marie scowled at Naoto and said, "My name is Marie Bell Breguet. I'm a Meister belonging to the Meister Guild.

This YD-01 RyuZU is my family's personal asset, you realize?"

"Personal asset...?"

Naoto threw his head back and yelled in surprise before standing up and saying, "So you guys were the worthless idiots who carelessly dropped a storage unit right above my apartment!"

"S-storage unit?"

As Marie faltered, flabbergasted, Naoto pressed on with an anger that showed on his face. "Thanks to you guys, I lost the home and all the tools my late parents left me and became practically penniless. To top off becoming a hobo at sixteen years of age, I met RyuZU and ended up entering into a contract with her you know and how are you going to compensate me huh-indeed-thank-you-very-muchhh!"

The boy of small stature yelled all that out in one breath before lowering his head. Marie looked at him with seeming disgust before turning to Halter. "Halter, is this idiot complaining? Or is he thanking us?"

"Who knows. I think he's probably doing both."

"In. Any. Case! As compensation for the financial losses as well as the mental anguish I suffered, I'm making RyuZU mine! I decided that just now that's right I've decided so leave already you cursed lumps of protein!"

"Stop babbling nonsense, you idiot!" Marie promptly shoute back, huffing violently.

Feeling a headache coming on, she pressed her hand against he throbbing temple. She slowly calmed her breathing before trying t pacify Naoto with a placid voice. "...Listen, okay? I sympathize wit your misfortune. The cargo falling off was due to the ineptitude of th airport; still, I'll apologize in their place as many times as necessa

Sweat immediately started to pour from Marie's entire body.

The angelic-looking girl looked like she had transformed into a man-eating tiger from the jungle. Marie couldn't even feel the blades that gently enveloped her neck, but she understood that they were literally ready to nip her throat like the fangs of a beast at any moment.

She only had one question—why was she still alive?

"...Ahh... Ahh."

She couldn't breathe. Her body wouldn't move one bit. Even so, she managed to move just her eyeballs to glance at Halter. He was pointing his gun and ready to shoot, a tense expression on his face.

But the muzzle wasn't aiming at the automaton.

It was turned towards—the petrified boy next to her with his mouth agape.

RyuZU was ready to kill Marie and Halter was ready to kill Naoto—as the two murderous intents intersected, a drop of sweat ran down Halter's face. He proposed in a tranquil voice, "All right, Miss, let's calm down, shall we?"

"At just whom do you think you are pointing that gun?"

Even as he was being stared at viciously by those golden eyes, Halter smiled gently and continued, "Let me apologize for my companion running her mouth. She was entirely in the wrong. Something unpleasant just happened, so she's feeling a bit hysterical, you see. She wasn't serious, just a tad irritated. Please excuse her."

RyuZU whispered softly, "If you don't even have the intelligence to read between the lines, then let me rephrase. If a patchwork piece of junk like yourself, more inferior than humanity who are themselves lowlier than fleas, thinks it is acceptable to point a toy like that at Master Naoto, then I shall collectively tear both of you to pieces. Are you fine with that?"

Her voice was cold enough to make a demon cower and cry.

Though her eyes were inorganic, her gaze clearly harbored murderous intent.

"I get it, I'll put my gun down. I wasn't serious. See, I didn't even release the safety." Halter slowly turned his gun around and showed its safety mechanism to RyuZU before discreetly lowering his weapon. "So please, could you not decapitate our princess in kind?"

It seemed like she accepted those words as Halter had hoped, for the black scythes folded up without a sound and returned back under her skirt in an instant. During that entire time, RyuZU didn't stir one bit.

"Haahh... Haah..."

Released from the mechanical murderous intent, Marie flopped onto her seat while rubbing her neck over and over again. Perhaps she couldn't believe she was still alive, for her emerald eyes seemed somewhat out of focus, and their lids were quivering.

"Wh-what just..."

"Listen here, princess..." Grasping Marie's shoulder with his hand to calm her down, Halter said, "I'm irritated as well, but these two *aren't* involved in our situation yet. Don't say something thoughtless like that a second time. Otherwise, you really *will* be bidding farewell to your head."

Marie angrily glared at him. "Halter! I was almost murdered just now! You know that, right?!"

"Yeah, you were. I'm glad you're quick to understand."

"Why can an automaton that isn't even military-use kill a person?!"

Without hesitating, Halter said something preposterous. "She obviously doesn't have a code of ethics programmed into her." He glanced at the automaton, who was putting on a placid face. "This Miss here hasn't taken her eyes off you for even one second since the moment you showed malice towards that boy over there. That's why I kept my guard up against her the whole time. Even so—I couldn't even react to the speed she just showed. ...Do you understand what this means?"

"...That's—"

It meant that even Halter, who had been reinforced with the latest cyborg technologies, didn't have a fast enough reaction time to make out this automaton's combat movements. Despite having kept his guard up the whole time, the best he could do was to take a hostage *after the fact*.

"To tell you the truth, if she really intended to kill you, I surely wouldn't have had time to make that boy a hostage."

In other words, that had been simply a warning. If RyuZU felt like it, that threat wouldn't remain just a threat. Marie and Halter would both be shredded into bits and pieces before they could realize what had happened.

And by no means would there be any way for them to defend against that.

Halter waited for that fact to sink into Marie's head before continuing, "...Understand? First, calm down. After that, forget the fact that she was the Breguet family's personal asset. Even if it angers you, bear with it. Those are the rules in this situation."

RyuZU smiled in a carefree manner and said, "I retract my words calling you a less-than-human piece of junk. You appear to be rather perceptive for a human."

"I'm glad you understand." Putting both his hands up, Halter said, "We apologize for our rudeness. Still, we want you to hear what we have to say. This is a momentous problem that doesn't just concern us, but the lives of the twenty million residents of this city."

After that, Halter explained the situation.

The abnormal fluctuations in gravity occurring here in Kyoto. The dispatch of the Meister Guild, which was too rushed no matter how one looked at it, and the conspiracy and motives behind that. The military abandoning all responsibility and planning to conceal the truth, and the design of some in Meister Guild to try to turn that into an opportunity for political gain within the organization. And above all, the hopelessly insufficient time they had to work with—

Naoto, who had finished listening to Halter's explanation, was left holding his head, speechless.

After a while, he barely managed to get himself together and said, as if gasping, "Wait, wait, this city will be purged? Letting the residents die? Are you saying this with a sober mind?"

"We couldn't say something like this as a joke." Marie continued, "I'm sorry to say that it's all true. The military and a portion of Meister Guild have lost their minds. There are eight hours left—no, seven now, I think? This city will collapse. It'll be annihilated, without a trace left behind. They're totally insane, aren't they?"

"That can't be... Can't you do something?"

"...To tell you the truth, we've got nothing."

Marie cast her eyes downward and made fists with her hands, vexed.

"At any rate, there's no time. I was divested of my authority, so just to return to the core tower I'd have to break through the military's beautiful silver hair.

She had no recollection of the boy. The girl was the problem.

Marie knew the face of that girl well. She had seen that girl's face many times since she was a kid. More specifically, it was the face that had slept in her family's treasure house. Since Marie had become a Meister, she would bring her out to the worksites, and whenever she had spare time, she would challenge herself by trying to fix her and make her move once more.

"A-a-ah..."

"Hm...?"

"Is something the matter, Master Naoto?"

A perplexed face turned toward her.

The stunningly beautiful girl—or rather, automaton, was unmistakably operating.

—YD-01, First Machine of the Initial-Y Series, RyuZU.

Seeing the flabbergasted Marie, the slim hope that could possibly overturn this situation tilted her head, looking puzzled.

The lobby on the first floor of Central Hotel had become something like a mall.

There were shops on either side of the entrance; on the right were fine-dining restaurants, and on the left were boutiques and brand-name shops lined up in a row.

In one of those restaurants, having moved to the café lounge from which the hotel's courtyard could be seen, the first thing out of Marie's mouth was, "I'll have you lend me your hand, RyuZU."

Without reservation towards the automaton sitting opposite her, Marie placed her hands on the table and bent forward boldly. RyuZU looked at Marie with indecipherable golden eyes and a somewhat cold expression.

Naoto, seated beside her, raised his hand and asked, "Er, could I ask something really quick? To begin with, who are you?"

"You don't know who *I* am?"

Naoto shrugged at Marie's suspicion.

"Not one bit. Are you someone in show business? I'm not the kind of person who watches TV and the like, so..."

Halter, who was sitting next to Marie, slapped his bald head and laughed. "Show biz, huh? That's a good one."

"Halter, is this the time to be fooling around?"

"You say that, but that isn't actually incorrect, is it? I forget whether it was for *Automata Fan* or *Technical Weekly*, but you modeled for the front cover of a magazine several times, didn't you?"

"That was only because Elder Sister ditched that project, so I was forced to do it instead."

"*Automata Fan*? If that's the case, then I should have seen your face before..." Naoto muttered as he tilted his head. That was a magazine he had unfailingly and devotedly bought every issue of for as long as he could remember, yet he had no recollection whatsoever of the golden-haired girl in front of him.

Naoto shrugged. "Well, I guess there's no way I could remember all the little details like cover models... So, who are you, then?"

"You keep asking who I am, but who are *you* supposed to be?" Looking displeased, Marie scowled at Naoto and said, "My name is Marie Bell Breguet. I'm a Meister belonging to the Meister Guild.

This YD-01 RyuZU is my family's personal asset, you realize?"

"Personal asset…?"

Naoto threw his head back and yelled in surprise before standing up and saying, "So you guys were the worthless idiots who carelessly dropped a storage unit right above my apartment!"

"S-storage unit?"

As Marie faltered, flabbergasted, Naoto pressed on with an anger that showed on his face. "Thanks to you guys, I lost the home and all the tools my late parents left me and became practically penniless. To top off becoming a hobo at sixteen years of age, I met RyuZU and ended up entering into a contract with her you know and how are you going to compensate me huh-indeed-thank-you-very-muchhh!"

The boy of small stature yelled all that out in one breath before lowering his head. Marie looked at him with seeming disgust before turning to Halter. "Halter, is this idiot complaining? Or is he thanking us?"

"Who knows. I think he's probably doing both."

"In. Any. Case! As compensation for the financial losses as well as the mental anguish I suffered, I'm making RyuZU mine! I decided that just now that's right I've decided so leave already you cursed lumps of protein!"

"Stop babbling nonsense, you idiot!" Marie promptly shouted back, huffing violently.

Feeling a headache coming on, she pressed her hand against her throbbing temple. She slowly calmed her breathing before trying to pacify Naoto with a placid voice. "…Listen, okay? I sympathize with your misfortune. The cargo falling off was due to the ineptitude of the airport; still, I'll apologize in their place as many times as necessary.

However, RyuZU is an irreplaceable, precious asset to our family. I firmly request that you return her immediately. The compensation that is properly due to you shall be processed as a priority under my na—"

"No way. I refuse. RyuZU is mine," Naoto cut Marie off and discarded her proposal childishly.

Marie, whose face had crumbled in disbelief, turned her head and looked at Halter.

"Let's kill this guy and bury him. That would solve everything."

However, Halter waved his hand, warning in a low voice, "...Cut it out, princess."

"What? We're in an emergency right now. We don't have time to waste on dealing with an idiot like h—"

"I told you to *knock it off,* Marie!"

Startled by Halter suddenly raising his voice, Marie shut her mouth.

Immediately afterwards, she realized.

"Wha...?!"

Just when had...?

Rising from underneath the table, two black scythes surrounded Marie's neck.

RyuZU, who seemed to have unleashed *those* objects from under her skirt without stirring at all, was reflecting Marie's stiffened face in her eyes, as unreadable as ever.

As someone who had disassembled her body for maintenance before, Marie knew that was the one and only weapon RyuZU was armed with—and also that it possessed the ability to easily sever alloy-armored military tanks, much less a human, in just an instant.

Sweat immediately started to pour from Marie's entire body.

The angelic-looking girl looked like she had transformed into a man-eating tiger from the jungle. Marie couldn't even feel the blades that gently enveloped her neck, but she understood that they were literally ready to nip her throat like the fangs of a beast at any moment.

She only had one question—why was she still alive?

"...Ahh... Ahh."

She couldn't breathe. Her body wouldn't move one bit. Even so, she managed to move just her eyeballs to glance at Halter. He was pointing his gun and ready to shoot, a tense expression on his face.

But the muzzle wasn't aiming at the automaton.

It was turned towards—the petrified boy next to her with his mouth agape.

RyuZU was ready to kill Marie and Halter was ready to kill Naoto—as the two murderous intents intersected, a drop of sweat ran down Halter's face. He proposed in a tranquil voice, "All right, Miss, let's calm down, shall we?"

"At just whom do you think you are pointing that gun?"

Even as he was being stared at viciously by those golden eyes, Halter smiled gently and continued, "Let me apologize for my companion running her mouth. She was entirely in the wrong. Something unpleasant just happened, so she's feeling a bit hysterical, you see. She wasn't serious, just a tad irritated. Please excuse her."

RyuZU whispered softly, "If you don't even have the intelligence to read between the lines, then let me rephrase. If a patchwork piece of junk like yourself, more inferior than humanity who are themselves lowlier than fleas, thinks it is acceptable to point a toy like that at Master Naoto, then I shall collectively tear both of you to pieces. Are you fine with that?"

Her voice was cold enough to make a demon cower and cry.

Though her eyes were inorganic, her gaze clearly harbored murderous intent.

"I get it, I'll put my gun down. I wasn't serious. See, I didn't even release the safety." Halter slowly turned his gun around and showed its safety mechanism to RyuZU before discreetly lowering his weapon. "So please, could you not decapitate our princess in kind?"

It seemed like she accepted those words as Halter had hoped, for the black scythes folded up without a sound and returned back under her skirt in an instant. During that entire time, RyuZU didn't stir one bit.

"Haahh... Haah..."

Released from the mechanical murderous intent, Marie flopped onto her seat while rubbing her neck over and over again. Perhaps she couldn't believe she was still alive, for her emerald eyes seemed somewhat out of focus, and their lids were quivering.

"Wh-what just..."

"Listen here, princess..." Grasping Marie's shoulder with his hand to calm her down, Halter said, "I'm irritated as well, but these two *aren't* involved in our situation yet. Don't say something thoughtless like that a second time. Otherwise, you really *will* be bidding farewell to your head."

Marie angrily glared at him. "Halter! I was almost murdered just now! You know that, right?!"

"Yeah, you were. I'm glad you're quick to understand."

"Why can an automaton that isn't even military-use kill a person?!"

Without hesitating, Halter said something preposterous. "She obviously doesn't have a code of ethics programmed into her." He glanced at the automaton, who was putting on a placid face. "This Miss here hasn't taken her eyes off you for even one second since the moment you showed malice towards that boy over there. That's why I kept my guard up against her the whole time. Even so—I couldn't even react to the speed she just showed. ...Do you understand what this means?"

"...That's—"

It meant that even Halter, who had been reinforced with the latest cyborg technologies, didn't have a fast enough reaction time to make out this automaton's combat movements. Despite having kept his guard up the whole time, the best he could do was to take a hostage *after the fact*.

"To tell you the truth, if she really intended to kill you, I surely wouldn't have had time to make that boy a hostage."

In other words, that had been simply a warning. If RyuZU felt like it, that threat wouldn't remain just a threat. Marie and Halter would both be shredded into bits and pieces before they could realize what had happened.

And by no means would there be any way for them to defend against that.

Halter waited for that fact to sink into Marie's head before continuing, "...Understand? First, calm down. After that, forget the fact that she was the Breguet family's personal asset. Even if it angers you, bear with it. Those are the rules in this situation."

RyuZU smiled in a carefree manner and said, "I retract my words calling you a less-than-human piece of junk. You appear to be rather perceptive for a human."

"I'm glad you understand." Putting both his hands up, Halter said, "We apologize for our rudeness. Still, we want you to hear what we have to say. This is a momentous problem that doesn't just concern us, but the lives of the twenty million residents of this city."

After that, Halter explained the situation.

The abnormal fluctuations in gravity occurring here in Kyoto. The dispatch of the Meister Guild, which was too rushed no matter how one looked at it, and the conspiracy and motives behind that. The military abandoning all responsibility and planning to conceal the truth, and the design of some in Meister Guild to try to turn that into an opportunity for political gain within the organization. And above all, the hopelessly insufficient time they had to work with—

Naoto, who had finished listening to Halter's explanation, was left holding his head, speechless.

After a while, he barely managed to get himself together and said, as if gasping, "Wait, wait, this city will be purged? Letting the residents die? Are you saying this with a sober mind?"

"We couldn't say something like this as a joke." Marie continued, "I'm sorry to say that it's all true. The military and a portion of Meister Guild have lost their minds. There are eight hours left—no, seven now, I think? This city will collapse. It'll be annihilated, without a trace left behind. They're totally insane, aren't they?"

"That can't be... Can't you do something?"

"...To tell you the truth, we've got nothing."

Marie cast her eyes downward and made fists with her hands, vexed.

"At any rate, there's no time. I was divested of my authority, so just to return to the core tower I'd have to break through the military's obstruction. Moreover, even if I arrive at the site, there are no prospects whatsoever of being able to repair the system in time."

"That can't be..."

"It's especially fatal that we can't locate the point of malfunction. Our observation squad calculated that it would take two weeks to find it. It goes without saying that we don't have that kind of time. But..."

Pausing there, Marie turned her face towards RyuZU, whose expression remained wholly unchanged even after hearing of such a hopeless matter. She hesitantly asked, "If it were you, couldn't something be done about this situation?"

Keeping silent, RyuZU didn't answer her.

As if to speak up for her, Naoto interjected. "Hey, wait up, now. From what you've said, you guys are a group of Meisters, right? What's RyuZU supposed to do on her own about something that would take you guys a whole two weeks at full force to accomplish?"

Without answering him, Marie peered into RyuZU's golden eyes and said, "I know your legend. The Initial-Y Series. The supreme automata that the creator of this Clockwork Planet, the legendary 'Y,' left behind. You're one of them. A mysterious automaton girl that wouldn't budge a millimeter, even though nothing should have been broken..."

RyuZU gazed back at Marie without a word. Recalling the sensation of having almost been killed not too long ago, Marie stiffened her body and continued as if muttering to herself. "A little more than two hundred years ago, you suddenly stopped functioning. Afterwards, several thousands of clocksmiths, including me, took on the challenge of repairing you, but were left frustrated. Y's ultimate treasure—the First of the Initial-Y Series. It's said that he who gathers all the automata of the series will rule the world, will inherit Y's legacy, but...well, let's suppose that that's just idle gossip. In any case, we, the Breguet family, have some fragmented information on you, as the ones who have had you in our custody."

RyuZU didn't reply. Marie licked her dry lips and continued, "The automata of the Initial-Y Series each have their own unique inherent abilities. You, the First, have the 'Acceleration' ability—it's said that you're an automaton specialized for ultra-high speed movements."

Naoto's eyes widened. He had been listening to everything from off to the side.

I see, if that's the case, it would explain all the questions I had.

The movements that allowed her to escape the apartment while holding Naoto right after starting up. The ultra-high speed movements that peeled the clothes off the three playboys in an instant, and the action earlier that didn't allow Halter to even react.

That is undoubtedly the inherent ability that Marie was talking about.

The high level of functionality she displayed that left even current military aircraft in the dirt would make sense if the great "Y" was her creator—I buy it.

Marie said, "You see, with the limited information I had, I interpreted the existence of you and your sisters thus: As this Clockwork Planet's—*maintenance machines*, left behind by Y for posterity."

"I'm right, aren't I?" Marie asked. She sounded like she was praying.

The Clockwork Planet that replicated the planet's mechanisms in their entirety was simply too complicated.

A mere human couldn't possibly—no, not even a single one of the clocksmiths who had devoted themselves wholeheartedly to their profession in the last one thousand years had caught up to "Y." None of them could understand the technology he left behind. With all their efforts, humanity had just barely been able to reproduce a portion of the Clockwork Planet through imitation, and even that process wasn't perfect yet.

In order for this planet to never perish again after his own death, did he not perhaps create his own successors, ones that would neither grow old nor die?

"The children who inherited the now-lost technology of 'Y.' The stuff about 'inheriting Y's legacy' was probably derived from that. The fact that you're operating now when this city is about to collapse is—"

Marie looked at RyuZU, eyes filled with expectation. "The very proof of that."

"Oho...!" Halter's eyes widened in admiration at Marie's deduction.

Naoto turned towards RyuZU as well, unable to conceal his excitement.

I see. If what Marie's saying is true, then there would be no doubt that it's this very silver-haired beauty who will become the angel of salvation for this city facing the imminent danger of collapse.

However.

Having gazes of expectation and admiration from the three of them turned towards her, the legendary automaton in question put on a somewhat out of place expression, like the one contrarian to laugh at a joke that fell flat with everyone else. She informed them thus: "I am clueless as to what you are speaking of. With all due respect, the current situation is gravely perilous—regarding your sanity, that is."

•••●•••

A queer silence befell them.

Marie had frozen solid mid-smile, and Halter was digging into his ears with an indescribable expression on his face. Baffled, Naoto was repeating a sequence going back and forth, comparing RyuZU's and Marie's expressions and cocking his head in confusion.

Halter managed to mentally reboot the fastest out of the three of them.

"...Ah, excuse me, Miss." He tilted his neck slightly as he calmly asked, "I want to confirm, just in case. Basically, are you saying that everything the princess here just said is wrong?"

"Yes." RyuZU faced Halter and nodded. "She looked so exceedingly confident and smug as she graced us with her grand hypothesis that it was terribly difficult to speak up, but—yes, her conjecture was a complete whiff. It is almost comical how it fails to even scratch the truth."

Marie's face slammed onto the table. Her body was twitching and trembling while her face remained buried into it. Perhaps she had become unable to bear all the shame.

RyuZU continued dispassionately, "It is true that I was made by the one you call 'Y' and that I possess an inherent ability that belongs only to me. That I'm the world's supreme automaton is, well, a self-evident truth that goes without saying."

Marie's head flew up, and she opened her mouth as if reciting a prayer. "I-In that case...!"

"However, it is not really my mission to maintain the planet's mechanisms. I have neither the knowledge and skills necessary, nor was I given an order along the lines of, 'protect the city.'"

Taking over for Marie, who had stiffened up again, Halter asked, "Then what are you actually here for?"

"'The Follower,'" RyuZU uttered, placing her hand on her chest and casting her eyes downward, as if to nonverbally assert that this was the most important thing of all. "That is the categorical imperative etched into me—to serve my master, Master Naoto, at his side, and devote all of my being to him. That is my one and only reason for existing."

Halter kept silent, his face indescribable.

Glancing at Marie, who was on the verge of fainting, RyuZU added, "Also, I would like you not to call my native ability a trivial contrivance like 'Acceleration.' Regardless, I don't have the ability to locate a malfunction, and as for the problem you are facing—frankly, I have no interest in it whatsoever."

After RyuZU declared that with a very pleasant smile, there was a drawn-out silence.

Marie looked up at the ceiling, holding her face with both hands, while Halter hung his head with an exhausted expression on his face. Seeing a scene before him that could be titled "Despair," Naoto couldn't find any words, so he simply stayed silent.

"...However, there's just one person." RyuZU muttered softly, causing Halter to slowly raise his head.

"There's just one person who may be able to fulfill your expectations."

"Who would that be?!"

Marie turned towards RyuZU with a start as she vigorously latched onto the automaton's words.

With their eyes on her, RyuZU slowly pointed—

At the dumbfounded boy on her left, before casually informing them, "I'm speaking of Master Naoto."

"Hah?"

"Huh?"

Being mentioned so abruptly, Naoto pointed at himself in a fluster, looking confused.

RyuZU nodded at him in response, then turned towards Marie and said, "Based on what I have heard from you, I believe that Master Naoto, who was able to repair me, may also be able to save this city."

"Wait a second—he *repaired* you?!" Marie yelled out in astonishment. "What are you saying?! You weren't broken anywhere!"

She was supposed to be the mysterious automaton precisely because she wouldn't move even though she wasn't broken.

"That simply means that you all are even more incompetent than Master Naoto."

"Ah—I was just casually called incompetent as well. That's fine, I guess..." Naoto grumbled in a small voice.

Ignoring him, Marie spoke up angrily. "I-Incompetent, you say...?! Are you insinuating that the Breguet family, which has continually turned out many hundreds of Meisters generation after generation, is below that chump over there?!"

RyuZU curled her lips as if scoffing.

She continued speaking with a smile that was different from the ones she showed Naoto—one that clearly contained anger.

"Yes. 'This chump over here' corrected the fault in my body that the members of that lofty family of yours failed to even detect, despite wringing the knowledge out of their flea-sized brains as hard as they could for over two hundred years—*in three hours*."

Being told this so forwardly caused the gears in Marie's head to stop turning for a moment.

Looking stupefied, she pointed at Naoto. "...This dumb-looking chump did?"

RyuZU wordlessly held up the hem of her skirt. Marie shook her head in a fluster and cried out, "I-I get it, I take that back! ...No, it's true that RyuZU is operating... Why was a clocksmith like him hidden in this city...?" Muttering to herself, Marie flopped onto the chair with a thud.

On the other hand, Naoto, the one who had been nominated, was breaking out in a cold sweat. "No, erm—Miss RyuZU? I appreciate your flattery, but you went a little far in suggesting that I'd be able to do something that a hundred great Meisters combined couldn't mana—"

"You can," RyuZU asserted. "As the one who was able to repair me, Master Naoto is, without any room for doubt, currently humanity's greatest clocksmith."

"No, I'm honored to hear you say that, RyuZU... but—"

It's impossible.

There's no way I could do it. To begin with, I'm a total amateur who isn't even an apprentice yet, you know?

Words of repudiation immediately surfaced in Naoto's mind, but he was unable to put his thoughts to words when he saw RyuZU's all-too-serious face.

He agonized and hesitated, but just when he thought he had something to say and opened his mouth to respond—

"...!!"

The city trembled furiously from a shock of unprecedented scale.

Clockwork Planet

● Chapter Four / 19 : 30 / Conquistador

The air crackled as it shook.

Assaulted by the fierce impact, Naoto was thrown out of his chair and tumbled onto the ground. His body stiffened as he crumpled to the floor. Standing up would be impossible.

Even in the present day, where the entire planet had been replaced by gears, there were still earthquakes.

Those frequently occurring micro-tremors just barely perceptible to humans were the result of the city mechanism expelling the pressure that had built up in its systems.

However, this shaking wasn't as simple.

The shock was of such magnitude that it felt as if space and time itself was being violently rocked. It was enough to make one think that the city was going to be smashed into smithereens if things continued like this.

The cupboard by the café lounge's counter collapsed.

The gigantic chandelier in the hotel's lobby had fallen.

Cars on the boulevard in front of the hotel collided in a line like billiard balls.

One after another, thunderous roars and explosions made it through Naoto's headphones and into his ears.

Meanwhile, the quaking still showed no signs of stopping.

And that's when Naoto saw it.

A teacup had been blown right off the table, yet it didn't fall to the floor; instead, it was *floating* in the air. The contents that had spilled out had split into big drops of water and were also gently drifting.

...What is this?!

As if to answer Naoto's question, Marie yelled, "A gravitational disorder...!"

Marie had crawled under the table and was lying face down on the floor. Next to her, Halter, who had thrust just his head underneath the table (because he was too big), exclaimed in a fluster, "Don't tell me that the collapse has already begun?!"

"Halter, how much time is left?!"

"Seven hours and twelve minutes—there should still be plenty of time..."

Marie's eyes widened. "Don't tell me that the military expedited the purge...!"

"No, calm down. If it's true that they've come to an agreement with Meister Guild's leaders, then they won't try to bury our Meisters along with the city."

"Even so, an omen of this scale should be outside their calculations. If the pandemonium spreads, we can't rule out the possibility that they'll take firm measures against it...!"

A short while after, the quaking settled down.

Even so, a numbing sense of foreboding markedly lingered

prominently in the air, as if lightning were about to strike.

Driving the cries and angry bellows he could hear from afar into the corner of his mind, Naoto stood up.

And then Marie addressed him. "You—"

"Huh?"

"You, what's your name?"

Serious-looking emerald eyes stared straight at Naoto.

Unable to ignore her, Naoto answered, "...It's Naoto. Naoto Miura."

Hearing that, Marie let out a deep sigh.

She looked down, hanging her head before raising it back up with a look of resolve. "Very well, Naoto. As I mentioned earlier, my name is Marie. I won't admit that you're a better clocksmith than I am even if it kills me, but—"

Her words were cut off. Before she knew it, RyuZU was standing behind her with a threatening look on her face.

With a tight smile, Marie continued, "B-but because my life is dear to me, I'll admit it! Listen, okay? Humility and modesty are unnecessary, so answer me clearly. Do you possess even the slightest potential to do something about this situation?!"

Naoto was at a loss for words. "That's..."

"He can." RyuZU immediately replied for him.

She turned to Marie and continued indifferently, "Based on what you have told me, the essential problem you have should not be 'there is not enough time' but rather 'the source of malfunction cannot be located.'"

After hesitating a bit, Marie said, "...Well, you could say that too, but aren't they the same thing?"

"It is a difference of heaven and earth. Conversely, as long as the cause can be located, then there is no problem."

Marie wavered a little again before nodding. "You're right. If the source is located, then things would be in the bag, but..."

"In that case, there is no problem whatsoever—master Naoto."

"Wh-what?"

"You should already know. The origin of this city's disorder—*the source of the sound*."

Marie tilted her head. "Sound?"

Well, if it's just that...

Naoto nodded.

"But, it should be no surprise that I can't tell exactly where it is like this... I'd have to actually go to the twenty-fourth floor for that."

"Wai—wait a second!" Marie cried out. She questioned Naoto, "How do you know that the twenty-fourth floor is where the problem is?!"

"Wha?"

Naoto looked befuddled as Marie pressed him so vigorously it looked like she was going to bite him. "Neither Halter nor myself said anything about the current repair site being the twenty-fourth floor. So how do you, who hasn't ever even entered the core tower, know that?!"

"How, you ask...?" Naoto said with a blank look on his face. "Obviously because dissonance is coming from around there."

"—Hah...?"

"I had thought that it was really annoying, making that racket all the time, but then it got *really* bad two days ago, so I was convinced that the military guys were ditching their maintenance work..."

"Two days ago—"

An "Ah" escaped from Marie's mouth. She thought back to the gravitational fluctuations that had suddenly occurred before dawn that day.

He noticed that irregularity—the one that took ten members of the observation squad to measure—wait, *dissonance*?

Halter stepped forward from Marie's side and asked cautiously, "Naoto, I want to confirm something with you—In other words, is it like this? Through just sound, you can perceive a disorder seventy kilometers underground from the surface, and with just your ears to boot. Is this what you're saying?"

"Hm? Yeah, what about it?"

Seeing Naoto nod his head nonchalantly, Marie and Halter froze. They were astonished.

Even though they could understand the meaning of what was said, that only made it more unbelievable.

They felt uncertain as to whether the short boy in front of them was really human.

In a trembling voice, Marie yelled, "L-look here, you! What kind of absurdities do you think you're saying so casually?!"

"I mean, even you guys can pinpoint it this far, can't you?" Naoto looked like he wanted to answer "of course" for them.

Marie shouted back at him with abandon, "...Yes, that's right. But it was information that we had to force out of someone from Technical Force, since it took us an entire day to inspect down to only the second floor!"

Naoto tilted his head, his mouth agape. "Why would you do something so troublesome? Ah, was it to make extra sure?"

"Because we couldn't have found that out if we didn't do at least that much..." Halter let out a sigh that seemed like it was squeezed out from the bottom of his artificial lungs.

"Hah? I just have ears that are a little sharper than most, you know? You guys should at least also have some parabolic reflectors to gather sound with, right?"

"...Look here, if the analysis could be completed with just sound collectors, no one would be worked up—" Halter groaned while pinching the bridge of his nose.

"Hold up."

Talking over Halter, Marie said with a tense face, "I just realized. Don't tell me that *those are a pair of noise-canceling headphones*?"

"Hm? Yeah they are, what about them?"

"You're kidding me!" Marie yelled. Her voice had grown hoarse. "You—*how are you able to hear us* while wearing something like that?!"

"You can ask that, but, uh, because it was cheap, I guess?" Naoto scratched his cheek as if he was unsure before continuing, "I don't really listen to things like music, but it's more relaxing when things are quiet, so...

"They give me peace of mind," he added.

Marie glared at him and pressed, "Peace of mind? Nowadays, even any cheap product should make good on being '100% soundproof.'"

"Even if you say that, I really do hear you."

"I'm saying that that's weird! You know that you're cutting out all information that enters through the ears right now?! Just what are you saying, that you can 'hear' like that?!"

"I-I mean, you say that, but..."

"...No, never mind. It doesn't seem like you're lying."

Marie let out the largest sigh she could. Then, to make sure, she continued, "In short, you can tell the source of irregularities by just listening to their sounds. If we take you with us to the twenty-fourth floor, you'd be able to identify the point of malfunction. As long as you can do that for us, we can manage to do something about the rest—are you fine with me construing things this way?"

As Marie looked at him, Naoto scratched his head as if troubled.

He understood that she was placing her expectations on him.

It was just that, to Naoto, this was an unfamiliar sensation—it might even be the first time he'd felt something like this. Because of that, he was unable to simply give an immediate reply.

Sounding less than confident, he answered, "Ah... Before you become disappointed in me, I want to mention beforehand that I'm just a high school student, that fumbling with machines is just my hobby, and that I'm a total amateur who isn't even an apprentice, much less an actual clocksmith."

"Thanks for that depressing information." Marie groaned, closing her eyes halfway as she shrugged. "I don't know you, but I do know how complicated RyuZU's design is. If you fixed her, if you're saying that you found the fault in her with your ears, then that's all that matters. I'll believe in that reality."

Naoto stayed silent.

After thinking a bit, he properly faced the blond-haired girl in front of him for the first time.

He asked, "...Tell me, why would you do so much?"

They could hear screaming outside that sounded like it was coming from the lowest level of hell.

There's no reason whatsoever for me to stay in this city now that I know it's going to be purged. To be honest, I want to get the heck out of here already.

"According to what you've said, you're surrounded in all directions by enemies and the future looks hopelessly bleak. Why aren't you running away?"

Naoto thought that that was what most people would decide to do in her situation.

However...

"I'm someone who hates thinking that something's impossible," Marie stated. "There're limits, no doubt, but setting them myself and giving up on my own? No thanks. I've come this far by constantly challenging someone, whether it be Father, Elder Sister, or myself in becoming a Meister."

Naoto couldn't understand her thought process. "...Why?"

"Because this world is a challenge. Our planet died a thousand years ago. It had reached its limits and come to an end. *But because there were clocksmiths who challenged themselves, we are alive today.*"

Marie smiled sweetly and continued, "Things that are irreplaceable always lie beyond one's limit. That's why I don't want to give up. If I run away here—I could never be proud of myself again."

"......"

"That's why," Marie whispered, as if making a wish, "Please—lend me your hand."

Naoto didn't answer her.

The boy who was born an ordinary person, grew up at the bottom of society, and had lived his life up to now savoring the bitter taste of his circumstances, and—

The girl who was born a genius, had her talents polished, and had lived her life up to now bearing noble ideals.

The two of them were oil and water.

For the two of them to come to understand each other in this short time was hopeless; their values were separated by far too large a gulf.

"......"

Naoto believed that if this city was going to collapse, he and RyuZU should get the heck out of there already.

Fortunately—or perhaps not, they were homeless right now. It made no difference where they went.

To begin with, even if I were to trust this incomprehensible creature called Marie and bring RyuZU along with me to a do-or-die situation like that, just what would be in it for me?

"...Sorry, but—"

"Ah—Master Naoto. I have something I would like to report," RyuZU spoke up, interrupting him as he was trying to refuse Marie's plea. "As I am but Master Naoto's follower, I was troubled over whether I should mention this, but..." began RyuZU, glancing in the direction of the core tower through the window before continuing quietly, "If she has not been moved, at the bottom of Kyoto's core tower should be...*my younger sister*."

Thump.

Naoto felt his heart pound vigorously.

He stopped breathing for a moment as the word that RyuZU had uttered echoed in his head many—no, countless times over.

Yanger sistur...younger, sister...younger sister... Eh? Younger sister...?

"Younger, sis...ter?"

Naoto staggered and clung to the table that had tumbled to its side next to him as he looked up at RyuZU.

RyuZU's...younger sister.

At the bottom of the core tower?

In other words, here in Kyoto?

In this city that's on the brink of collapsing in a purge and sinking down into the dead planet below?

His lungs sought oxygen savagely, and he felt an illusory sensation run through him, like his blood had reversed its flow.

"...In other words, that is to say..."

Naoto tried his best to feign composure somehow by taking deep breaths, but it just made his panting louder.

However, his valiant efforts were negated by his shrill voice as he exclaimed, "A-a-an automaton made after RyuZU?!"

"Yes. The Second of the Initial-Y Series, AnchoR, 'the one who destroys,' should be there."

"W-w-wait, in other words, umm, an automaton...more advanced... than RyuZU?"

RyuZU furrowed her eyebrows. "There is no automaton with greater overall functionality than me, but I have capable younger sisters who possess abilities that exceed my own under specific situations and whom the inferior creature that is man cannot even hope to compare to."

Naoto staggered to his feet.

His body temperature was flaring, and his blood pressure was skyrocketing with such force that it felt like his blood vessels would rupture.

"Err, umm. Could I ask you something just to be sure?"

"Yes, what is it?"

"Umm...was it 'AnchoR'? ...What kind of girl is she?"

"Let me think. She has pretty black hair in a bob-cut, and though she has visible white beneath her iris, her pupils are a vivid red. In terms of human appearances, I would say that she looks to be about twelve years old. She's about a hundred forty centimeters tall at most, and has trouble expressing emotion. True to her title of 'the one who destroys,' she possesses the strongest mobile fighting ability and armaments of all automa—"

"Hm? Whaaat are we just sitting around for? Let's get going!" Naoto straightened his back with a snap and raised his fist high into the air. Sounding determined, he declared, "If there is even a slight chance that someone like me possesses the means to save twenty million lives, then we mustn't let go of that chance! After all, I suspect that that's—my destiny!"

Naoto spoke forcefully. Unlike before, his eyes were now full of radiance, like they were burning with passion.

His emotions were typically called 'ulterior motives' and 'selfish desire.'

However, people—especially women; in other words, Marie—didn't know.

That men can risk their lives for transient emotions like that.

That men are foolish, yet noble creatures like that.

"...Say, princess. Is it really a good idea to count on these guys...?" Halter whispered to Marie.

"Could you not ask...?" Marie groaned as she shook her head.

Once Naoto decided to go to the core tower, the group of four began to advance briskly through the corridors of the hotel.

They were heading for the underground parking lot. Naoto and RyuZU were told that Halter had a car parked there. They cut through the lobby, which was in a state of pandemonium from the chandelier falling down, and entered the stairway.

There, Halter stopped and turned around.

"Now then, first, what should we do about *them*? Though we already know, there'll be nuisances trying to hinder us so long as we try to head to the core tower," Halter said, squinting one eye ever so slightly as he glanced suggestively at the wall.

Understanding what Halter was alluding to with his gaze, Marie nodded. "...We need to do something about that. If we're captured on our way to the core tower, the staff left underground might be taken hostage." She sighed and shrugged in irritation.

Naoto spoke up from beside her. "What now? Aren't we gonna head to the core tower?"

"Yes, we are."

"There's no time, right? So let's get going."

"...I'm telling you that at the moment, we're thinking about what to do from here so we get to the core tower safely. Understand?" Marie clicked her tongue in displeasure.

Seeing her reaction, Naoto tilted his head and looked puzzled. "Are you referring to those guys keeping watch on us over there? Are they really a problem that we have to stop moving for?"

Hearing a keen observation out of Naoto made Marie furrow her eyebrows sourly. "...If you've already noticed, then could you use your brain a bit more? Do you think they're only here to watch us and they'll just silently see us off as we leave?"

"Well, I mean," Naoto continued as he looked up at Halter's giant frame. "This old man is a cyborg soldier, and RyuZU is here as well. Aren't we good if we just dispose of them before they send out communications?"

Halter smiled wryly, somewhat taken back. "...Now that you're on board, you've become awfully aggressive, eh, mister."

Marie let out a sigh before saying in a subdued voice, "If we could, I'd want to do that as well. But this isn't such a simple problem. Politics are involved. The military's clocksmiths may be incompetent, but their ability to organize effectively is—"

"I'm not talking about that. When all is said and done, what are you trying to do? Play political house?"

"Ngh."

Marie raised her fist at Naoto—then stopped herself. She glared at him with her pair of blazing, emerald eyes as her body trembled all over with anger.

Her voice loaded with indignation she wouldn't be able to conceal even if she tried, Marie spat out, "...Just what could *you* know."

"I don't know. That's why I'm asking, isn't it?" Naoto replied. "This stuff about politics and organization, is it more important than the urgent mission of going to the core tower and repairing it?"

With a sunny expression.

Without any other considerations whatsoever.

Without any bonds or fetters, possible precisely because he was just an ordinary citizen.

The boy who had resolved to act freely for nothing but his own desires stated his concise and straightforward philosophy:

"Frankly, isn't everything aside from that *simply 'whatever'*?"

•••●•••

Marie closed her eyes and turned her brandished fist toward the wall, punching it mightily.

After that, she let out a grand sigh before turning to the giant man standing next to her and saying, "Halter."

"Yo."

"To lose an argument to someone like—someone like this *dimwit* is mortifying beyond belief. What am I supposed to do with all this frustration within me?"

"Hey, don't call me a dimwit."

Ignoring Naoto's protest, Marie continued, "But I'll still ask. Looking at things fairly, who's right?"

"Who knows... Well, if you're looking for an argument an adult would find sound, you're probably in the right, princess." Halter stroked his chin and shrugged his shoulders. "But, I don't think there's anything wrong with brats agreeing with each other as brats do, you know? Cleaning up after brats is a job for an old man like me, after all."

...*Brat*, Marie muttered inside her mouth before nodding. "Oh—I see. Now that you mention it, I am a brat, aren't I."

"Yep, you aren't even a clocksmith right now; you're just a sheltered, cheeky little princess, no?" Halter grinned broadly. He extended his bulky palm towards her and teasingly asked, "Will you give me some work to do, Marie?"

"...I suppose." Marie nodded lightly as she smiled bitterly.

From her side, RyuZU interjected coldly, "Is everything settled then? As we speak, precious time is being squandered. May I expect you to have the ability to at least reflect on that?"

"I know already. ...I'm going to ask just in case: I can count you as part of our combat force, yes?"

To Marie's question, RyuZU smiled gracefully as she curtsied and said, "Slashing down obstacles blocking the path of Master Naoto's will is my job."

Marie nodded at RyuZU; next, she turned back towards Naoto. "Naoto, after running your big mouth to the great Marie Bell Breguet like that, you'd better lend a hand as well."

"Let me just say beforehand that I'm super bad at fighting."

"I'm not expecting anything from you in that department. More importantly—" Marie placed her hands on her hips and threw a challenging glance at Naoto. "Your 'talent' that RyuZU mentioned—I'll have you show it to us, got it?"

Naoto nodded and quietly let out a small sigh.

Then, he slowly removed his cheap, fluorescent-green headphones.

Immediately after...

A noise so colossal it was nauseating assaulted Naoto, and he stumbled forward.

"Ghh...ngh." He grimaced, clenching his teeth. He felt as if everything around him was crawling into his ears.

It must have been because of the gravitational fluctuation. There were not only the sounds of malfunctions ringing from the city's gears, but also of the damage being caused by the fluctuation and of the hysteria of the people. Together, they reached Naoto's ears as a blasphemous symphony.

"Master Naoto." RyuZU gently supported Naoto, who was about

to collapse involuntarily, with her hands. "You're fine. If it's Master Naoto—it can be done."

"Yeah," Naoto spilled out a sharp breath. "If I couldn't live up to the faith of the world's greatest automaton, my reputation as a machine geek would be ruined."

He closed his eyes.

In the midst of the raging storm of noise was a clear melody in a hidden calm. It was the sound of RyuZU operating. A beautiful, elegant, perfect—and fateful melody.

With RyuZU's melody as his auditory pillar, Naoto began to pick only the things he needed from the massive stream of information infiltrating his brain.

And then—

"...Now—let's go."

Naoto began counting *them* up.

Marie descended with an elegant stride down the spiral stairwell as they headed towards the underground parking lot. Naoto walked gingerly behind her. However, two men showed up standing on the landing ahead so as to block their path. Both were big and brawny, and side by side, they gave off an aura intimidating enough to flatten someone like Marie.

One of the men glared sharply at her and said, "I take it that you're ex-Meister Marie Bell Breguet?"

Marie grinned, saying, "If I said I'm not, would you believe me?"

The men didn't laugh.

"We're from the military. We want to ask you about the disappearance of Ryoji Nijima of the Technical Force."

"I seeeeeeee, so you're going to use that as the pretext. How well prepared you are."

One of the men stepped forward and grabbed Marie's wrist. That instant—

Marie's body sank.

With a sweep of her foot, she tripped the man who had grabbed her, toppling him, then pulled her foot back and kicked his head as it came falling down from above. It was an intense blow, so much so that the sound of his cranium cracking was audible.

Looking down on the man who had been knocked down unconscious before he could even speak a word, Marie clicked her tongue.

"Who gave you permission to touch me, huh? Know your place, won't you?"

The other man became enraged and reached out to grab Marie. "You bitch! Do you intend to resist—?!"

Marie brushed his hand away coolly with a simple stroke. She traced an arc with her hand as she followed through, punching the man's chin with her clenched fist. The man couldn't help but stumble forward, covering his torso as he lost his footing.

In that instant, Marie danced.

At the end of a sharp spin, she gouged the man's temple with the heel of her boot using the ample centrifugal force she'd gathered. The blow knocked the large man over, and a thud echoed out as the heavy lump of meat hit the floor.

"......"

Marie landed as her coat fluttered about. Without even taking a look at the men she'd brought down, she fetched a piece of candy from her pocket and tossed it into her mouth, crunching it into pieces. Naoto, who had been watching from behind, reflexively knelt down.

"I'm sorry for the conceited things I said, so please don't use those moves on me," Naoto pleaded.

"Good, I'm glad you understand." Marie nodded, then turned around.

Her gaze was turned towards the corridor at the bottom of the stairwell that led to the parking lot. There, she saw a military automaton that had gone unnoticed until now.

It was a lightly armed, bipedal model. Its silhouette was close to that of a human, but its arms bulged awkwardly. The muzzle at the end of its right arm was pointed precisely where they stood.

When she saw the weapon, which could easily turn two living children into mincemeat, Marie's eyes widened.

"You're kidding me. It's almost scary," she muttered; however, she wasn't addressing the automaton. Despite currently being exposed to mechanical murderous intent, her face showed no signs of fear. "Halter."

As if to answer her, Halter leaped down the center of the stairwell.

Boom. The heavy sound of impact thundered.

With the full momentum from his free fall, Halter's fist smashed into the automaton, greatly mangling its body all the way down to its frame. As it stumbled forward, Halter landed so he was shielding Marie and the others from the automaton's muzzle.

The automaton instantly recalculated the threat level of the enemy target that had abruptly assaulted it. Judging from the targets' physical capabilities and the distance between them, the automaton acknowledged that the full-body cyborg soldier was its greatest threat, and as such, turned its muzzle away from where Marie and the rest were.

However, by that time, Halter had already slipped up against the automaton's chest. Grappling its bulging right arm, he leveraged his own weight in addition to using his full strength, and tore it off.

"...!"

Upon being severed, its wires swung down with a jerk, and its gears and springs flew and scattered everywhere.

The automaton retreated as it stumbled—however, Halter crouched down fully, and then kicked off from the floor, sending himself flying towards it.

The automaton swung down its remaining arm as quickly as the blade of a guillotine.

The blow would have flattened and burst a human with a body of flesh—but Halter easily stopped it with one hand.

"..."

Its upper body jittered. Halter sneered as he pinned down the military automaton operating at full throttle with all his might.

"What a pathetic combat algorithm you've got, jeez. Did you really think you could take on a complete cyborg like me with the power of a lightly armed model? You lookin' down on me?"

Crack. The automaton's arm was being crushed flat.

Halter pinned down the arm with his hand. He squeezed with his fingers, warping its plating, breaking its shaft, and crushing its structural frame.

"You—idiot!"

Immediately after, Halter stomped down on its body, and massive fissures radiated out from where his foot landed. Then, after drawing it back all the way, he unleashed his fist. His punch came so quickly that the fragments that had broken off from his stomp hadn't even flown into the air yet. With all his internal gears working together, Halter smashed through the military automaton's plating with his fist and destroyed its nucleus, forcing it to shut down. He tore the central spring out and tossed it onto the ground; the cracked cylinder clattered as it rolled around on the floor.

As Halter tossed the automaton, now nothing but scrap metal, Marie addressed him from behind. "As expected, Halter. Thanks for your hard work."

Looking back at the girl walking down the staircase, he shrugged his shoulders. "Not a problem. However—" Glancing at Naoto, Halter spilled out, "Calculating both the number of enemies and their positions this perfectly... Are your ears a sonar system or something like that?"

That's right—the information that Naoto had gauged with his ears had been frighteningly accurate and precise.

Though Halter couldn't even begin to comprehend how Naoto could discern who and what bore hostility towards them in the first place, the boy had known everything in advance—the number of enemies, their positions, and even their weapons.

Just how advantageous is that, strategically...?

However, the boy in question didn't answer. Instead, he asked him with a somewhat excited look on his face, "Hey, old man! You're not just a military cyborg, are you?!"

"Oh, you can even tell that much? That's right. As you can see, I'm a stud on the outside, but I'm just as great on the inside, you know? My body is the 'Eighth Generation' model made by the Breguet Corporation."

"Huh, eighth? The current ones on the market should only go up to the 'Sixth Generation'..."

"It's a prototype a generation above the next model to be released on the market. This is as high-end as it gets." Halter took a pose, flexing his forearms to show off his muscles. "I'm the princess's bodyguard, so I get to use the Breguet Corporation's top-secret technology because of my affiliation with her."

"Hah—! Hey hey, show me what your arm looks like disassembled lat—"

"What are you two men chattering between yourselves for? About disgusting things no less. We're going already!"

Urged on by Marie, Naoto and Halter shut their mouths.

Walking down the stairs and through the corridor, they exited into the parking lot in no time. A black car was parked right next to the entrance to the corridor. However, when Marie approached the vehicle's doors—

"Don't move!" A booming voice echoed from a megaphone and through the underground parking lot. Marie zoned in on where the sound had come from.

A short and stout steel giant appeared as it turned off its optical camouflage. It was blocking the tunnel leading to the surface.

"A VS-08 Goliath—an armored soldier! Seriously? You've gotta be kidding me," Halter muttered, as his face broke out in a cold sweat.

Developed by the Vacheron Corporation, it was a clockwork mobile suit piloted by a live human aboard it. Because of its thoroughly sound-dampened mechanisms, it operated silently, and its thermo-optical camouflage gave it an invisibility function—its trump cards for battles in special environments. It possessed overwhelming power that the lightly armed automaton they had encountered earlier would be no match for even if it ganged up with other automata of the same model. Its cannon could pulverize even the cutting-edge artificial combat body that Halter used.

With a smooth motion, its muzzle turned towards Marie's group.

It roared.

•••●•••

The report he'd just received on the phone made Limmons swallow his breath.

...What did this clown say just now?

He felt sweat slowly seep from the palm that was holding the receiver.

"...Could you repeat that for me one more time?"

"I'm saying, because Marie Bell Breguet and her bodyguard resisted vehemently, I had no choice but to shoot the two of them dead. Aside from them, a civilian was caught up in the combat as well—"

"I don't care about that!" Limmons clicked his tongue loudly before continuing, "Who gave you permission to kill her?! I believe I told you to restrain them!"

"Yes, however—"

Feeling irritation boil within himself at the ambiguous reply, Limmons spat out in a low voice, "You guys were borrowing our corporation's Goliath and you couldn't even capture what is, at best, a single brat?"

"...With all due respect, to compare the target to an ordinary civilian is a little..."

"She's just a brat," he stated sharply. While tapping the phone with his index finger, Limmons curled his lips. "Yes, a brat. That's all she was in the end. She was but a brat who had quick hands when it came to handling machines, at most.

"Shot her dead, you say... I see, so she died, huh?" Limmons licked his lips as he breathed in and out once. "Considering that you showered her with rounds from the Goliath's machine gun, I take it that her body wasn't left in one piece, yes?"

His voice seemed to harbor some sort of expectation, and the one reporting answered in the affirmative. "...Yes. As the corpse has been severely mangled, it'll take a bit of time to confirm its identity—"

Limmons said, "That's just fine. In that case, dispose of the corpse as is. A written report is unnecessary. The story will be that Marie Bell Breguet was caught up in the city's collapse and has been missing since then."

"...Are you sure you're fine with that?"

"It'll be a serious problem if it becomes known that the daughter of the Breguets was killed by someone working for the Vacherons. Besides, this city is going to sink in a few hours, anyway."

"Understood."

And with that, the call ended.

Limmons quietly put down the receiver—then flipped the entire table over.

He glared and ground his teeth as he raved, "Idiots! Those incompetent fools...!!"

Having her die was a problem.

Marie Bell Breguet was supposed to be forced to take the responsibility for the forthcoming purge and drown in censure for it, consequently dampening the Breguet family's influence.

But that could only happen if she was alive.

A dead person couldn't be made to take responsibility, and the Breguets, their daughter having been killed, would naturally take a hard line. That would go against the script of the Vacheron head house.

"That wretched bitch! Disgracing me even in death...!"

But above all, he couldn't humiliate her if she died so easily. Limmons wanted to ruin Marie Bell Breguet. He couldn't contain his desire to have been able to see how her face would have distorted after she'd lost both her pride and her reputation.

If he had baited her with promises of restoring her position, or leniency at the hearing, perhaps that haughty girl would have serviced him like a prostitute and cried all the while—a future like that might have been possible.

But even a vulgar desire like that was meaningless if the girl was dead. He was full of spite.

Still, there was nothing he could do. He wanted to at least be able to kick her corpse once, but there was no time left even for that at this point. The gravitational anomaly was growing faster and faster, and the time limit until the purge was pressing closer even now.

While spewing foul curses, Limmons headed towards the helipad on the rooftop in haste.

•••●•••

Click.

"...And stop. Are you sure this is what you wanted?" Halter asked as he flicked the recording device's switch, turning it off.

Marie nodded happily while grinning from ear to ear. "Yes. 'The daughter of the Breguets was killed by the Vacherons.' We were able to catch that on tape without a hitch."

"To be honest, I think this plan is full of holes..." Halter groaned as he stroked his chin.

"Don't worry. This voice recording will become the truth. Whatever those pet soldiers of theirs say afterwards will only be seen as an attempted cover-up without any credibility whatsoever."

"If you die, their plan almost completely falls apart... Well, that'd be the case in theory. Still, feigning your own death was quite an idea..." Sighing, Halter discreetly turned his head and glanced at what was behind him: a heap of scraps RyuZU made when she'd deftly dismantled the mobile suits.

Fishing through the wreckage, the boy—Naoto—muttered while looking bored, "This is the feature product of the illustrious Vacherons, one of the Five Great Enterprises...? There isn't even a hint of artistry."

Standing beside him, the girl—RyuZU—rebuked Naoto in a whisper.

"Yes. However, Master Naoto—even if it were simply trash, if a child did his best to make something out of building blocks, you would have to praise him, like this: 'I see that you put a lot of effort into this.'"

While gazing at those two, Halter grumbled, "...Two human soldiers, a lightly armed automaton, a mobile suit, and a communications officer. *It was all just like Naoto heard with his ears, wasn't it?* Still, I thought that the mobile suit had to be a mistake..."

"If it becomes known that the Goliath Stealth the Vacherons are so proud of was seen through so easily, I wonder what their arms development department would think. Keheheh, serves them super riiight."

"You sure look happy..." Halter tossed away the communicator, stood up, and sighed. "As an ex-soldier, I still don't want to believe it even after a demonstration like that. Just how did he catch even the sounds of dampened mechanisms that were underground?"

"It's not like there's any room to doubt him after this, though, right? He's—*the real deal.*" Marie narrowed her eyes.

It wasn't actually impossible in theory.

For example, the animals known as "elephants" discerned sounds not with their ears but with their feet.

By stamping their feet, they could sense vibrations in the ground and communicate with faraway comrades. Whether in the earth, the floor, or the air, vibrations are all the same—"sound" is essentially vibration, and vibrations interact with anything and everything they touch, causing resonance.

It's true that the sound of the footsteps—in other words, the vibrations in the air—wouldn't reach above ground. However, the air would cause resonance in the walls, and the walls would transmit the vibration to the rest of the building.

Based on that principle, animals that can even perceive a coin being dropped several kilometers away definitely exist. Radar and sonar are technologies that were invented by applying those very principles.

However—

Marie threw Naoto a scrutinizing glance.

Naoto Miura.

He's human. For him, that shouldn't be the case.

It would make sense that he was still able to hold a conversation even while wearing noise-canceling headphones if he was using his entire body. For example, if he was using his bones to conduct the micro-vibrations of speech to his ears, the logic would check out.

But how was Marie supposed to grasp the fact that someone who could do that not only really existed, but could put it to such good use? There was no way one could dismiss something like this as just someone's "special talent."

If Marie were to give a name to something like this based on all the knowledge she had been able to acquire, it would be—a "superpower."

In this world where everything was composed of gears, this ability and the value it held implied consequences far too heavy for it to be dismissed as just someone's personal makeup...

"Marie?"

"Ugh." Having her name called brought Marie back from the vortex of her thoughts. "Wh... What?"

"Well, you were spacing out, so I was wondering if something was wrong. We need to hurry, right?" Naoto asked as he tilted his head, studying Marie.

"Yes, you're right. I'm sorry," Marie apologized quietly and set her interrupted contemplation in a corner of her mind.

It's fine for now.

What's important at the current moment is the fact that this boy Naoto is just as RyuZU said—an existence worth putting our hopes in. And also...

"...Now then. Are you ready, princess?"

"Yes, Halter, if you would."

Marie tore off the chrono-compass by her coat's chest pocket. That was the proof of being a Meister. It was a medal a girl called Marie Bell Breguet had once obtained.

With a grunt, Marie flung it up into the air.

At the same time, Halter raised his gun and fired. The shot was on target, piercing through the chrono-compass.

"…"

Destroyed by the bullet, the chrono-compass smashed into countless gears as it fell.

"That's right—being a Meister? Who cares about that," Marie muttered, like she was finally spitting something unpleasant out of her mouth.

The incredibly intricate timepiece with nine clock faces, big and small, broken into bits and pieces. The proof of being one of the very best clocksmiths in the world. There were clocksmiths who devoted their entire lives to earning one.

Excellent character, outstanding talent, and unremitting training—just as in the past, the present world continued to overflow with despairing clocksmiths who had all those areas covered yet still couldn't become a Meister. Even Marie, who had been called the Breguets' greatest treasure, had only obtained it after herculean efforts.

"…"

However, Marie didn't care about that at all.

If it was no help to her in accomplishing her current goal, if it was only going to get in the way of the ideals she was trying to protect—then it was absolutely worthless.

"From here on, I'll be doing as I please." Marie lifted her head and surveyed everyone's faces.

She clenched her hand into a fist before continuing emphatically, "I want to save this city. I don't care about what happens after, and things that are of no use to me are the same as shit. I don't care who you are, if you're gonna get in my way, I'll crush you and force my will through. Got a problem with that?!"

Halter answered Marie's bold declaration with suppressed laughter. While covering his smile with his hands, he gazed at her tenderly and said, "Well, I don't have a problem with that, Dr. Marie, but I do think it's questionable for a lady to say 'shit.'"

"Shut it, iiidiot." Marie replied in a vulgar tone as she placed her hands on her hips. "The Meister Marie Bell Breguet no longer exists. I'm just Marie. A brat with no obligations or responsibilities whatsoever." She smiled. Her eyes were full of fighting spirit.

She turned towards Naoto and RyuZU. "With this, we're on equal terms now, for better or worse. I'll be working you to the bone without any qualms, so you'd best prepare yourself."

"Ah—well—right, I'll try my best, ma'am." Naoto nodded as he drew backwards slightly.

As they had been talking, Halter quickly checked whether there had been any explosives or traps planted in the car. Confirming that there weren't any, he unlocked the doors before cheerfully saying, "Come on, get in. I'll take you guys on the ride of your lives."

Marie took the front passenger seat, while Naoto and RyuZU sat in back. Once everyone had buckled up, Halter stepped on the gas, a ferocious smile on his face.

After explosively speeding up the underground parking lot's ramp, Halter turned the steering wheel sharply. The car drifted as its tail violently veered to the right, causing Naoto to grab the assist grip on the ceiling in a panic. The gravitational engine roared as the car accelerated.

"How horrible," Marie groaned, pained by the sight outside. Even if one were to put things mildly, it was total hell in downtown Kyoto right now.

Dark clouds covered the skies as thunder boomed. In the distance, several tornadoes could be seen casually ravaging the city, as if it wasn't even worth their time. Things caught in the gravitational anomaly and funneled up into the air included houses, junk—and people. With things as they were, it looked like the anomaly would only grow more powerful.

The intense view looked just like a scene from a disaster film. Those were the kind of streets the car Halter was driving bolted through.

They were headed towards the center of the city—the giant core tower that pierced both the heaven and earth. It was the vast nucleus of the city that governed all of its weather and other natural phenomena.

"Hurry, Halter!"

"Right!" Halter responded.

There were accidents everywhere on the main road, but Halter managed to weave through the gaps by turning the steering wheel left and right as he continued to accelerate.

Naoto had taken off his headphones and was listening attentively. He quietly mentioned, "Ah—if you already noticed, then I might be giving unwanted help, but—there seem to be two cars with menacing vibes approaching from the left."

"Whaaat? Is it the military?!" Marie exclaimed.

"No! I don't think so?" Halter answered.

Naoto nodded, and just then, two gray cars leaped out from the cross street behind them. They were autonomous vehicles with machine guns installed on top of their flat bodies. The two vehicles drifted as they changed their directions, then chased after the car Halter was driving at a fierce speed.

"Warning! Warning! Pull over at once!" a jagged, robotic voice rang out from one of them.

"These aren't pursuers from the military. They're unmanned police patrol cars. They're something like a vehicular type of automata, and it seems like they're chasing after us at their own discretion."

"Haah? Why are the police chasing us?!" Marie yelled.

After thinking a bit, Naoto suggested, "Isn't it probably because this car is going way over the speed limit?"

"You've gotta be kidding me!" Marie shouted angrily, kicking the dashboard. "Trying to catch someone for speeding at a time like this, are the Japanese idiots?!" Turning to face Halter in the driver's seat, Marie inquired, "Can you shake them off?"

"Looks difficult. They're a little faster than us. It'd be troublesome if they continue to hinder us like this."

"Got it." Marie unfastened her seatbelt and bent to the side, pulling the lever to raise her seat. "Naoto, just to confirm, they're unmanned, right?"

"Yeah, no mistake, but what do you plan to do?"

"Lower your head and grab on to something."

"Huh?"

"Master Naoto, lean towards me." RyuZU pulled Naoto towards herself so she could cover him. Hearing the sound of the pursuing patrol cars getting closer, Naoto stiffened.

Marie opened the car's sunroof and popped out up to her waist. In her hand was an object that looked to be about twenty-five centimeters tall...

"Wha—?!"

It was a submachine gun.

Ignoring Naoto's gasp, Marie fired at the car on the right. A full-auto volley of bullets showered the unmanned patrol car. However, the sprayed shots merely scratched the car's armored exterior as they were deflected.

"...Bulletproof armor? How cheeky for a measly patrol car." Marie clicked her tongue.

Naoto spoke up. "Umm, I don't know if it's appropriate for me, who would be playing 'Ordinary City Resident A' if this were an action movie, to say this, but..."

"What?"

"The car you just shot at has two-wheel drive. The right front wheel seems to be unstable, so if you aim there, then probably—"

Before Naoto could finish and, Marie rotated the submachine gun one revolution with the flick of her wrist, causing it to swiftly transform.

A Coil Spear.

Using the weapon, which had transformed into a small rifle, Marie aimed and fired in a flash. The bullet ricocheted off the asphalt and up into the suspension of the right front wheel—which immediately popped off. The patrol car shook violently.

It began to spin, and the other patrol car collided with it from behind, making them both roll over before smashing into the guardrails and landing on their sides.

"...Your ears sure are handy, aren't they." A sigh of admiration escaped Marie's lips as she refastened her seatbelt.

"Are you seriously required to know how to snipe like that to become a Meister...?"

"Don't base your assumptions off this princess." Halter laughed as he turned the steering wheel sharply.

Their car drifted a great deal as it turned at the wide intersection, then began to race forward at an even more ferocious speed. They had entered the administrative district and were on a broad boulevard that traced a straight line and was surrounded by high-rises. If they just continued right to the end of this road, they'd arrive at the entrance to the core tower.

"...Everything's gone well so far, even though I figured there'd be an inspection point along the way somewhere as well," Marie said uneasily.

"Sealing the city off requires forces too, after all. They might have actually pulled out already," Halter answered.

Right after Halter finished speaking, Naoto felt a chill run down his spine. But before he could tell the others about it—

"Excuse me, Master Naoto."

RyuZU, who had been sitting quietly until then, began to move. She pulled Naoto towards herself forcefully, embracing him tightly.

"Mph—hmphngh?!" Naoto's voice was muffled as his face was buried into RyuZU's soft chest.

"Huh? What're y—" Marie turned around and began to ask, but

was so shocked she stopped mid-speech.

That was because RyuZU's skirt had fluttered slightly. As someone who had a grasp on RyuZU's construction, Marie knew what the sign she'd just seen meant.

The one weapon RyuZU was armed with—*the black scythe extending out from under her skirt*—had been swung down at a speed so fast that even Halter, a cyborg, couldn't perceive it. Immediately after, there was a *crack* as the car was cleaved cleanly in two down the middle, like a gag in a cartoon.

The two halves drifted apart and started to lean outward and away from each other, tracing a straight line as they continued to move forward in accordance to the law of inertia.

"What the hell do you think you're d—?!"

As Marie and Halter cried out, a deafening *boom* ran right past them. Something sharp and heavy pierced the air right between the two halves of the car.

Even Naoto's super-hearing couldn't capture that "thing," which had bolted past faster than the speed of sound.

The blast that sounded behind them afterwards, however, revealed its identity. It had been a shell—a high-explosive projectile with overwhelming firepower—that had fallen from the air and hit the ground.

The blast of air from the explosion caused the halves of the car to fall onto their exteriors. Sparks scattered everywhere as the metal grated against the asphalt. Carrying Naoto in her arms, RyuZU escaped from her half of the car with a skip.

While bearing another person's weight, RyuZU danced down from the skies. She continued falling, just so, before landing gracefully.

RyuZU looked down at the bewildered Naoto, whose eyes were darting about between her breasts.

"Master Naoto, were you injured anywhere?"

"Uh, shouldn't you worry about the two over there more than me...?" Naoto said as he slipped down from RyuZU's arms.

The halves of the car had continued to slide and crashed right into the guardrails. Their bodies were practically demolished, and their respective wheels faced the sky and clattered pitifully as they spun fruitlessly in the air.

If they were caught up in that...

Just as Naoto was thinking that, he noticed a white lump lying face-down on the ground right next to him—Marie. With her summer coat soiled, she stood up with a vengeance. It seemed that they had escaped just before the crash.

"RyuZUUUUUUUUUUU!! Are you trying to kill us?!" Marie shouted, her beautiful emerald eyes brimming with murderous intent.

However, RyuZU tilted her head and looked puzzled. "You sure do say some odd things. Looking at things objectively: Did I not just incidentally save your fleeting, precious life as I was protecting Master Naoto? I would not mind if you bowed your head and offered me blessings of gratitude, you know."

"There were other ways to do it, weren't there?!"

Halter staggered toward Marie from her side. As one would expect, his clothes were dirtied as well. He threw a glance behind himself. Seeing that the road had been reduced to a crater, he groaned quietly.

"...Hey, Marie. The more important thing is that they fired a shell at us in a downtown area."

"Urghh, God! Is every last one of them totally insane?!"

"It seems that Mistress Marie has a tendency towards emotional instability. Lack of composure is the sign of an infantile mind. Would it not be a good idea to become more of an adult and keep your childishness limited to your figure?"

Marie lowered her head and looked down, her mouth flapping open and closed repeatedly. "I feel like I could smash even a military-use automaton into pieces right now with the hatred I'm feeling towards this unreasonable treatment."

"That so? Then without further delay, could you give it a try?" Halter jested. Marie looked up at Halter, intending to retort, but was left speechless when she followed his gaze with her own eyes. There was a red light shining in the center of the road about three hundred meters in front of them.

It was an eye. A single eye that belonged to a body towering imposingly over the road, blocking it and casting a giant shadow onto the ground.

It had an enormous frame with a total height of roughly six meters, and two legs with reverse joints. Its silhouette was akin to that of a hare standing halfway up or an ostrich with short legs, and its abdomen was armed with a 120mm cannon.

Cold sweat gushed out of Marie.

"How does it look, princess? Could you do something about this with that vaunted punch of yours?"

"You're saying that while knowing full well what that is, aren't you, Halter?! That's a heavily armed automaton!"

A heavily armed automaton.

It was an unmanned mobile weapon developed for subjugation

through force. Equipped with a powerful cannon, durable alloy armor, and the ability to run, even on uneven surfaces. Because it was more maneuverable than a tank, it was undoubtedly one of the most powerful weapons in modern-day urban warfare.

Furthermore, there was more than just one of them.

Behind the first mobile suit she saw, Marie made out two, three... She was able to confirm sixteen of them in total just from what she could see by squinting her eyes.

"...My, is this finally the end of the road for us? What a bummer. I still haven't fulfilled my dream of hitting a jackpot in Vegas and hiring a blonde model to wait on me."

"Discard that vulgar delusion of yours," Marie muttered as she glared at Halter contemptuously. Despite the tangent, neither of them looked in the least bit relaxed.

"Unmanned weapons... They've probably been set to automatically intercept anyone who tries to approach the core tower."

The reason the mobile suits weren't shooting right now was because the distance at which they recognized a moving object like a car, versus the distance at which they recognized a human who was standing still, were set at different target-intercept intervals.

"To think that they'd use a force almost on the scale of a battalion as disposable chips. What happened to their spirit of not wasting things?"

"If they're going to make things look like an unforeseen accident, they'd need to suffer some losses too, wouldn't they?"

As the two exchanged banter, an air of despair began to drift between them.

RyuZU quietly stepped forward and asked, "In short, the two

of you are going to give up here... Are you fine with me construing things this way?"

"Wellll—yeah," Marie groaned with her eyes half-closed, looking agitated. "Breaking through that from the front is impossible. We have to somehow find a blind spot in the region they were set to guard and make an invasion route based on that—"

"If you think we have the time for that, there would be a need for me to re-categorize you from small fry to less than small fry..." RyuZU spewed out a derisive line dripping with venom, after which she began to walk forward.

She walked straight towards the throng of mobile suits positioned like avatars of violence and murderous intent.

"RyuZU? Just what are you planning to do?" Naoto asked worriedly, but the answer he received was succinct.

"I'll eliminate them," RyuZU replied as she took half a step backwards. She scowled as if the obstacle she saw before her was something exceedingly displeasing to her eyes. "Of all things, those pieces of junk without even a shred of artistry, so miserable that I can barely stand to look at them, fired a shell at Master Naoto. Given that that is the case, they are enemies that I should eliminate," RyuZU declared gallantly.

Marie yelled in a strained voice, "Wha! Stop right there! Those are the latest military-use automata, you know?!"

"What about it?"

"'What about it?' You...!"

"If you are trying to say that an antique made a thousand years ago cannot win against a state-of-the-art weapon..." A small, audacious smile surfaced on RyuZU's face. Her golden eyes were focused only on what was in front of her. "Let me answer you like this." She looked up at the skies. "Even after a thousand years, you humans still have not graduated from those brains of yours that are below those of mites, unable to create anything but toys that do not best even me—the weakest among us sisters."

A sound spilled out from RyuZU. It was not her usual light and melodic voice.

In a mechanical, businesslike manner, RyuZU said—or rather—RyuZU *proclaimed,* "Definition Proclamation—the First of the Initial-Y Series, RyuZU YourSlave."

That's right, she properly *proclaimed.*

"Inherent ability—'Dual Time.' ...Initiating start sequence."

It was a declaration of mutiny.

This is what her statement expressed: Right now, from this moment onward—

I shall break the laws of physics.

Naoto's eyes widened.

He heard a faint sound from within RyuZU that would be absolutely impossible for an ordinary person to hear.

Tick-tock, tick-tock, tick-tock.

The sound of a clock's second hand demarking time.

Loosely, definitely, irregularly, irrationally—but also beautifully and naturally—the sound distorted. At the same time, the sound of gears clicking into place against each other rang out, and in a cascade like a chain of dominoes being knocked over, RyuZU's black, formal dress transformed in shape and color. The naked, pale skin of her arms was laid bare, her face was covered by a fluttering veil, and her dainty torso was wrapped tightly in a pearl-white wedding dress.

Her golden eyes flared into a brilliant, ruby-like red.

"Commencing shift from the first timepiece, 'Real Time,' to the second timepiece, 'Imaginary Time.'"

The shutter of the timepiece above RyuZU's chest was lowered and, immediately after, *a second timepiece* revealed itself. The sound of a second hand ticking that Naoto couldn't hear made his eardrums vibrate.

There wasn't a single alteration in this space, this time, or this universe, but the supernatural sound RyuZU was producing was refashioning the time she was in and her very existence according to aberrant laws of physics.

It was incomprehensible.

But Naoto's perception chased the continual changes in the sound assiduously.

"Initiating Chrono Hook—jumping from normal operation to imaginary operation."

RyuZU suddenly turned around, surprising him. He swallowed his breath. On the surface of her deep crimson eyes, turned towards Naoto, were complicated patterns that glowed brilliantly, yet ephemerally.

RyuZU whispered in a sing-song voice, "Master Naoto."

"Y-yes?"

"The reason I stopped functioning for over 206 years was because of just a single gear, the one that you fixed for me. I am now going to initiate that gear, the 'Imaginary Gear.' It will only seem like a moment to you, but on my time axis, several hours will have passed."

What are you saying? Naoto simply couldn't seem to grasp the gist of it, and his face showed it.

Regardless, RyuZU cast her eyes downward apologetically and continued, her voice dispassionate. "Once this function is initiated, it cannot be turned off until my spring is fully unwound. I shall definitely return, so when I do, please—take care of my spring."

"Y-yeah."

"Well then, though it will only be from my perspective, please forgive me for leaving your side for *so long a time as three hours*."

With an elegant gesture, RyuZU made a curtsy and bowed deeply.

She announced the name of the maneuver she was about to undertake: "'The Relative Maneuver, Mute Scream'—"

At that instant, in Naoto's consciousness, everything had come to an end.

Naoto wouldn't be able to say *what had happened* coherently.

As for why, it would be because to Naoto's—no, to *any* human's imperfect vision, everything would appear to have happened simultaneously.

And that—that was, in fact, true.

It was just like an illusion of a film flying past in five minutes at a theater. An unnatural sensation of seeing a transformation process that should be there, entirely omitted. An absurd reality in which everything was altered instantaneously.

A wholly inexplicable, blasphemous phenomenon.

If one were to try to describe what happened anyway—it would be like this:

First, the sixteen heavily armed automata blocking Naoto's way had been pulverized all at once. Underneath their remains were several hundred lightly armed automata whose necks and feet had, without a single exception, been severed from their torsos.

The self-propelled artillery that had occupied a key position had been cleaved in two from front to back. The ten-odd silent helicopters that had dominated the skies, intimidating Naoto and his group from above, had their rotors torn off and were helplessly plummeting downwards.

That was the conclusion of things.

The unmanned force, about the size of a battalion, which had been deployed to seal entry to the core tower had been, in a literal instant, wholly transformed into a gigantic heap of scrap iron.

"Wh-what's up with all this...?" Halter muttered, dumbfounded.

"...RyuZU did all this by herself?" Naoto said as he noticed the pleasant sensation of something pressing down on his feet.

Looking down, there was RyuZU, snuggling up to him with a face like a child sleeping in her parent's arms.

"Th-that's right. I've gotta wind her spring!" Recalling the task he had been entrusted with, Naoto turned RyuZU on her side in a hurry.

Holding her slender, dainty waist under his arm, he parted her silver hair. He reached his hand towards RyuZU's spring—whose teeny little grip lay slyly hidden a little above her neck—and began to wind her attentively.

As he was doing so, Marie cried out, "Imaginary...? Did she say *imaginary time*—?!" Her eyes were overflowing with terror. "N-no way... Time control is a technology that we don't even have a hypothesis for! How does she have such an ability?!"

"Ah—sorry to bother you while you're all excited, but can I ask for an explanation? I don't understand what just happened." A groan spilled from Halter's mouth.

While winding RyuZU's spring, Naoto also looked at Marie as if deeply interested. Marie audibly gulped.

"Imaginary time. It's like the time that passes in dreams... For example, you've had a dream long enough that it felt like several days had passed even though you had only dozed off for a few minutes before, right?"

In dreams, time doesn't simply flow. There, time has no continuity or regularity. The time observed in dreams can speed up or slow down or freely move between past and future. What that shows is that the concept known as time is actually *relative*, not absolute.

The concept of time as absolute, flowing from the past to the future at a fixed rate is flawed—in reality, clocks, arguably the best symbols of that school of thought, do nothing but delineate what events happen at what point inside the continuous consciousness that humans possess.

What exposes that truth is the axis of time whose existence can only be proven mathematically that lies perpendicular to the axis of real time.

Delineated by imaginary numbers that don't really exist.

A fictitious time conjured by one's imagination.

Namely—imaginary time.

"Umm, sorry, but I don't speak French."

"Every word and sentence I said was proper Japanese!" Marie huffed and puffed after yelling with all her might.

Beside her, Halter spoke up, sounding perplexed. "...Even if you say that, does something like that really exist? Sorry, but I didn't understand any of what you said, either. I would think that as a Geselle I'd be able to understand...though I may not look the part at times."

"...It doesn't. Rather, even if it did, it would be impossible to observe."

Observing imaginary time would require an object that existed in imaginary time, something that is only possible in mathematical models. As long as human consciousness remains something that only flows continually in one direction, humans can never observe it, let alone understand it.

However—

"Hmm?" Naoto tilted his head.

Stopping the hand that was winding RyuZU's spring, Naoto gestured toward the automaton and pointed out, "Isn't there someone right here that fits the bill?"

"I'm telling you that that's impossible!!" Marie raised her voice.

Halter summed things up for Marie to pacify her. "In other words, this young lady used her control of this so-called 'imaginary time' to move on a different axis of time from ours, and by doing so, she was able to create this terrible spectacle, right?"

"No—that's impossible." Shaking her head, Marie firmly rejected Halter's explanation of things. "It's impossible. Taking in positive energy and outputting negative energy... Unless something that exhibits that kind of impossible behavior exists, it can't be explained. I'm sure that 'imaginary time' is just a moniker and that whatever RyuZU did just now works on a different princi—"

"C-could that have been it?" Naoto spoke up suddenly as if he had just recalled something.

Marie looked at him suspiciously, "What, do you have a clue of some sort?"

"RyuZU mentioned something earlier, didn't she? About the malfunctioning gear that caused her to stop running."

"Ahh, now that you mention it..."

"RyuZU was broken because of just that one single gear," Naoto announced, "which outputs counterclockwise rotational energy, *even though it turns clockwise.*"

"...Huuhhhhh?"

After an ample silence, Marie furrowed her eyebrows sharply and stared at Naoto. "Wh-what did you just say?"

"I mean, just like I said, there was a gear like that. It was the only one that wasn't tur— "

"How did you fix something like that?!"

"Eh? I mean—is it that strange?"

As if she was about to bite him, Marie exclaimed, "Of course it's strange! Rather, it's impossible! Do you have loose screws in your head?!"

"Uh, err...?"

"Use some common sense!! Are they teaching you nothing at school?!"

"Ah—well... I'm always sleeping, except for during practical exams. Tee hee~!" Embarrassed, Naoto stuck his tongue out to one side while Marie stared on in silence.

Sensing a sign of danger in her eyes, Naoto hurriedly followed up, "Ah—I mean, you couldn't fix it because you assumed it turned counterclockwise."

With an icy cold gaze and tone, Marie asked, "Do you think it's possible for a ball thrown forward to fly backwards?"

Naoto tilted his head and looked puzzled. "...Ahh, now that you mention it, it's strange, maybe?"

"Right? So—"

Marie let out a sigh of relief. *You finally get it, huh.*

"But if that's how it is, what can we do but accept it?"

"Stop messing with me! ...Aaarrrgh!!" Marie screamed, throwing her head forward so hard that her hair flew everywhere. Trembling all over, she uttered, "For the Breguet family's thirteen-hundred-year lineage to lose to a, a loose-screwed, perverted jackass like this... Just what kind of joke is this...?! Goddamn it!"

Marie clenched her teeth.

The idiot in front of her was literally and truly *absurd*.

If you're saying that someone wouldn't have been able to fix this automaton without that irrationality bordering on madness of yours... I see, if that's the reason every single clocksmith born to the Breguet family has failed, I can accept that.

I can accept it, but—

"...I don't want to acknowledge it. What's with this absurdity that violates all reason...?!" Marie groaned in agony.

Seeing her like that, Naoto tilted his head and said, "I mean, you keep saying stuff like 'common sense' and 'that's impossible,' but frankly, isn't it a bit late to worry about those things?"

"...What are you trying to say?"

"I mean, RyuZU was made by Y, right?"

"Yeah, so what?"

"*Well*—getting the idea to try to make an entire planet function with gears is pretty out there itself, don't you think?"

"..........."

"Rather, isn't it obvious that an automaton made by a guy like that would be more or less out of the ordinary?"

"................."

Marie couldn't respond. Her tongue had frozen.

"Y."

The legendary clocksmith whose true name no one knew, he was the designer of this planet—the Clockwork Planet—and also RyuZU's maker. Marie had never doubted that legendary figure until now.

She had respected him as a fellow clocksmith, and had devoted herself to her studies in an attempt to one day catch up to him and fully understand the technologies he had left behind.

But—but—

Today, for the first time, Marie thought that his existence was an anomaly.

He was a monster who had invented technologies that no one understood even a thousand years later; he'd created the blueprint for this planet, and on top of all that, had even mastered relative—or imaginary—time.

"How silly. There's no way such a feat can be done."

But whatever he had been, anomaly or not, his technologies and his product were right before her eyes. She had no choice but to acknowledge them. Just as Naoto had said, as far as this was concerned, there was nothing they could do but accept it.

...Even so, the nasty chill she had felt wouldn't dissipate.

The false sensation that the ground beneath her was rattling as it crumbled wouldn't disappear, either.

"..."

Just then.

"...Good morning, Master Naoto."

With her spring wound, RyuZU had restarted.

Seeing that, Marie and Halter instinctively took a defensive posture. The emotion swimming in the two's eyes, as clear as day—was terror.

It was an exceedingly natural response for those clocksmiths, who had just witnessed firsthand the nonsensical functionality possessed by the automaton known as RyuZU.

Dual Time—and the Relative Maneuver Mute Scream.

Just as its name suggested, it was an ability that sprayed silent death everywhere. RyuZU was an automaton that could destroy everything in frozen time, her targets unable to even resist.

There was no guarantee whatsoever that they wouldn't be classified as targets in her sights.

If she were just a weapon, then there probably wouldn't have been a problem. But RyuZU was an automaton. She was an autonomous being that didn't take orders from them. Furthermore, she wasn't programmed with the ethical code for artificial intelligence. In other words, that meant she could kill people. If she felt a need to, this automaton could very easily murder humans.

There wasn't any human who wouldn't be afraid of her if they knew those facts. There couldn't be.

However—

Seeing her slowly get up, Naoto said, "RyuZU." He paused, taking a deep breath.

"Please—please be my wife!" He yelled.

•••●•••

RyuZU's reply was almost instantaneous.

She blushed ever so slightly as a modest, yet sentimental smile came to her face. In a light, clear, sing-song voice like the sound of a music box, she replied, "You seem to have lost your mind, Master Naoto. How about you know your place?"

……

Mercilessly cut down in a single stroke, Naoto crumbled, falling prostrate onto the ground as his body spasmed.

A painful silence fell.

Marie looked up at Halter. He was looking back at her with half-closed, vacant eyes. Seeing the cold, sour look on his face, Marie nodded at him. They were thinking the same thing.

Namely: *The hell is this kid saying?*

"Naoto..." Marie sighed as she addressed the boy who trembled groveling on the ground. "Are you sane? Of course not, I knew that, but have you finally completely lost it? Just what train of thought led you to say that, just now?"

Still shaking, Naoto answered with a voice as tiny as a fly's. "Dat's not it... It jus' came outta me..."

I mean—I can't help it if I see something like that, you know? Naoto thought as he quivered in embarrassment.

He had lived up to now liking, loving, romanticizing machines. In his life filled with gears, RyuZU was unmistakably the supreme mechanism.

She was an automaton who possessed the greatest functions; her exterior was that of a girl so cute he could die; the sound of her operating was like the singing voice of an angel; and of all things, her master happened to be someone like him.

How could I not fall in love with her? And now, that transformation—

If I don't confess my feelings after seeing the most precious girl to me in the entire universe wearing a wedding dress, when am I ever going to?

It wasn't reason. It was his soul crying out impulsively.

That was why RyuZU's words pierced his heart so lethally.

"Master Naoto, I conclude that you have lost your mind." RyuZU repeated. "Even if I am a supreme work of art and a peerless automaton, a proposal is something done between a man and a woman of equal standing. To request marriage from a clockwork servant is, to put things modestly, absolute nonsense, and frankly, aberrant."

"Stop! My HP bar already fell below zero a long time ago!" As he traced small circles on the ground with his finger, still prostrate, Naoto said, "Heheheh... No, right, I get it... Yes, that was rash of me. I knew that RyuZU was embarrassed to have me as her master from the start. I couldn't think of appropriate words to express how I felt upon realizing that she had gone from being the treasure of the world to my personal treasure... I was reckless. I'll reflect on this solemnly. I'll go bury myself in a hole."

Naoto trembled in anguish. Perhaps even Marie felt some sympathy seeing him in such a sorry state, for she glanced down at him from behind and said, "W-well... Don't be so down, yeah? I mean sure, anyone would recoil at being suddenly proposed to by someone like you, but I mean, there'll be good things too if you liv—"

"I am sorry, but with all due respect, Mistress Marie." For some reason, those words made RyuZU respond. In a tone that sounded somehow menacing, as if she were issuing a threat, she said, "You are but slightly shrewder than most among the base lifeforms known as humanity, who possess intelligence below that of fleas. If you think you are in a position to look down on Master Naoto, I would suggest that you reflect on your own irrelevance instead."

"Huh? Wh-why do you have to insult me so badly just for agreeing with you?! Also, you're not sorry at all, are you?!"

"Say, miss," Halter interjected. He seemed puzzled as he stroked his chin. "... It seems that you're not programmed with the code of ethics, considering that you tried to kill our princess, but don't tell me that you aren't even programmed to obey your master—Naoto—unconditionally?"

RyuZU answered, "I am YourSlave, the one who follows—the only rule that I have been programmed with is to follow my master. Is there a problem?"

"...*I see.* In other words, you aren't programmed to show favor towards your master."

Those words became the final nail in the coffin for Naoto as he wailed, heartbroken.

However—

"There seems to be a misunderstanding, so let me rephrase. I am programmed to obey my master as a 'follower,' but my having feelings for Master Naoto is of my own free will. It would be great if you did not treat me the same as a sex toy who spreads her legs unconditionally as soon as the confirmation of her master is complete."

"...*Free will*? Did an automaton just say something like 'free will' just now, Halter?!" Marie cried. However, Naoto, who had abruptly stopped crying, ignored her.

RyuZU said it just now. She definitely did.

And that she 'has feelings' for me.

...Oookay, calm down, don't panic, Naoto told himself.

Naoto slowly stood up before asking gingerly, "Could it be that... you don't hate me... RyuZU?"

"Me? Hate Master Naoto?" RyuZU had a blank expression. However, Naoto didn't let it slip past his eyes—or rather, his ears.

Now that he had taken off his headphones, he definitely heard it—

The sound of RyuZU's gears shifting ever so slightly.

"What reason would I have to dislike someone like Master Naoto, whom it would be a challenge to find anything but fault with?"

In other words, she had no reason to like or dislike him.

Marie and Halter probably heard it that way. If Naoto had taken her words at face value as well, he probably would have smashed his head against the ground and buried himself.

However, by now, Naoto was convinced.

RyuZU had showered him with heaps of verbal abuse up until now—and strangely, he didn't find it unpleasant. That was probably, most likely, maybe, not because Naoto was a pervert with particular fetishes.

...No, perhaps he had no choice but to frankly acknowledge that at the moment that he, being the machine geek that he was, proposed to RyuZU, an automaton—but that's not at all what we're talking about here—

"RyuZU, c-can I ask you why you won't be my wife?" Naoto's voice was trembling.

"I am Master Naoto's follower, so... That is, to be your wife would be—in other words, to be husband and wife with you..." RyuZU's expression was as graceful and elegant as always. At first glance, one couldn't see any difference in it from usual.

However, Naoto didn't let it slip past him—RyuZU's eyes were wavering slightly.

"A husband and a wife—are two people of equal standing. It's true that whether you consider looks, brains, intelligence, or class, I surpass Master Naoto to the point that it's meaningless for us to be compared, but you are my master, and I am your follower. A thought like us being of equal standing... Please know your place."

Naoto was convinced.

He asked, "Say—RyuZU, could it be...that you're loaded with an abusive speech filter?"

RyuZU tilted her head. Then, she scrutinized him as if hurt by his words.

"Abusive? Me? For me, who sits at the zenith, to spend effort doing something unproductive like verbally abusing Master Naoto, a creature on the lowest level of the hierarchy? There is no way that I would conduct myself in a manner that damages my own character, like spewing venomous words, do you not agree?"

"She doesn't notice it herself!" It wasn't just Naoto who yelled that. Marie and Halter also joined him in a chorus.

Naoto's breath had become ragged, and he placed his hand on his chest to calm it.

"C-c-c-calm down, Naoto Miura...! You're at the ultimate crossroads right now!"

If RyuZU had an abusive speech filter (Naoto's provisional hypothesis), then everything she's said up to now was questionable.

Naoto had to somehow evade that hypothetical abusive speech filter and extract RyuZU's true feelings, which had been deftly hidden, out from her.

In the end, did RyuZU like or dislike him?

The answer to this one question would mean either heaven or hell for Naoto...!!

Naoto said, "Th-then, let's try this. Nod for 'yes' and shake your head for 'no.'"

RyuZU nodded.

...All right, it seems I can bypass her abusive speech filter if I make her keep her mouth shut.

Confirming that, Naoto turned the gears in his head—which usually saw so little use that it wouldn't be surprising to find cobwebs there—at full strength, cautiously selecting the contents of his question so he could get a definite answer.

He asked, "Then, first... Is the 'free will' that you mentioned something you're programmed with that activates unconditionally upon a request by your master?"

RyuZU shook her head from side to side.

Nice! It's going well. Naoto took a manly pose, raising his fists up in front of him.

He was happy at the content of her reply as well. In other words, RyuZU was programmed to follow her master, but having feelings for her master wasn't automatic.

However.

"Then...have those feelings of your own free will ever been directed at anyone besides me?"

Naoto's tactics, which he had taken a brief pause to come up with, began with a cautious—one could even say cowardly—question.

Considering that her abusive speech filter operated outside her consciousness, her free will might also have been receiving the same sort of interference. If so, Naoto wanted to analyze previous examples from which he could infer some sort of interference with her will that RyuZU wasn't conscious of. He could use that to deduce the interference's activation conditions.

However.

RyuZU simply shook her head.

"Huh? It hasn't happened before?"

Nod.

"Uh, umm. So, you're saying that, even though it's never happened before—you have feelings for me?"

Nod.

...The whole thing was becoming more and more baffling to Naoto.

Not to parrot Marie, but what is it about a dimwitted pervert like me that could have flipped that switch within her?

Actually, before that...

RyuZU's eyes had grown moist, and were wandering unsteadily. Her pale cheeks were tinged with scarlet, and her lips, just barely parted, were trembling. Her back, which she had always kept gracefully nice and straight, now seemed fragile somehow as she fidgeted bashfully.

She looked just like—right, just like a maiden troubled by love.

Could this mean... No way. That expression on her face, though. Could it really be...?

Was he just seeing things differently now because he had been constantly showered with streams of abuse? Or was this the real RyuZU that had been hidden behind her words, one that he hadn't been able to see until now?

...He had to make sure of it.

"Then, umm, I've got just two questions left... I want to...*confirm* something. Is that okay?"

Nod.

"First—in other words, you...have feelings for me by your own will and judgment, and not because anyone programmed you that way... Is this what you're saying?"

RyuZU nodded meekly.

Now that her wall of vilification had been demolished, the feelings that had been hidden within her words were laid bare. She exhaled as if in pain. She was holding both of her arms as if pleading for mercy. Her eyes were cast downward meekly, yet as his follower she couldn't turn her face away from him.

Naoto struggled to breathe. His mouth was as dry as a desert, and his heart was beating so fast that it felt like his veins would rupture. Something hot welled up from deep inside his heart. He was terrified of facing the girl in front of him. He wanted to yell, to run away—but even so, he held his ground.

His field of vision trembled.

He uttered the last confirmation. "Then, as for how strong those feelings are...could you nod your head as much as you see fit to describe how much you l-like me?"

It'd be more accurate to call it a want of his than a confirmation.

Comprehending her master's wish, the automaton's face turned red, then slowly began to move.

Once, twice, thrice...

Nod, nod, nod, nod, nod, nod, nod, nod, nod.

Naoto gazed up at the heavens. Hot tears spilled out in big, non-stop drops, wetting his cheeks.

He was happy. Right now, he was faced with the fact that the most precious treasure in the world loved him. His heart felt full from that alone. At this point, what did questions like whether this counted as love or not or whether love between machine and man was proper matter?

Ahh, the world is so beautiful.

It was like the daybreak that slowly lightened the deep darkness of the night sky. Like scenery that came alive upon the sun peeking its face through a gap in the clouds. Like a newborn that opened his eyes for the first time after crawling out of his mother's womb.

Naoto simply continued gazing at the sky as he yelled internally.

I won.

My time has come.

My life was anything but decent. To put it bluntly, I was a loser in life. There were times that I wanted to cry, too. There were even times that I wanted to die. Really, I always thought that my heart would be snapped in two one day.

Ahh, but I'm glad I kept living.

Nod, nod, nod, nod, nod, nod, nod, nod, nod, nod.

Seeing the scarlet-cheeked RyuZU continue to nod and nod as if it still wasn't enough, Naoto spontaneously fell to his knees. He clenched his teeth in an effort to hold back his unstopping tears and clasped his hands together, raising them with great reverence towards the sky high above as he bowed his head.

He prayed.

It was a prayer of gratitude.

For the first time since he was born, Naoto thanked the Almighty One of this world, whoever they might be, from the bottom of his

こくっ

heart.

Ahh, thank you, thank you sooo much...! I love you!!

...And then RyuZU, who had finished nodding for the two hundred and fifty-fifth time, suddenly asked, "Are you satisfied now, master?"

Her voice was cold.

"Considering that you evidently have a humiliation fetish as well, I am going to run out of category slots to assign for your personality analysis before long. Would it be all right if I summed things up and made a dedicated 'celestial-tier pervert' category to assign you to?"

However, because she was blushing, even those venomous words had no bite.

Wiping away his tears, Naoto smiled brightly and said, "Please, do as you wish. Right now, I'm busy savoring the joy of having been born."

"Is that so?" RyuZU nodded. "If you plan to stay here and savor the joy of life, then that joy will last for about six more hours. I would appreciate it if you could spend the remaining time in a way that does not leave you with any regrets."

...Hmm?

"Six hours left? Was there something going on?" Naoto tilted his head.

Marie, who had been flabbergasted by the developments until now, screeched, "The time left until this city's and our fates are sealed, you dumb perverted bastard!"

When he heard that, Naoto looked up at the soaring tower in front of him, taken aback.

Recalling the situation that he had completely forgotten as he was being deeply moved, he yelled, "Ahhhhhhhhhh!! Crap!! The repair of the core tower!!"

RyuZU spoke in a voice below freezing. "Ah, had you forgotten? I thought you were astoundingly bold to set a functional restraint on your automaton and indulge yourself in your humiliation kink in this situation, but I see that you merely have a case of tunnel vision."

Sensing her words were even thornier than usual, Naoto asked gingerly, "Ah…Miss RyuZU, are you mad at me, or…?"

"Mad? Why should every single word Master Naoto says jolt my emotions?"

"By all means, do as you wish."

Witnessing a conversation that for some reason seemed sweet, Marie screeched, "Do your romantic comedy routine afterwards! Do you guys really understand the situation?!" She glared at Naoto and RyuZU with searing eyes hot enough to melt titanium alloy.

Behind her, Halter let out a deep sigh. He looked exhausted as he pinched the bridge of his nose. "Give me a break, please. If we die because of this, it won't even be funny in the afterlife."

They were rushing towards the core tower, but Marie's mind was on something else. A deep suspicion was stuck in her mind.

"Y."

The clocksmith who had created the world, and also RyuZU's maker.

Imaginary Gear, the technology that shouldn't have existed in reality.

An automaton with free will that looked like she was in love, no matter how one sliced it.

The one-of-a-kind genius that no one else in all of human history could compare to had created those things over a thousand years ago.

But that was simply too much to believe...

"Was he really human...? Did he even really exist in the first place?" Marie inadvertently muttered.

No one answered her.

Seventy-two thousand meters deep underground, there was a vast space filled with gears.

In that space was a central corridor, where the aisles that led to all the different sections of the floor intersected. The corridor had a height of a little more than three hundred meters and a length of at least two hundred meters, but even this broad space was but a teeny-tiny piece of the entire twenty-fourth floor.

The rest of the area was entirely buried by the gears that governed the city's functions. Above the ceiling, behind the walls, and even underneath the floors, there were countless gears intertwined in ways complex beyond imagination.

That space was deserted, with no sign of even a single person's presence. Aside from the four who had stepped into the area just now, there were neither any shadows nor forms here.

"...Seems like no one's here. Did the military take everyone away?" Halter muttered as he picked a sheet up from the documents scattered on the ground.

With the equipment and papers left behind, only the clocksmiths themselves were missing. If they had voluntarily evacuated, they surely would have collected the reusable equipment, so one could surmise that their disappearance wasn't something that they had willed themselves.

Marie sighed as she nodded. "If that's the case, it might have been for the best. At the very least, it means that everyone's safe..."

"Hm? No, wait." Halter raised his face. "Looks like there're people here after all. They're coming back."

As he said that, silhouettes emerged from an aisle leading to the back of the floor.

It was a group of ten-odd people. Upon noticing Marie's group, they yelled in surprise. "Dr. Marie?!" As they called out her name, they ran towards her.

They were an elderly group of staff members who were all wearing fatigues; Service Chief Konrad was among them.

The service chief stepped forward as their representative and said, "Ahh, thank goodness! I see that you made it out safely."

Marie's eyes widened. "What do you mean by 'made it out safely'?"

"Right after you went back to the surface, a group from the military came spewing nonsense and ordered us to withdraw immediately. I wanted to tell them to get lost, but they started to say something bizarre like 'the Meister Guild has already agreed to this,' and considering that you were detained as well... Left without a choice, I had just the youngins evacuate."

Marie said in surprise, "Why didn't you guys evacuate as well?!"

"'Why'? You sure ask some strange things." Stroking his goatee, the service chief snorted. "How could we possibly run away when there's still plenty of work left to be done?"

"Speaking of which, Dr. Marie, I thought that the entrance had been sealed by the military. How were you able to get here?" Observation Chief Hannes asked.

Marie smiled bitterly, then shook her head. "Ah—let's leave that for later. We don't have time right now. The gravitational anomaly has already become terribly severe on the surface. We have to finish the repair as soon as possible."

"...About that," Hannes said with a dark expression. "Dr. Marie, sorry to tell you this when you've just rushed your way here, but we'd like to have you hurry and evacuate as well."

Marie's eyebrows shot sharply downward. "What are you saying?!"

"We're serious. A chain reaction occurred just now." The observation chief hung his head with pensive eyes. "If you stay as well when things are already this hopeless, then you'd... If you evacuate now, you should more than likely be able to escape."

"You're still young and have more talent than we do. We won't accept having you commit suicide here with us senile old fools," the service chief interjected from the side.

However, Marie glared at the two of them severely. "I came back to save this city, not to hear a tearful plea from a bunch of old bones."

"But...realistically speaking, there's no hope anymore..."

"There's no need for concern. We have a secret weapon."

"Secret weapon?"

A perplexed look spread among all of the staff, the two chiefs included.

Marie nodded with a smile, speaking confidently. "Yes, let me introduce him. He's a resident of this city, and—" As she turned around, her lips froze.

Where her gaze and the palm of her hand were directed was *the thing* she had begun to introduce as her secret weapon.

"A resident of this city, and..."

Her smile stiffened.

That *something*—namely Naoto—was looking at the ceiling ecstatically with an intoxicated expression on his face.

His delirious, feverish eyes were glittering brilliantly, like an addict's. The incoherent "weehehehehehehe" he kept repeating clearly proved to the onlookers that he was severely ill, beyond a shadow of a doubt.

On top of that...

"Wow, how beautiful..."

"...What?"

So absorbed that he didn't register Marie's voice, Naoto staggered towards the wall of gears. He ogled the countless moving parts on it and the ceiling with a gaze that was clearly one of love.

"Gorgeous...! I haven't seen mechanisms so complete and perfect since I saw RyuZU's internal workings...! It's simply too amazing. Dammit, just who was it?! Who was the unbelievable god that designed such pretty, bewitching, exciting, and wonnnderful moving parts...?!"

Seeing the deviant spewing nonsense as he wriggled his body gave Marie a chill, causing her to inadvertently take two steps backward. She was repulsed.

Behind her, one of the staff members inquired doubtfully, "...A secret weapon?"

"No, er, could you give me a sec?" Marie said, then groaned and shook her head as she beheld the over-the-top sight before her once more.

"Master Naoto."

Perhaps RyuZU had become unable to watch on any longer as well, for she told him in a severe voice, "I do not think that that is what you should be worrying about right now."

"R-RyuZU! I see that you're someone reasonable after all... That's right! Stop ogling the gears and—" Marie's face relaxed; she was practically moved by RyuZU's words.

RyuZU nodded deeply to Marie in turn, before continuing in a voice filled with refinement. "More importantly, blurting out that you haven't seen such perfect mechanisms since mine as you look upon this stale, moldy antique—I cannot let such an insult pass."

"It's not that, either!" Marie yelled tearfully.

Meanwhile, Naoto was acting suspiciously like he had been hit right where it hurt.

"Eh, b-b-but, I mean! No, well, of course I know just how amazing you are, RyuZU, but, but—"

"No buts or butter cakes. You said my body was 'very pretty' the other day. Were those words lies?"

"Your body?" Marie muttered, dumbfounded.

Naoto denied it in a fluster. "A-a-absolutely not! As if that could be a lie!"

"Then why are your eyes being drawn towards antiques like these? I demand an explanation."

I don't know what's going on anymore... Marie thought as she held her head. RyuZU's tone and attitude are the same as always, and her wicked tongue aside, she's wearing a gentle, highly refined smile. *But something seems...off.*

Almost like—a girl rebuking her boyfriend for being charmed and following another girl with his eyes.

"Look at it, this was something made a thousand years ago! Yet it's still operating perfectly, and on top of that, everything down to the details are visible! Despite having been daringly laid bare, this framework, this beauty remains just as magni—"

"I understand now. In other words, you are telling me to strip."

"Haah?!" Marie cried out, bewildered. Ignoring her, RyuZU began to unbutton her dress.

"H-h-h-hey, you! A-a maiden shouldn't show her skin in front of a gentleman!"

"Worry not, for I am an automaton, not a maiden. More importantly, even though I am superior in every way, whether it be number of parts, the precision with which they were made, or functionality, to suggest that I am inferior to mass-produced antiques like these is on a different dimension from actions that can be forgiven by claiming ignorance or stupidity."

"Ahh..." Marie finally understood.

I see... So in other words...

During an emergency like this...

At a time like this, when the fate of this metropolis and the lives of twenty million people are on the line...

This automaton is acting jealous.

And then, RyuZU clutched the hems of her dress. Seeing that, Marie yelled, "AHHHHHHHH!! CUT IT *OUT* ALREADYYYYYYYY!"

She'd snapped.

Rumble. As her roar rang out, it shook the space buried in countless gears.

"Consider the situation, you two! In four hours, we'll all be buried alive!"

Perhaps the roar that she had put all her might into had done the trick, since the two of them had shut right up.

They nodded in unison at Marie.

"Yeah, you're right."

"I apologize for Master Naoto failing to understand the situation."

"Eh, it's my fault?!"

"I don't care whose fault it is! Listen up! In four hours—ahh, it's already past that point!"

Marie pointed at her pocket watch as she continued, yelling, "In three hours and fifty-seven minutes, approximately twenty million people will all be purged and sink to the earth's core, including us! Are you two telling me I have to die watching your lunchtime soap opera?!"

...Where did the serious atmosphere of a few momets ago go off to?

Marie panted, her shoulders heaving as she was assaulted by the desire to strangle her past self from just a little while ago to death for believing in this pervert and this automaton.

Seeing her furious expression, Naoto batted his eyes as he wiped the blood off his face. He'd just had a massive nosebleed.

"Ah—yeah, sorry. I guess it's about time that we get serious, RyuZU."

"Yes, Master Naoto. We shall continue this conversation afterwards."

"I'm begging you, seriously..." Marie groaned, nearly sinking down to the floor then and there.

Service Chief Konrad called out to her from behind. "Ah—Dr. Marie? ...Just who are these people...?"

"I know what you want to say, service chief. I know all too well! But—" Marie turned around with her face red from violent fury and embarrassment. The service chief's face had the words "fed up" practically written on it, and when Marie saw him, she continued, nearly crying. "Please give him some time, out of respect for me. I'm sure that it hardly seems believable, that you don't even want to believe it...but they're our one and only hope."

The service chief seemed earnest as he looked at Marie.

He had been on this Earth for as long as fifty years now. During that time, he'd seen clocksmiths who had burned out from the severe workload, as well as genius clocksmiths who had retired early, crushed by the weight of their own talent.

That's why he had suspected that the girl in front of him had snapped in this all-too-hopeless situation, but...

Marie gazed back at the service chief fixedly. Her eyes had become a little puffy, but they still had life in them. Her gaze was a sane one, harboring the light of reason within it.

Sighing, he nodded slightly. Though he certainly wasn't short on questions, he concluded that he could, at the very least, trust the girl in front of him.

"I understand. I shall believe you for now."

"Thank you," Marie said, smiling with tears in her eyes.

She turned her gaze back to Naoto. She caught him just as he lowered himself to sit down where he was.

He crossed his legs, straightened his back, and took a deep breath. He silently took off his pair of fluorescent-green headphones and tossed them to RyuZU.

"Take care of those for me, please."

"Certainly." RyuZU bowed.

Naoto gave her a smile in return before facing forward once again and sinking into silence.

Like that, he proceeded to stare off into space without moving at all.

It may have been another story for Marie, Halter, and RyuZU, but the staff who had just met Naoto for the first time had no clue what he was trying to do.

One of them spoke up restlessly. "Err...? Just what are you trying to—"

"Be quiet," Naoto said sharply.

His terse words carried neither gravity nor impact. However, the sharpness of his tone made the staff member hold his tongue.

The heavy silence continued.

The sound of the gears meshing together, grating against each other, and brushing the air aside quietly sounded.

So intimidated that she even struggled slightly to breathe, Marie inadvertently thought, *What do these sounds sound like to this guy?*

The sense of hearing that could catch the disorder in the twenty-fourth floor from above ground. A superpower that anyone would scoff at in disbelief, should he confess it to them.

What did this world full of gears sound like to someone with a gift like that? Marie wanted to know the answer to that badly.

Unaware of Marie's thoughts, Naoto continued staring into space without even so much as a twitch.

Nothing happened as time simply continued to flow.

The staff were visibly antsy. In about four more hours, they were going to sink to the bottom of the earth along with the whole metropolis and twenty million other lives. And yet, they were to remain silent, without doing anything. Such a task was no less agonizing than torture.

However, anytime someone tried to open their mouth or leave—the automaton standing next to the boy stopped them with a sharp look.

Don't speak.

Don't move.

Recognizing the overt message encoded in her gaze, the staff stayed nailed right where they were.

Two minutes, four minutes, six minutes—a seemingly eternal amount of time passed.

Before finally...

"I've got it," Naoto muttered quietly. The tense atmosphere instantly relaxed a few degrees.

Released from the suffocating, anxiety-inducing pressure, a commotion stirred among the staff who had been constrained to silence until now. They sounded suspicious.

Among them, Observation Chief Hannes raised an eyebrow.

"You've got it, you say?" he questioned in a chilly tone. "Just what did you get? That you wasted precious time? If it's the fact that we're already done for, we've known that for quite some time," the observation chief said sarcastically; however, Naoto paid no mind to his words.

While gazing at something seemingly far away, almost as if his soul had left his body behind, he declared, "Eighteen spots."

"What...?"

Marie interjected to fill in the blanks left by Naoto's insufficient words. "You mean that if we repair eighteen spots, the system governing gravity will be normalized, right?"

"Right." Naoto nodded lightly.

Hearing Naoto's reply, the observation chief became enraged, shouting at him, "Such nonsense! How would you know that?! Don't tell me you plan to say that you grasped the structure of this floor's mechanisms just by sitting over there?!"

"That's right," Naoto immediately and clearly replied.

The observation chief was about to shout at the kid in front of him again, but was flabbergasted upon seeing Marie rush up to Naoto with a diagram of the floor.

"Where are those eighteen spots?" Marie asked as she spread it on the ground.

Naoto peered intently at the diagram, but alas, he shook his head.

"Sorry, this is too difficult for me to read. I'll tell you where they are verbally, so look for them in my place."

"Got it, leave it to me." Marie nodded.

All of the staff present had been watching their exchange as if it were something terrifying.

The observation chief asked Marie timidly, "...Dr. Marie, are you really serious? You're going to act based on the ramblings of a boy who just said he can't even read the layout of the floor?"

"That's right."

Exasperated, Hannes yelled, "Dr. Marie! For you of all people to tag along on a nasty child's prank like this, what are you doing?"

Marie turned around and said, "I know it sounds unbelievable.

But at present, we have no other means. If we have no other way, then I want to bet on a miracle."

"Dr. Marie!!" the observation chief screamed. He seriously thought that this girl, who had always been wise and composed, had snapped. Even while wavering, he continued to be driven by a sense of duty to somehow make Marie come to her senses and quickly evacuate.

However.

"43,985,047,245,908—that's the precise number of parts."

Naoto's words turned that sense of duty of his into a shivering chill.

The corridor fell silent. Even Marie and Halter, who had already known about Naoto's ability beforehand, got goosebumps.

His tone was such that one couldn't think he was simply spewing out a random number. He declared it as if he had actually counted—no, as if he were simply reading it aloud from a spec sheet. He had declared it dispassionately, as if he were simply stating an obvious and unmistakable fact—such was his tone.

"There are 4,047 parts behaving irregularly among those. However, of those, 4,029 parts have no immediate relevance to the current situation—so in other words, there are eighteen spots. If those are repaired, the gravitational anomaly will end."

Just what is with this kid?

The veteran staff of the Meister Guild were left speechless.

Even the service chief and the observation chief were simply dumbfounded.

Even though they could understand the simple words Naoto was saying, it appeared that their brains were refusing to acknowledge what that statement implied. There should have been no one who knew the structure of a core tower.

The total number of parts here was something that even the military, who had maintained the core tower for hundreds of years, shouldn't know, much less how each of the components related to one another—an epic feat like that would normally take several hundreds of average clocksmiths observing and analyzing the structure of this floor for several months.

Even they, who held pride in being the best clocksmiths in the world, would need two weeks, and that's *if* they came into the job completely prepared and worked themselves to the bone.

No matter how they struggled—it would have taken at least that long.

Yet here was a boy who had announced what would have been the result of all that work after he had simply sat down for around just ten minutes.

...There was no way that could be true.

It should have been just random crap, but—the scary thing was, it didn't sound that way at all.

It was almost as if they had heard the physical laws of another universe, or encountered an incomprehensible extraterrestrial lifeform.

It was an abnormal, bizarre, strange, peculiar, outrageous, exceptional, inexplicable, and irrational—truth.

Someone gulped.

What was the emotion that they felt at that moment?

At the very least, they were looking at Naoto with a gaze that was neither respectful nor scornful.

If one had to say...

"Did you not say that there is little time?" RyuZU spoke up in a freezing-cold voice that destroyed this atmosphere in which time seemed to have stopped.

She glared at each of the staff members one by one. They trembled with a start upon her gaze, and she whispered sharply, "You are free to remain stuck in a daze, but to do nothing but shiver in a situation like this where even the help of a cat would be welcome... Should I take that to mean that your skills are less than that of a cat?"

That rebuke caused heat to return to the staff members' eyes. They blazed upon having their pride injured, the pride that came from being referred to as "first-rate" and having done jobs worthy of that title.

The service chief sighed grandly as if he were resigned. "...I suppose. It's true that we don't have any other methods. If Dr. Marie insists this much, then I suppose I'll try putting my faith in this kid, considering that it doesn't seem like he's completely fabricating things, either."

"But service chief...!" the observation chief groaned. He objected even now, but unable to find words to continue with, fell silent.

Because he knew just how difficult the task of observation was from his job, it was more difficult for him than anyone else to accept the reality in front of him—but he lost to the service chief's chiding gaze and Marie's spirited, emerald eyes.

As if enduring something difficult, he ground his molars just a bit before nodding. "...I understand. Let's do this."

The service chief tapped Hannes's shoulder gently as he turned around and said, "—Now then, could we have your instructions, Dr. Marie?"

•••●⬤●••

After getting Naoto to describe where the eighteen spots were in as much detail as possible, Marie picked out the ones that matched Naoto's description from the list of the projected points of malfunction and made marks on the diagram of the floor.

She assigned each of the spots to different staff members according to their individual technical ability.

After the impromptu assignments and instructions were given, all that was left was the same familiar work as usual.

Each staff member took their own equipment and went off to the location to which they were assigned.

Marie sighed as she saw them off.

There's nothing to worry about now. They'll surely do their jobs right.

"Now then, all that's left is this right here... RyuZU! Come here," Marie shouted loudly.

RyuZU walked to where she was as asked and looked down at Marie with an austere face.

"What is it? Just so you know, Mistress Marie, I do not appreciate being casually summoned by someone as measly as you."

"There's just one spot that would be difficult for a human to easily access." Marie continued, ignoring RyuZU's venom. She had begun to learn how to handle the automaton in the short amount of time she'd known her. "Normally I would use a repair bot, but I'm leaving it to you. Move exactly as I say down to the millimeter, all right?"

"The only one who can order me to do something is—"

"RyuZU, listen to her," Naoto said.

RyuZU scowled as if she found it disagreeable down to her very core, but nodded begrudgingly in the end.

"...I understand. Feel free to direct me."

After taking a glance at the diagram, Marie looked at the gauge in her right hand as she quickly did some calculations in her head. She turned to face RyuZU and gave her instructions based on the result from her calculations.

"Turn 91.2 degrees to the left from your current position, then look up 47.5 degrees horizontally, then jump 22.3 meters in that direction; there, turn your body 180 degrees, then look down 75 degrees, then jump 14.25 meters in that direction and land vertically. From there, move 57 centimeters to the right. Find the thirty-third shaft from the right, then locate the seventeenth gear that's turning it, then look down and right from it 67 degrees. Stick this screwdriver inside the 0.2-millimeter gap that's there. Inside, there's a gear 0.7 microns in diameter with a bent tooth. Straighten it without letting the gear stop turning."

At that point, it would be more accurate to call them super-precise input commands than instructions.

RyuZU sighed when she finishing receiving the instructions Marie had reeled off in one breath.

"Understood."

She bowed; the next moment, she had already turned her head and jumped.

Naoto's eyes widened as they followed RyuZU's shadow slipping into the group of gears forming the left wall.

Marie stood up while folding the diagram. "Now then, we're going, too. There're three spots that are difficult to specify orally, so we have to go confirm their locations ourselves. Halter, you come with me while *holding onto* Naoto."

"Yes, yes. Well then, you'll have to excuse me."

As ordered, Halter reached out with his burly arms, grabbed Naoto, and put him under his arm.

Having been lifted up like luggage, Naoto groaned sadly. "I'm totally being treated like equipment, huh..."

Marie had begun to charge towards where the three spots were. While chasing after her, Halter laughed. "What else can we do? You're simply too weak. If you're aspiring to be a clocksmith, then gain some endurance. The job is a physically challenging one where two or even three consecutive overnighters are common."

"Gehh..." Naoto groaned before sighing; however, he wasn't confident in the slightest that he would be able to keep up with this blistering pace if he were to run on his own feet. He resigned himself to being baggage.

"Then again," Halter continued, "if we have your power, then that might not be the case in the future."

"Am I really doing something that significant...?" Naoto mumbled doubtfully.

To which Halter asserted emphatically, "You are. Rather, you're so handy it's almost scary. The observation chief was trembling pitifully, you know? He was wondering just what all the work he had done up to now was for."

"There's no need to feel dejected over seeing the perverse ability of a pervert like this," whispered Marie coldly. She had caught up before Naoto had realized it.

Halter slapped his own head. "...Princess. Though he leaves much to be desired, he's still the messiah that saved us from a huge crisis and absolute despair. You shouldn't call him a pervert."

"If someone who can discover all malfunctions in a three-kilometer radius just by sitting silently for ten minutes isn't a pervert, then who is?"

"...Meh, I'm used to being called a pervert, so whatever, but—hold up," Naoto said.

Marie and Halter stopped abruptly in their tracks.

Still being held, Naoto turned his head. "It's that gear over there. The fourth one from the right."

He pointed downward with his finger.

Marie bent forward past the walkway's guardrail and confirmed it.

There was a group of gears that moved up and down as they turned. The parts, which were moving like pistons, were all the same shape. Among them, just the fourth one from the right was half a second late. "Got it. It's that one, right?"

Naoto nodded in return, but his eyebrows were furrowed.

The faulty part was suspended in the air twenty meters directly beneath them. There was nowhere to stand, and because other mechanisms were in the way, descending on a rope wouldn't work, either.

He turned to face Marie, asking, "What should we do? Go back and fetch a repair bot?"

"You're joking. We don't have that kind of time." Marie answered succinctly as she tossed off her coat.

She continued to climb over the railing before jumping off with nothing but her clothes, falling towards the group of gears as they continued to turn.

"Hey—!" Naoto yelled out in a panic.

"Relax, there's no need to worry." Halter laughed as he gently pulled Naoto back by his shoulder. "Watch carefully. These are the techniques of the number-one Meister of our time."

And then, Naoto witnessed a miracle.

Marie landed silently on a shaft, then crouched down and jumped once again. Screws, cylinders, wires, springs, and gears all operated in complex style. She slipped through all of that with movements as nimble as a cat's as she approached the malfunctioning gear.

She moved at a terrifyingly quick speed, without stopping for even a single moment. The group of gears in operation were strong, heavy, and sharp enough to easily tear a human body to pieces should they come into contact with one, yet the girl flew past them without any hesitation whatsoever.

Lastly, Marie kicked off from a rotating cylinder before hooking her feet onto a single, thin grate.

As she swung into an upside-down position from her momentum, the fourth gear just happened to be passing in front of her. The slender, pale legs extending from her shorts were awfully dazzling.

However—perhaps she had gained too much momentum, as tools were falling right out of the belt wound around one of her thighs. At least, that's how it looked to Naoto.

However, those tools didn't fall. Marie would grab one, use it, and then toss it up. She repeated the maneuver continuously.

The tools danced through the air just like juggling balls, *revolving* around a fixed point *in front of her.*

Screws, wires, and gears traced an ellipse in front of Marie as they danced in the air like gravity didn't exist, then fell back down into her hands. She was moving so fast that her hands were forming afterimages. While upside-down, no less.

It was terrifyingly quick work. A superhuman feat. Naoto shivered and forgot to breathe as he was mesmerized by the sight in front of him.

He gasped, muttering, "Ama...zing... So that's a Meister...!"

Halter smiled wryly. "Don't try to mimic her. Even a Meister would normally use a repair bot here or assemble a scaffold to work from before starting the repair."

"...Then what's up with that?" Naoto asked, purring.

To which Halter answered, "Though her ability may be different from yours, the princess is a fine genius in her own right. Her title 'youngest Meister in the world' isn't just for show."

"...I can't get enough of this," Naoto moaned.

It was the peak.

The zenith.

Sure, her divine technique was a beauty to behold; that much was a given. But even moreso, what about the elegant tone of the symphony being conducted by her hands? It was music Naoto had never heard before.

Naoto had always found sounds made by humans to be unpleasant; they were nothing but uneven and irregular. Yet, in the composition titled "Marie" being performed in front of him at this very moment, everything, from her pulse to her breathing and even the squeaking between her bones and muscles, was in perfect harmony.

"Hahah...ahahahah!" He couldn't resist laughing.

A splitting sense of excitement boiled up inside his chest.

One day...

Will I be able to make such sounds?

Marie's work ended in what seemed like less than a minute. However, to Naoto, who thoroughly etched all of it into his eyes and ears, it felt like it had lasted several tens, no, hundreds of times longer.

She returned the dancing tools to her belt like a sleight-of-hand trick. The magician herself wore a nonchalant face as she silently climbed back up, as smoothly and swiftly as she had descended.

Marie flipped herself over the rails like a circus performer before landing back on the walkway, and then she glared. "What are you spacing out for? We're moving on to the next spot immediately!"

She broke into a squall-like charge again.

Breaking into a dash himself as he chased after her, Halter gave Naoto a wink.

"What'd I say? She's the best, right?"

Three hours later...

The staff, who had gathered back in the central corridor after finishing their jobs, gulped as they listened to the observation chief read out the values of various parameters from their gauges.

"...And Brownian motion, normal value. Items to confirm—all clear."

Marie muttered, her voice tense. "Then, this means that..."

The observation chief slowly raised his face up away from the gauges as the staff present all watched him. His expression was a strange, distorted one. Big teardrops had welled up at the corners of his eyes and were spilling over.

"The repair...is a success. I can't believe it...!" he reported with a shrill yell.

The staff looked at each other, their exhausted, sullied faces saying, *Is it really over? Did we really do it? Can we celebrate now?*

However, little by little, cheers began to erupt from among them… before exploding.

"*Yahooooooooo!!*"

The space was filled with loud cheering. With complete disregard for their age, tears wet their wrinkled, stoic faces. The elderly veterans yelled, their merry voices echoing throughout the corridor.

"You're kidding me! Can you believe it?! We actually did it!"

"Hahahahaha! Dammit, I better not be dreaming!"

"Dear God…! I'll be going to church when I get back! I'll dump all the cash I have on me onto the donation plate!"

While some were hammering the floor with their fists, and others were rolling about on the ground, a certain someone left the crowd.

It was an old man with a splendid goatee—Service Chief Konrad.

He came in front of the automaton leaning against the wall some distance from the commotion and the boy—Naoto—sitting next to her.

"Can I have a word?" he asked in a rich, gentle voice.

"Eh? Ah…ahh, yes."

"Thanks," he stated his gratitude concisely, then sat down himself.

Naoto looked a little tense. The service chief turned a tender gaze towards him before slowly lowering his head. "We were saved because of you today. My name is Konrad. What's your name?"

"Ah… It's Naoto. Naoto Miura."

"I see." The service chief nodded. He then straightened his posture and bowed once again, formally this time. "Mr. Naoto Miura. I deeply apologize for my colleagues saying disrespectful things earlier. Because of you, our lives, Dr. Marie's life, and above all, the lives of the twenty million residents of this city were saved. Thank you so much. I'm grateful from the bottom of my heart."

Naoto's eyes darted about. It was the first time in his life that he had been thanked so earnestly, and by a fine adult at that.

Becoming somewhat embarrassed, he looked away, saying, "Ah... No, you give me too much credit. I simply pointed out the places where I heard unpleasant sounds coming from. The ones who actually fixed them were Marie and everyone else."

"There's no need to be modest. Without your power, there's no doubt that we wouldn't have even known where to begin."

The elderly man's assertiveness made Naoto gulp.

He darted his eyes about, looking flustered, opened and closed his hands several times for no reason, and shrugged his shoulders meekly before turning to face the elder in front of him.

Naoto said timidly, in a quivering voice, "Umm..."

"Yes?"

He asked, "Was I helpful?"

The service chief cracked a smile. "No matter how many times I were to thank you, I don't think it'd be enough to convey how grateful I am right now."

Unable to bear it any longer, Naoto looked down.

His eyes burned. An urge to cry out assaulted him. Recalling the awe and frenzy he had felt when talking to Marie after seeing her skills a couple hours back, Naoto trembled. How he had felt then and how he felt now seemed similar, yet somehow different. In the end, he couldn't understand it, despite trying his best to.

What was certain was that it wasn't a bad feeling.

Naoto felt something soft being laid on top of his hands as they pushed against the floor.

Seeing RyuZU's face near his own when he lifted his head up, Naoto's heart skipped a beat. She was smiling gently, as if she had cast her usual venom off somewhere.

The service chief gazed at Naoto as if seeing something heartwarming. "Mr. Naoto. I have a proposal for you: Would you be interested in enrolling in the Academy?"

"'The Academy'? You mean the Meister Guild's?!"

Naoto batted his eyes in astonishment. The service chief nodded. "Right. The specialty school that's even sometimes called the gateway to success for becoming a Meister."

"Uhh...b-but if I remember correctly, holding the rank of Geselle is a prerequisite to enrolling there..."

"True, that's one of the conditions. However, if you have recommendations from two working clocksmiths, you can enroll as a scholarship student. I think the talent you've displayed for us today is more than befitting of that. I'll write one of your letters of recommendation, of course, and as for the other..."

"If that's the case, I can prepare one."

Hearing a sing-song voice from above, Naoto looked up. He saw Marie, whose face was one big smile.

"Letting your talent lay dormant would be too much of a waste. Go receive a proper education at the Academy, Naoto Miura. If you acquire the technique and knowledge—and also the character and dignity worthy of a Meister, then you really might be able to become the number-one clocksmith in the world."

"Marie... You just casually repudiated my character, didn't you?"

Naoto glared at Marie with his eyes half-closed.

From his side, RyuZU stated, "It seems that you are finally able to accept reality now, but I see that your understanding is still lacking, you worthless human. Master Naoto is already the greatest clocksmith of all humanity."

"My, is that so?" Marie put on an impish smirk as she closed one eye, the one closer to RyuZU. "Excuse me, but if he's going to call himself the number-one clocksmith in the world, he should at least learn to read the layout of a mechanism first. Otherwise, he'll just look silly, you know?"

RyuZU put on a surly face, but said no more while Naoto made a strained smile.

That was when...

A thunderous roar and shockwave seemed to pierce the core tower through to its very center.

Losing her balance, Marie fell on top of Naoto.

"Gwahh?!" Naoto let out a strange noise from below, but she ignored him and looked up.

"What happened?!"

No one could answer the question she had yelled out. Everyone was panicking from the sudden impact, their minds a mess. Among them, Halter, who had recovered the quickest out of everyone, dashed to the gauges. When he read them, he looked like he was on the verge of panic.

"Hey Marie, this is serious! We're dropping in altitude!!"

"What?!"

The analysis chief sprang up, practically frothing at the mouth as he pushed Halter aside and read the gauges himself. He immediately glared as his complexion turned paler than paper.

"The purge is beginning!!"

Hearing his scream, the central corridor broke into the very definition of an uproar. All of the staff members doubted their own eyes and sanity and were shrieking while trembling in shock, their complexions faded from terror.

"That can't be!!"

"This has to be a joke! The city's malfunction was repaired!"

"And even if it wasn't, there should still be an hour left before the purge!"

"Don't tell me that they don't realize it's been repaired?!"

"No, if they're executing the purge, they should have been observing the core tower's situation."

"Then why?!"

As the tumultuous furor continued, Halter, who was standing still having missed the timing to panic along with everyone else, said in a low voice as if he had suddenly realized something, "Could it be that they're trying to pretend that it was never fixed?"

A terrifying silence fell. The look on everyone's faces was indescribable.

...That can't be.

Everyone doubted their own imagination, but even so, they were forced to acknowledge the truth the gauges showed.

The sound of someone sobbing could be heard. The veteran clocksmiths, who were likely second to none when it came to mental strength, crumbled onto the ground, their hearts snapped in twain. The jubilation they had felt from succeeding in the repair only made the despair they were thrust into from the betrayal immediately afterwards all the more unbearable.

"You're kidding me..." Naoto muttered in a daze.

He couldn't believe it at all.

There's no way someone who could think up such an evil thing and seriously execute it actually exists.

However, cruelly, Naoto was able to perceive it. Around the heart of this metropolis, the linked shafts that connected the city were being uncoupled, one after the other.

Naoto's hearing caught the booming sounds as it happened.

...Was it all over at this point?

Naoto fell to his knees, heartbroken. He felt the word "despair" slowly penetrate and spread throughout his heart. The warm feeling he'd had just before steadily cooled down as its heat dissipated.

Even though...

Even though I was finally able to see something.

...

Just then,

"Doooon't meeeessss with meeeeeeee!!" Marie screeched.

"Like I'll let it end like this!!" Marie shouted, her voice so loud that it echoed throughout the corridor. While everyone was sobbing on their knees, just one person was spitting fire as she stood on her two legs, her emerald eyes blazing.

Marie dashed to a nearby table and fiercely began to draw a blueprint. While doing so, she shouted, "Service chief! When this planet was reconstructed, the gravitational controls should have been replaced with clockwork in the city's mechanisms, right?"

The service chief, though perplexed as to where she was going with this, still nodded and answered, "Y...yes, that's correct.

"Is the location of that mechanism known?!"

"It should be on this floor. However, what do you plan to do with that knowledge?"

Marie didn't reply, instead turning to address RyuZU next, shouting, "RyuZU! Do you know the principle behind gravity being generated by gears?"

"...By means of the heat and kinetic energy from the gears' operation, a massive amount of energy is generated," RyuZU answered dispassionately.

Seemingly satisfied with RyuZU's answer, Marie bared her canines as she laughed, "Thanks for the explanation. Indeed, gravity is a phenomenon that occurs from space being bent towards masses and energies that are greater than other ones nearby! As such, can't you output negative energy with your Imaginary Gear—and cancel out the current gravity?!"

"...It is possible, in theory." Under Marie's stare, RyuZU answered in a voice full of hesitation before quickly casting her eyes downward. "However, if I use my one gear to reverse the gravity that is covering the entire city right now, I do not know just how long my gear will last."

"Can you give me an estimate?"

"...Thinking wishfully, about thirty minutes, I believe."

"That's more than enough. If you can buy us that much time, we can relink the shafts by manipulating the controls opposite of what they're doing from here!"

Marie cracked her knuckles as she curled her lips.

However, Naoto jumped up and wedged himself between Marie

and RyuZU.

"Hey, wait up. What are you saying? Just what are you planning to make RyuZU do?"

Marie met his gaze with her own. She said in order to confirm his understanding, "Listen up. The reason this city is falling in the purge right now is due to gravity. And that gravity is being generated and governed by a mechanism on this floor."

"...And?"

"If we interfere with that system by generating a reverse gravity proportional to the one causing the city to fall, we can avert the collapse of this city temporarily. All that'd be left to do would be to hack into the system responsible for the purge and relink the shafts in the meantime."

Despite Marie's explanation, Naoto looked suspicious. "Hold up... hacking into the system responsible for the purge? If you can do that, then why didn't you do that from the beginning?"

"I couldn't, though." Answering Naoto's question readily, Marie continued, "I only became able to do so just a little while back. I was able to deduce the root structure from the layout of this floor that you described to me. As for the concrete details—I can finish this diagram within five minutes."

The veteran staff members' eyes widened at Marie's statement. Even the service chief looked like his jaw was about to fall off as he stared at Marie. Such a feat of technical prowess was something that sounded impossible even for Meisters like themselves.

Naoto consciously exhaled to calm himself. "Then, what's this talk about there being a chance that RyuZU won't be able to endure the process?"

"...It means that we jam that small Imaginary Gear of RyuZU's into the center of a system that manages gravity and a large amount of energy. If we fail, her gear will break into pieces on the spot, and even if we succeed, her gear will still break if things go on for too long."

"That's a no, then." After cutting down Marie's proposal on the spot, Naoto turned around towards RyuZU. "RyuZU, would you make it if you escaped starting now?"

"That is impossible."

"What are you saying? If it's just you by yourself, you should be able to escape with the maneuverability you demonstrated when you wrecked those military automata—"

"I said that that is impossible. The option to leave Master Naoto behind and escape by myself does not exist within me."

"We're all screwed either way then, aren't we! What are you suggesting that I do?!" Naoto shouted angrily.

However, RyuZU shook her head and pointed at Marie. "That is not true, Master Naoto. If I sacrifice myself as this self-proclaimed girl genius proposes, we can overcome this crisis."

The observation chief, whose face was thoroughly pale, latched on to RyuZU's words.

"!! Can you really do something like that?!"

Naoto turned around. "No she can't, you dumbass!!"

"I can," RyuZU declared dispassionately.

It seemed like Naoto had touched a nerve, for the observation chief shouted as his forehead creased. "What are you talking about?! If there's a way to save the city, then—"

"I told you that she can't! Did you not hear the part where RyuZU will be sacrificed?!"

"But—a single automaton against twenty million lives—"

"I don't care whether it's twenty million or two hundred million!! Are you telling me that you would kill the most precious person to you in the world without hesitation if you learned that the world would be saved if she died?!"

Naoto looked like he was going to lunge at the observation chief any time now. The observation chief quailed from seeing Naoto's menacing expression.

"P-please calm down. 'The most precious person to you in the world'? ...She's an automaton."

"Yeah, she's an automaton, so what?" Naoto said with an expression that couldn't be more serious. Ignoring the flabbergasted observation chief, Naoto turned around and stated sharply, "This is an order, RyuZU. Escape right this moment."

"I refuse."

An automaton refused a clear order from her master.

RyuZU paid no mind as everyone was left speechless. She continued, "An unthinkable action like letting Master Naoto die—I shall firmly refuse by exercising my free will."

"RyuZU." Naoto's voice had become rough.

Notwithstanding, RyuZU said with a joking look on her face, "How about you think about it this way? Just by leaving me in a dysfunctional state, you will obtain a magnificent automaton—my little sister AnchoR—though not as magnificent as me. Aside from that, you will be able do whatever you want with my remaining body by taking advantage of my not being able to move. If you consider the twenty million human lives equal to a large heap of refuse that will also be saved as a cheap bonus to all that, then how about it? It is just barely worth it, no?"

"It isn't worth it at all." Naoto immediately answered, without so much as the hint of a smile.

RyuZU bowed once, saying, "I see. Then, how about this?"

RyuZU curtsied as she lowered her head again, saying, "An extremely incompetent automaton proposed something that threatened Master Naoto's life, and chose to destroy herself to atone for her incompetence, so you should at least make good use of her parts... What do you think?"

"Whaaat?"

Faster than Naoto could get a sense of suspicion from those words.

Correction, faster than those words could reach his brain.

The black scythe that flew out of her fluttering skirt left time itself behind—

As it pierced RyuZU herself.

"........."

He couldn't understand.

His brain refused to comprehend the sight in front of him.

"Master Naoto...I have no doubt—that you can do it."

RyuZU quietly stopped operating right in front of Naoto with a smile on her face.

Hooked onto the tip of the scythe that had pierced her chest was a small gear as black as night.

The Imaginary Gear.

"...Don't...mess with me..."

Naoto, whose brain had finally taken in the reality in front of him, squeezed the air from his lungs, yelling, "Don't mess with me, damn it! What do you think you're doing, leaving me behind as you please?!

I—I didn't come here for an outcome like this! Screw this!!"

No sooner had he yelled than he seized RyuZU's Imaginary Gear.

...He had no confidence that he'd be able to fix her.

It wasn't like before, when she was just hibernating. It wasn't just the damage from the black scythe piercing her chest. Because she had forcefully extracted an important part of herself, its sympathetic resonance with her other gears had been forcefully interrupted, causing micro-deviations throughout her entire body.

However, even so—Naoto reached his hand toward RyuZU.

"Naoto." Marie grabbed his hand before he could reach her.

"Let go of me! If, if I don't put this back where it was immediately—"

Marie yelled at Naoto, who had practically been reduced to a state of derangement, "Naoto Miura!"

"I told you to let go, didn't I?!"

"Just listen to me!!" Marie shouted back, as she clutched Naoto's collar and held him up.

While glaring into Naoto's ashen eyes like she was going to bite, she whispered in a low voice. "Listen. Pound this into that empty head of yours. I didn't say a single word about sacrificing RyuZU. I only outlined my current plan and its risk."

"That's the same thing!"

"It's totally different. Risks are risks. They're just possibilities. In reality, things will never come to that. Trust me, I'll fix RyuZU back to how she was. So you lend a hand too, all right?"

"...You need me too?" Naoto muttered, looking like he didn't believe her.

Marie asserted emphatically, "That's right. I was able to grasp the layout of this floor thanks to you, but to make this plan succeed, I have to understand the *entirety* of the Core Tower. For that, I need your ears—your 'talent'—no matter what."

Naoto sank into silence. Marie lowered herself onto her knees and held his face with both of her hands as she continued, "I trusted you earlier. This time, you trust me."

"......"

"I promise: If you lend me your strength, everyone will be saved. Whether it's you, RyuZU, or this city, I'll definitely do something about this and save them all."

"...I don't see any basis for your claims."

"There is a basis. It's—" Marie paused, squeezing one hand into a fist and placing it against her chest.

She adjusted her breathing before firing herself up—and yelling, "Because—I'm Marie Bell Breguet!!"

Naoto's ashen eyes opened wide.

Marie's emerald eyes shone bright. "Believe in my ability, Naoto Miura! I am a daughter of the Breguet family. A daughter of the man who used to be the number-one clocksmith in the world. The younger sister of the woman who is the current number-one clocksmith in the world. I broke that woman's record in becoming the youngest person to ever become a Meister!"

"......"

"I'm a woman who'll never believe that something's impossible!!"

As a chilling sense of awe ran through Naoto's chest, he thought: *She's dazzling.*

Ahh, goddammit, I don't have any talent after all. Who's the genius? This girl's the genius. A real genius—a real genius's talent is something that glitters brilliantly, like this.

He lowered his gaze to the automaton in his arms. Even now, when she had stopped functioning, RyuZU's golden eyes continued to reflect Naoto inside them. She was wearing a gentle smile on her face, without a single cloud of doubt; it displayed trust, no, even conviction.

Naoto groaned quietly, then sank into silence.

A true genius, who was so talented that it was frightening, had told him this:

"If you lend me a hand, I'll definitely save everyone."

RyuZU had given her absolute trust in entrusting her gear to him.

"Master Naoto, I have no doubt that you can do it."

"Really."

If I have that kind of power...

Naoto grasped the Imaginary Gear in his hand tightly and raised his face.

Facing Marie, whose eyes were blazing in emerald flames, head-on, he bit his lips.

Light wavered in his ashen eyes.

"...Please, tell me, Marie." He inquired, "What should I do?"

The periphery of the heart of Kyoto Grid was a large framework that supported the enormous moving part that was the city.

The gigantic cylinder of twenty-seven floors, extending fifty thousand meters in diameter and ninety thousand meters in height, was connected to four million shafts which linked the entire city. In the periphery of that cylinder were mechanisms that had been installed to allow the shafts to be released. Those mechanisms were a system originally intended to be used in emergencies as a last resort.

Even if some gears were to fall out, the Clockwork Planet had been made so it could maintain its systems by making the remaining gears mutually compensate for those that were missing. However, if gears were to continue to be lost, the number of remaining gears would decrease. Each individual gear would thus have more burden placed on it, which would cause it to heavily wear down.

Therefore, a purge was a last resort and nothing if not the worst method to contain malfunctions that could shorten the planet's lifespan.

However...

Right now, in the periphery of this city of Kyoto, that worst method was being continuously executed.

"...The release of all shafts connected to the twenty-sixth floor is confirmed!" an operator wearing a military uniform exclaimed.

A large man stood in the center of the control room. He yelled in a loud, echoing voice, "Good! Begin the release of the last set of shafts!"

Obeying his words, the group of twenty Technical Force clocksmiths operated the interface of the purge system. All of them had dark looks on their faces. They knew what their actions would result in, that the twenty million city residents would be killed. They also knew that the purpose of the purge was to conceal the military's blunder.

This was, unsurprisingly, too much for even them, despite having been trained to loyally obey orders. They were unable to feel pride and a sense of duty in executing such an operation.

Seeing their expressions, the man in the center of the floor—the commanding officer—clicked his tongue lightly.

My goodness, youngsters these days.

This operation couldn't be dismissed as a simple cover-up. The military's dignity and authority, as well as the public peace they protected, were at stake—In other words, it was a noble mission to maintain "order."

To lose their bearings over a sacrifice on this level, they absolutely lack resolve!

That brat from the Meister Guild was the same. Obsessing over the lives of a mere twenty million, does she not even have enough of a brain to realize what kind of harm injuring the military's dignity will cause? What 'genius'? A sixteen-year-old kid being a Meister? *Please, it's obvious that she used her connections. Filthy scum.*

"All signals confirmed. Connection to the release system complete. Preparations for the last stage complete," the operator said.

The commander raised his head. He sneered as he handed down the order.

"All right then, begin the countdown!"

"Understood. Beginning countdown. Five, four, three..." A dispassionate, emotionless voice counted down.

The clocksmiths who had completed their work gazed at the gauges with largely blank expressions. Though the commander's lips were pressed together, the corners of his mouth curved slightly upward.

"Two, one—release the last system of shafts!" the operator yelled in an ever so slightly shrill voice.

And then...

"..."

"..."

...

"...What?"

The metropolis didn't fall.

At least, no response showed on the gauges, and the rumbling that should have begun to some degree was also absent.

"What's the problem?! What's going on?!" the commander yelled. The clocksmiths and the operator checked their operation logs and the gauges once again.

After a short time, the operator exclaimed, "It's a gravitational anomaly!"

"What?" The commander tilted his head, looking perplexed. "Shouldn't that be the malfunction in the city mechanisms? What does that have to do with the failure of the purge we just did...?"

"Yes—I mean, no. This is a colossal gravitational response coming from the bottom of the city... No way! It's lifting the city!!"

"...What are you saying?"

"I-In other words—"

"I can only think that someone is obstructing the purge by manipulating the gravitational controls."

A heavy silence fell.

After which, the commander suddenly screeched, "Don't give me that crap!! Just who and how—" All of a sudden, his eyes, bloodshot from rage and agitation, opened as wide as they could.

He ground his teeth, looking shocked. "Don't tell me that it's that brat—?!"

•••●•••

The mechanism that controlled gravity was in the 289th control block on the twenty-fourth floor. It lay in a deep location where even the illumination from the light gears installed throughout the floor didn't reach it well. The sum of a great number of thick shafts that were joined together, its majestic appearance looked not unlike a giant, ancient tree that had lived for several thousands of years. Its nucleus lay in a place that was partially hidden by its roots.

Marie grappled with a circuit board that looked as complex as the anatomy of a living creature as she stared at the gauges. Naoto, who had taken a seat by her feet, held the automaton that had stopped moving in his arms. A wide, hollow hole was exposed in that automaton's—RyuZU's—chest. The Imaginary Gear that had been inserted in her chest was now crammed into the nucleus of the gravitational mechanism in front of them.

Naoto whispered quietly, "Marie, three military helicopters are approaching."

"Where are they?"

"Thirty-five degrees northwest, around 24,906 meters away from us."

"That's above the 192nd ward... They must be planning to obstruct the relinking." Marie fiddled with something by her hands. Immediately after, Naoto's ears caught the splitting roar of three explosions.

A cry rang out from the intercom on the wall.

"Dr. Marie! Explosions detected near the 192nd ward—!"

"Is there a problem?" Marie answered dispassionately.

"N-no. It doesn't impede our work in any way."

"Then please continue working. It was just some military helicopters falling due to a slight disturbance in the atmospheric pressure. There's no problem."

The voice from the intercom was left speechless.

Paying that exchange no mind, Naoto again announced in a quiet, detached voice, "Marie, this time it's twenty-four degrees southwest, around 24,589 meters away."

"Roger." Marie answered quietly as well.

Naoto's ears again perceived explosions in the far distance.

The staff must have detected those explosions too, for a gulp could be heard from the intercom. Marie faced the intercom and said quietly, "Can you hear me?"

"Y-yes..."

"We'll eliminate the hindrances that the military send. We have our hands full here between that and managing the gravitational controls, so I'm leaving the relinking to you guys. Please reconnect the shafts as soon as humanly possible."

"Un-understood...!"

"Naoto. The fifth floor's circuit won't seem to connect. What's going on?"

"The fifth cylinder in operation right now isn't in place. A different system that sits a meter right above it is causing interference. To sidestep it, turn the first cylinder clockwise by thirty-four degrees."

"Got it, the water collection system, right? Okay, connection successful."

The values on the gauges fluctuated dramatically, showing that yet another system had been connected. Naoto observed, and Marie handled the controls.

This unknown system output reverse gravity, something that hadn't even existed until now. By changing the levels, Marie was keeping the super-enormous mass that was this great metropolis level. Acting as her eyes, Naoto was constantly observing the core tower's structure and the situation of the entire city through sound.

Naoto waved the baton to which Marie played her instrument. Their two differing talents meshed together tightly, increasing each other's potential. This on-the-spot jam session was producing music that made it seem like the two had been playing together for years. It was almost like a symphony only they could perform.

"..." Seeing such a sight, Halter's eyes widened as he remained silent.

Seizing city functions one after another, resisting the purge, and eliminating the military's interference by manipulating the atmospheric pressure controls on the twenty-fourth floor—causing turbulent air to burst downward and spawn a dustdevil.

Seeing the duo's "performance," Halter only had one thought on his mind. "Is this really a human feat...?"

He had witnessed the evolution of Marie's genius many times before. It was also true that he had been startled by Naoto's unusual ability that, at this point, might as well have been considered ESP.

However, this composition they were performing, hand in hand—

Seizing, ruling, controlling, and manipulating a metropolis—a microcosm of the world—were *humans* really performing this feat?

What surfaced in Halter's mind was just a single, certain letter.

The rebuilder of the planet whose very existence was questioned due to his preposterous enterprise beyond all imagination. The initial of the figure whose real name was unknown, extolled as the supreme genius in all of human history—"Y."

People had forgotten how absurd his feat truly was, because a planet run on clockwork was just "normal" now. Indeed, this planet that had met its end had been recreated by a human. It had been designed by someone who had been neither a convenient magician nor a god, but just a human.

However, at this very moment, Halter could see two small figures who had conquered even gravity, dictating it as they held the lives of twenty million people in the palms of their hands.

At this very moment—What objection could there have been against calling them "gods"?

...He had nothing to base it on, but he was certain. More than likely—no—surely, undoubtedly, this right here—

—Was the figure of the one who had reconstructed the world—"Initial Y."

"God, I can't get enough of this."

Seeing the two gods who had the city under their thumbs, Halter got the feeling that that *impossibility* had just been thoroughly repudiated. As he stroked his bald head, Halter could only smile wryly.

"Marie, the gear has started to creak."

When Marie heard that, her eyelids twitched. Having continually negated an enormous amount of energy, RyuZU's Imaginary Gear was reaching its limits.

Without looking away, Marie tapped the console's controls. "...Not yet. I need ten more seconds."

A sharp voice rang from the intercom. "Dr. Marie! The main balance wheel is off by 0.2 degrees!"

Again, Marie tapped the console's controls.

"...! The alignment matched! Angle adjustment complete. Connecting the circuit!"

"Marie! The gear's at its limit!!"

"Give me six more seconds, I'll start the countdown!"

Five.

Naoto stood up.

Four.

Marie turned around.

Three.

Their eyes met.

Two.

Emerald eyes and ashen eyes exchanged a message that couldn't be put into words—

One.

A thunderous boom pierced through the Core Tower.

"Linkage complete!!"

Naoto had pulled the Imaginary Gear from the gravitational system before the voice even reached his ears.

He screamed, "Marie!!"

"Hand it over!!"

Snatching the gear from Naoto's hand, Marie lunged towards RyuZU. The gear was slightly bent. However, given that it had been able to generate reverse gravity to the very end, it should have no problem functioning.

Marie moved her hands about savagely. She quickly amended the slight bend and adjusted its lattice, before threading a wire through the gear and placing them into a cylinder as fast as lightning. Despite being a deeply rational person, she ignored the cries of her reason and logic against this clockwise-turning gear that output counterclockwise energy. That was just how this thing worked. She simply accepted it and continued working. She inserted a spring into place and screwed it on.

Marie closed RyuZU's artificial skin. "Wind her spring!"

Without having to be told to do so, Naoto had already reached his hands towards the screw.

"......"

As an ominous silence fell, only the sound of Naoto winding her spring rang shrilly.

...Could it be that she won't wake up anymore?

That terrifying fear crossed Naoto's mind.

Each time the spring turned fragilely, a cold sense of loss seeped deeper and deeper into his heart.

...Eventually, after what felt like an eternity had passed,

"...Ah."

RyuZU opened her jeweled eyes. They glittered like gold and shook unsteadily, and she blinked over and over. Her indecipherable gaze slowly began to shift before settling on Naoto. As the lips that were like those of an angel moved, a high, ringing voice like a music box spilled out.

"Ahh—Master Naoto."

She smiled gently.

"Your face is already unappealing to begin with. If you weep your eyes out on top of that, no one will be able to look at you, you know."

While spewing venom with her sharp tongue, RyuZU gracefully reached her hand towards Naoto. However, contrary to her sharp words, her eyes were glistening and her cheeks had reddened sweetly.

Seeing her like that, a gentle smile came to Naoto's face. He stroked her hair, then took her hand.

They began to cry at the same time.

The abusive speech filter inside the girl made a small, pleasant sound.

Clockwork Planet

● Epilogue / 00 : 00 / Restart

Naoto and RyuZU held hands as they descended the steps. Marie and Halter followed behind them.

They were on the spiral staircase that extended from the deepest part—the twenty-seventh floor of Kyoto Grid's Core Tower. The steps that seemed like they extended all the way to the center of the Earth were narrow and dimly lit, as there weren't many light gears. It was like the mouth of a gaping pit that led to Hell.

"This is where she is, right RyuZU?!"

"Yes. There is no mistake."

Unintimidated by the bottomless pit in front of him, Naoto plunged into it triumphantly. The reason why was clear.

It was because...

While briskly descending down the spiral staircase, Naoto wore a stupid smile on his face, his cheeks slack.

"Beyond this—lies RyuZU's little sister AnchoR! A super-advanced automaton!"

Every pore of Naoto's body was exuding avarice.

"Master Naoto!" RyuZU yelled abruptly.

"Huh—? What the?!"

RyuZU grabbed his hand. However, Naoto had been running and had too much momentum to stop. He lost his footing on the spot, falling down—and his body dangled in the air beyond the last steps.

"......"

Holy crap. Cold sweat poured from his entire body.

Right now, Naoto was suspended in midair, the only thing supporting him being RyuZU's one hand. The spiral staircase had ended midway and become a literal pitfall. If RyuZU hadn't grabbed his hand, Naoto would have already plummeted into the pits of hell.

"Hey hey, be careful, man. You just saved your own life after a great ordeal, you know?" Halter teased Naoto as he yanked him up by his collar.

"Y-you saved me..."

While feeling relief from the sensation of something solid underneath him again, Naoto spoke up and asked, "W-wait a second. This staircase only has a single path, and at the bottom of it is RyuZU's younger sister, right? If that's the case, why do the steps end here?"

"...It would appear that part of it collapsed from the shock of the purge." Marie answered. She had just been examining where the steps left off in a crouch.

Naoto paled as if his world had ended. "No way—that can't be... Don't give me that... When, just a step further—damn it! No! *Nooooooo!!*"

It was the wailing of his soul. Letting out a heartbroken cry that seemed like it would drag those who heard it to the realm of the dead, Naoto collapsed onto the ground.

He cried. Without any regard to how he looked, he punched the step beneath him as he wailed and wailed. The deep, bitter sorrow caused by the endless, Stygian abyss in front of him tortured the sixteen-year-old boy's heart.

He didn't care if his lungs gave out. A useless person like him who couldn't save RyuZU's younger sister should just be blown to pieces. The boy who had saved twenty million lives was disappointed in himself for failing to save a single automaton. Unable to bear that shame, he bawled and bawled.

Seeing him so sad, Marie muttered, "You don't have to cry and shout *that* much..."

"Shut up, leave me alone! I just lost a supreme treasure of humanity that no number of measly human lives, be it hundreds of millions, can match—!"

"Well, the yammering about her being the supreme treasure of humanity aside—" Marie pressed her fingers against her temple. "If there's something waiting beyond this point, wouldn't it have been retrieved long ago?"

"Eh?" Naoto stopped crying and lifted his head.

While looking up at what was above the spiral staircase, Marie said, "Kyoto's purge was decided in advance. If there was an Initial-Y Series automaton here, the military should know how precious it is as well... It's hard to think that they would leave it here."

RyuZU nodded in agreement. "Yes, they may be a beyond worthless bunch who reached for the easy solution of purging the city to cover up their blunder, who even imbeciles would be outraged to be compared to, and who could never hope to be worthy of owning AnchoR, but if they cannot even understand how precious she is, then I would really have to question whether they actually have brains. As such, I believe it is likely that they moved her."

Noticing an incongruence from her words, Naoto asked, "...Wait a second, RyuZU. If you say that, then wouldn't you have expected this from the beginning?"

"Ahh, I apologize, Master Naoto. I assumed that them lacking brains at all was precisely the case, so..."

Seeing RyuZU bow to him with a nonchalant look on her face, Naoto slumped his shoulders.

"...What am I doing...trying so desperately, even putting RyuZU in harm's way."

"It's fine, isn't it? At the very least, you saved twenty million lives."

"It isn't fine at all!" Naoto yelled while glaring at Marie resentfully. He reflected on what had happened today.

Things were great during the day. I had a date with RyuZU where I saw her wearing cute clothes and was verbally abused just the right amount—it was truly a period of supreme bliss. A heartwarming experience worth commemorating.

Yet, the moment I met this cursed, crappy, walking landmine, I fell from heaven to hell. I was wheedled into doing this and that, dragged into the maelstrom of a storm, forced to overcome countless, desperate situations, and ended up being left in this sorry state.

"All my blood, sweat, and tears were in vain... Damn it."

"Stop sulking. If nothing else, you altered the fate of this planet today. And on top of that," Marie said cheerfully, "You *forced me to resolve myself*."

"...Haah?" Naoto sounded puzzled.

However, Marie didn't answer him, instead turning her gaze towards the big man besides her.

"Halter."

"Hm?"

She announced with a tender smile, "I'm going."

Halter sighed.

"...I won't stop you. I guess I'll ask just in case, though—are you fine with that?" Halter asked solemnly.

However, Marie's expression was refreshingly clear.

With a firm step, she widened her stance, stuck her chest out proudly, put her hands on her hips, and straightened that small back of hers with all her might as she faced Halter. Her emerald eyes were brimming with hope and confidence.

It was a dream of hers. A foolish yet dear one that only children would be allowed to dream—a noble intent.

While feeling so much as envy of the unwavering radiance of those eyes, Halter put on a bitter smile as he nodded. "...All right, I'll be taking the liberty of accompanying you then, Dr. Marie."

"Very well." Marie nodded.

By her feet, Naoto tilted his head. "What are you guys even talking about...?"

"Something that only concerns the two of us—no, perhaps it does concern *all* of us." Marie laughed impishly as she gazed at Naoto. "Sorry Naoto, but could you forget what I said about recommending you to the Academy?"

"...Wuh?" Unable to follow this conversation in the slightest, Naoto did nothing but make a stupid sound.

Seeing the boy like that, Marie smirked and she turned on her heels.

Her summer coat fluttered, and she began walking gracefully

away. Halter followed behind her small, yet somehow large figure.

"Hey, Marie?"

"It's okay."

Without turning around, Marie waved her hand, tracing a small arc.

With a happy looking face, she said, "See you soon, Naoto."

"Master Naoto, this is the part where you say 'ahhh.'"

...Now then, how should I explain this situation?

Naoto was at a loss.

It was something that happened at lunchtime on weekdays in Tadasunomori High School.

The students who preferred boxed lunches over what they served in the school cafeteria ate lunch huddled in groups wherever they liked. Naoto and RyuZU were two of them. They had taken up seats in the middle of the classroom.

It was a week after the purge.

The purge, the conspiracy between the military and Meister Guild, the crisis RyuZU had faced, and what had happened to her younger sister. In just one week, everything had returned to how it was before, like it had all been a bad dream. Indeed, everything was the same as before.

Naoto was used to his classmates looking at him with cold eyes and clicking their tongues. It was just his everyday life. Everything had been rewound to the way it had been back before he met Marie.

If anything...

"Master Naoto, is it your ears, eyes, or brain that is in poor condition right now?

Naoto cast his eyes downward.

RyuZU had pushed their tables next to each other, laid out her homemade boxed lunch, and glued herself unnecessarily close to Naoto. Brewing up a saccharine mood simply oozing with sweetness, she picked up a piece of broccoli with her chopsticks and said, "Now, say 'ahh,' Master Naoto."

Go blow yourselves to smithereens.

That's what the gazes of his classmates were silently telling him in a secondary audio feed. Unable to bear it, Naoto hastily stuffed the broccoli into his mouth.

Indeed, if there were two things that *were* different, it would be that RyuZU was attending school with Naoto like it was natural, and the around-the-clock reporting on the great scandal that had been going on for days now.

The attempted premeditated purge of Kyoto.

The fact that the government, military, and Meister Guild had all conspired to destroy an entire city and massacre its 20 million residents had come to light, throwing society into a state of turmoil.

The disclosure included not only information directly relating to the incident, but even authentic spy documents and reports of shady dealings, and in large numbers at that.

The truth behind a historical assassination, records of conversations between the government and private industries, a list of spies in sleeper cells within a certain country, secret military bases that weren't marked on any maps, the possession of weapons that were banned by the international arms treaty, the top-secret human experiments done by one section of Meister Guild, and so on...

While the incumbent Japanese prime minister *did* acknowledge responsibility for the military's failed premeditated purge...

"This is undoubtedly terrorism," he'd said, his voice trembling with anger.

A famous commentator on a certain talk show had remarked, "It's true that trying to purge a city is horrible, but no matter how you look at it, isn't the one who disclosed all that top-secret information even worse?"

He had received a grand bashing for that comment.

And one news program had played a recording of a conversation in which a public relations representative of the Meister Guild by the name of Limmons ordered the murder and cover-up of the young genius clocksmith, Marie Bell Breguet (sixteen years old). In wake of this revelation, Limmons fainted and was taken to a hospital; the Vacheron Corporation, considered his sponsor, now faced a fervent uprising in the form of a boycott. Their finances went into the red for a long slump.

The tragic daughter of the Breguet family suffered a premeditated murder for endeavoring to save the city to the very end. In the midst of this tempestuous scandal that swept the entire world—and because of this moving narrative—the Breguet Corporation came out unscathed.

Naoto inadvertently recalled the smug face of the blond-haired girl, smiling ferociously behind the scenes of this chain of events.

"...Well, it's fine, I guess."

To Naoto, who was distant from others to begin with, what had happened to her didn't particularly interest him. When all was said and done, everything had returned to the way it was before, except for RyuZU.

...However, *that* was the biggest problem.

"Master Naoto, if you are not learning, then as I suspected, it must be your brain that is in poor—"

Seeing RyuZU hold out another piece of broccoli in front of him, Naoto's face twitched, and he smiled lopsidedly before unloading, "Look here now! Would you be so kind as to pay a little attention to the looks we're getting?! If I'm going to die from stress like this, then I'd rather—"

He swallowed the words he was about to say.

RyuZU was the same as usual. She was smiling with a face full of refinement and composure.

However, back then, he had come to understand that her free will—the subtle signs of the automaton's "heart"—read like this: "I made this for you, yet you won't eat it?"

"I apologize. I'll eat everything without leaving a single grain of rice behind."

"You should have just said that from the beginning. Were you teasing me to gratify yourself?"

"No! Our classmates look like they want to kill me right now, you know. Jeez—"

Just then...

Naoto saw something that absolutely shouldn't have been there, and he froze.

A bald, middle-aged man had been standing by the front entrance of the classroom for who knew how long. He had eyes a little too fierce to belong in a high school. He was glowering at the students.

...Who is he?

His silent, intimidating aura caused the chatter in the classroom to immediately cease.

Eventually, he walked in and lumbered his way onto the podium.

He wasn't a teacher.

Furthermore, he wasn't even Japanese.

Actually, *further*-furthermore, one could say that half of him wasn't even human.

The man wore dark sunglasses and a gray suit over his well-built body. His lips, which were pushed together cynically, exuded the allure of a man who was dangerous, like a wild beast.

And furthermore, the operating sound of a reinforced cyborg body that only Naoto's ears could hear came from him.

The man spoke. "Ahh—my name is Vainney Halter. I know this is sudden, but starting now, I'm your new homeroom teacher. I'm not into brats, so spare me the love letters and date invitations. Any questions?"

"...Whatterya doin'?" Naoto asked, inadvertently slipping into his native dialect.

Getting a vague sense of déjà vu, Naoto held his head, but the scary thing was that the joke didn't end there.

Accepting the silence of the overwhelmed students, Halter nodded once. In a manner that was somehow reminiscent of a soldier, he said, "Well then, without further ado, I'll be introducing a transfer student to you guys. Come in."

"Okay."

The sun has arrived, Naoto thought.

The one who entered the classroom was a blond-haired, Caucasian girl.

Her skin was like velvet; her bright, golden hair tied up in twintails fell to her shoulders; and her big, vibrant, emerald-jade eyes were shining with vigor.

The girl looked graceful wearing the school's uniform as she stood on the podium majestically. She was about as petite as Naoto, but her confident, imposing air made her look much, much larger than she actually was. Even now, her charismatic aura seemed like it would materialize as a halo around her entire body, and the students' jaws dropped as they stared in amazement. Naoto was speechless as well.

The girl smiled sweetly as she spoke in a brisk, lively manner.

"I'm Maëribell Halter. I often get told that I look like a certain celebrity, but I'm not her, so please feel free to just call me Marie for short. I look forward to learning with everyone."

She bowed gracefully. In doing so, she snuck a glance at Naoto. Her emerald eyes were gleaming as she looked at him like a predator eyeing its prey.

Of course—no matter how one looked at it, the girl was none other than Marie Bell Breguet.

Naoto gazed at her figure, dumbfounded and unable to move even a single finger.

"...No, really, whatterya doin'?" he blurted out in his native dialect.

The rest of this scene shall be omitted.

After school, the four had gathered on the desolate rooftop of Tadasunomori High School. The Equatorial Spring was traversing the red sky, and the Core Tower, illuminated by the setting sun, produced a dark silhouette.

The girl who had claimed to be Maëribell Halter was gazing down at the streets of Kyoto from the rooftop fence. Facing her back, Naoto called out to her with a sigh. "...So, I'm wondering if I could get an explanation."

"Oh, didn't I say that I would see you soon?"

"Expecting me to understand that to mean that you would transfer to my school is beyond unreasonable."

Marie turned around and grinned. "Did I surprise you? I surprised you, didn't I?"

"Wow, you're super annoying."

Frowning slightly, Naoto squinted his eyes and looked away.

"If you don't know, then I guess I'll tell you: the world thinks you were killed."

"Of course I know that. After all, I'm the source of those leaks." Spreading out her hands, Marie smiled deviously with her entire face. "The world is in uproar thanks to those leaks, isn't it! Seeing those imbeciles who can't do anything but sabotage others trip left and right as they try to lay the blame on each other, what joy! It's euphoric! Mweheheee."

"Oi, lower your voice," Halter muttered, as he slapped his bald head. "...I knew that you would divulge everything about the incident this time to the media, but I never thought you'd breach your NDA with the Meister Guild and dump all the classified information. What are you, a devil?"

"Are you stupid? There aren't any NDAs that bind the dead."

"You know that politicians and military officers throughout the world were furiously forced to resign?"

"Like I care what happens to those scum. I'm doing these things for the sake of what I want to accomplish.

"...So just what is your objective?" RyuZU said to Marie, looking suspicious. "I do not have even the slightest interest in the things you choose to do, but if you try to use Master Naoto for something suspicious, then I shall respond with physical retribution."

"My, treating me like I'm a monster. I'm just looking for a little cooperation."

"Cooperation...?" Naoto muttered. It was clear from his voice that he thought Marie's words were fishy.

Marie raised her index finger and smiled.

"It's simple," she announced, "I just want you to come save the world with me for a bit."

"...Huhhh?" After a lengthy pause, Naoto knit his eyebrows sharply.

Marie continued cheerfully, "I dumped all the dark secrets I knew this time, but that was just the tip of the iceberg. There are countless more vile conspiracies in the world. In their wake lie people being trampled underfoot, and city malfunctions that are being neglected."

"...And...?"

"Charging into situations like that freely, tearing both politics and conspiracies into shreds, repairing mechanisms as we please, and stopping attempts to sacrifice people just like the one this time. We probably wouldn't be praised or thanked by anyone, but it would definitely feel great, right?!"

"What's up with you? Have you been hit with Middle School Syndrome two years late?"

"More like I've reached my rebellious stage. I'm going to revolt against this rotten world. Rock'n'roll, baby."

Marie took a pose twanging an air guitar.

Naoto asked, "...That's fine and all, but why did you transfer to my school?"

"Well, there're several reasons, but the main one is to camouflage myself."

"Camouflage...?"

Naoto tilted his head, and Marie grinned. "Do you know what the most convenient position to pursue an ideal from is?"

Naoto shook his head. "Nope."

"You see—it's as a terrorist," Marie stated. She was smiling sweetly, yet her face looked menacing. "Terrorists have no responsibilities or restraints whatsoever. They can just make a big racket as they hoist up their absolutely nonsensical ideals."

"...Doesn't that reasoning go a bit too far?"

"It's fine. After all, being allowed to say things like this is a privilege reserved for children."

Marie Bell Breguet didn't speak her heart. There was no way she could.

It was a vision that was so far-fetched that she hadn't even dreamed about it until now.

I might be able to save this Clockwork Planet.

I might be able to entirely overhaul this planet that's repeating a pattern of suffering failures and prolonging its life only by purging the affected grids.

I might be able to reproduce this planet's blueprint that was lost long ago.

I might be able to someday do what no one has done before, and finally reach the same level as "Y."

If Naoto is with me, I feel like I'll be able to do it—I think I will.

"Well, that's how it is. So becoming a student here was purely out of convenience. To make up for revoking my promise to recommend you to the Academy, I'll be personally whipping you into a clocksmith, so you better be thankful, got it?"

"Okay... I mean, I'm happy that you want to make it up to me, but—wait, huh? I have to be your student?"

"Isn't that obvious? Also, I'll be making sure that you pay your lesson fees punctually with those ears of yours."

"Even the hard sell has a limit, you know!"

•••●•••

...Gazing at the pair's exchange—

Halter thought, *Does that princess realize—*

That what she's saying is equivalent to "I'll become God"?

But it was true that the genius and that ESP boy had stepped one foot into that territory already. While that truth did make Halter fondly recall his own dreams from back when he was a lad himself, he felt a tinge of unease from that fact must have meant what he had suspected.

"Jeez, I wonder if I've become an old man myself..."

He sighed while scratching his head. He then said to the automaton watching Naoto and Marie from a short distance away, "... Say, miss—RyuZU."

"I would like to express my displeasure at being addressed by you in an awfully familiar manner, but yes, what is it?"

"How much of this did you foresee?"

"Is even your speech center broken down, you patchwork piece of junk? Or did you not learn that you should make the subjects in sentences clear?"

While smiling bitterly at her abuse, Halter asked, "You asserted that if it was Naoto, it could be done. Doesn't that mean that you knew how this chain of events would turn out?"

It was all too convenient to be coincidence.

Marie's genius. Naoto's superpower. RyuZU's Imaginary Gear.

If any one part was missing, this city would have sunk into the earth. Beginning with the storage unit conveniently falling into Naoto's apartment, if even a single thing had been different, they wouldn't have been able to arrive at this result.

More than anything, the one who had guided Naoto to the Core Tower was this automaton. The conclusive piece of evidence was her mentioning AnchoR's existence, which is what led Naoto to his decision.

However, the truth was that this automaton already knew that AnchoR wasn't there anymore. That should have been the case.

"It seems that you are misunderstanding something. I am YourSlave, the one who follows—not the one who leads the way."

...Can an automaton ever lie?

Seeing Halter narrow his eyes in suspicion, RyuZU's lips curled. "However, let me see. Do you know of this expression? 'The Gear of Fate'?"

"......"

The source of power that spanned the sky and turned all of the planet's gears.

RyuZU looked up at the Equatorial Spring, that turns by utilizing the moon's gravitational pull. "I believe that, in this world made only of gears—it would not be that strange for such a gear to exist. Just like how there are no coincidental elements in my mechanisms, everything is inevitably the way it must be—or so I, an automaton, think."

An automaton's philosophy.

Those words crossed Halter's mind, a man who was half-robot himself.

Before his eyes were two geniuses who might change the world, frolicking all the while.

"Ahh, Naoto. Rejoice, for intelligence is already coming in. It appears that there some sort of anomaly in Tokyo."

"...Could you please explain why I have to rejoice for an anomaly?"

"To tell you the truth, it seems that AnchoR was transferred there."

"All right, let's break out the champagne! There's gonna be a party tonight! And also preparations for the trip!!"

...Good grief.

Halter smiled bitterly.

"Well then, I suppose I'll try putting just a little faith in the guidance of this gear called 'Fate' or whatever."

Halter thought back to the day the world had ended—and been remade anew.

While looking towards the future that seemed just ever so slightly auspicious with both doubt and expectation, he glided his hand across his buzz cut.

Click, clack, click, clack,

The gears turned and turned.

Systematically, mechanically, inexorably.

They marked the march of time, effortlessly, just by fulfilling their function.

Even if a clock were to stop ticking, it wouldn't matter.

Even if the cogs of time became broken or twisted, they would surely simply continue to turn.

Systematically, mechanically, inexorably.

Click, clack, click, clack—

The gears simply continued to turn in the direction that they ought to turn.

(Fin.)

Clockwork Planet

AFTERWORD (JOINT)

The beginnings of this novel go back to more than a year ago.

"Say, aren't analog timepieces cool?" Yuu Kamiya said out of nowhere in a Skype call one day.

To which Tsubaki Himana replied, "...You're undergoing treatment for cancer. And I'm still going to college at this grand old age, so I have to start searching for a job to line up with my graduation."

Tsubaki was hinting at the fact that neither of them had time on their hands. However...

"Now now, stop playing Sk*rim's s*x mod and listen for a sec."

They hadn't been friends for over ten years for nothing. It seemed that Kamiya hit the nail on the head, for Tsubaki didn't retort.

Kamiya continued, "It was precisely when I was overseas for treatment that I caught sight of some analog watches at a duty-free store. The pamphlet they handed out was amazing."

"Oh, I see... Well, pocket watches possess a kind of romance, don't they?"

"Lul, you know as little as I expected. I'll send you some pictures I took—take a look."

"Good grief," Tsubaki said as he opened the JPEG image he was sent.

His hands stopped moving on the keyboard.

...

"Ohh... Such functional beauty. My crotch is getting h[censored]."

It was a small universe in itself. Delicate gears were crammed together in a single structure based on minute calculations; the metal was as polished as a mirror and emanated a sensual luster. Any man's senses would get aroused if he were to gaze upon this beautiful, mechanical contrivance.

Seeing Tsubaki's reaction, Kamiya had nodded as if to say, *that's exactly how I feel*, before continuing, "So yeah, I wrote out a plot, actually."

"A plot, you say?"

"And the grand title is—*Clockwork Planet*! A world in which the planet has died and been remade using only clockwork!"

Tsubaki tried imagining it.

...I see. A world composed of the moving parts of this beautiful watch. A clockwork planet that floats about in the dark universe—it's true that it inspires one's imagination.

"It's difficult for me to have to point this out to you, but...aren't you writing *No Game No Life*?"

If Tsubaki's memory served him correctly, his friend was in a weakened state from cancer treatment and as such, was taking a break from doing manga. He had switched to being a light novel author to replenish his wallet, which had been emptied to pay for advanced medical treatment, and here he was, currently writing his maiden series—he should have been in the middle of charging through this chaotic mess of a life, one that simply had too many points to quip about.

However, Kamiya didn't answer his question and instead continued, "I tried writing out the plot, but I found that it doesn't fit my style. Its world is rather dark, after all."

"You don't think before you act, do you?"

"So anyway, won't you try writing out this plot from the beginning, yourself?"

"I see that you don't listen to what others say, either! I said I'm going to college right now. I'm studying. I have to look for a job soon, too—"

"Well, it doesn't really have to be now. You're graduating next year, right? How about then?"

"Hmm..."

And so, he had been handed the plot. It was interesting, true.

Ever since they had met each other in high school, they had shared ideas, consulted, and collaborated with each other on their works, whether they be doujin or published, up to now. When Kamiya had been a manga author, Tsubaki was his assistant.

He did want to see what this plot would be like fleshed out into a full story. As for time...well, he'd make some, but—

"All right, but if I'm going to do it, I'll be writing it the way I like, okay?"

Indeed, what Tsubaki had been handed was, in fact, nearly a finished product.

The world, characters, plot, and ending were already there; he only had to flesh them out. However, simply writing them out as they were wouldn't be interesting for Tsubaki. There would be no point in him being the one to write it.

If he was going to do it—he would have to enjoy it himself first and foremost.

To his surprise, the reply he was given was short and carefree.

"Sure, do whatever you want. Just make it interesting."

As expected of an old friend who had known him for over ten years.

...Half a year later..

"...Ah—Mr. Kamiya. Could you spare a second?"

"What? I'm busy editing the second volume of *No Game No Life* right now," Kamiya replied; his tone lacked composure, as if to say that it was *he* who didn't have time for other things now.

"Umm, when I tried changing the plot to my own tastes, I ended up a bit lost... In other words, could you help me out?"

"No umm, really, I don't have that kind of time right n—"

However, as the one who started this fire in the first place, Kamiya found himself unable to simply refuse. "...All right. Then when I'm done with the second volume of *No Game No Life*, let's revise the plot together once more. I'll adopt your ideas and rework the plot points it breaks, so I'll be leaving the writing to you."

"Leave it to me."

Yet another half a year later...

"This is what it became as the result of leaving it to me."

Kamiya scratched his forehead and groaned, "...I mean, it *is* more interesting now than the edited plot I sent back to you. But how do you plan to end this?"

"What do you think I'm talking to you for, huh?"

...Though Tsubaki had wanted to punch Kamiya, he was thwarted by the physical distance between them, as Kamiya was in Saitama and he was in Kyoto.

"I'm not in a position to criticize others, but don't you act in the spur of the moment too much?"

"I really don't want to be told that by you, Mr. Workaholic-Receiving-Ongoing-Cancer-Treatment."

"...All right. Let's do it ooone more time with this as the base! I'll edit the plot. You write it out."

"Yessir."

A few days later...

"Whaaat! Why did you ignore my edits again?!"

Once again, the sound of Kamiya screeching rang through Skype from Saitama to Kyoto.

"But it's more interesting now, isn't it...?" (In a trembling voice)

"Yes, it's more interesting now, but how are you going to tie this up?!"

"Oh, you tease, with the help of the great Kamiya-sensei, of course~!" (Wiggle wiggle)

Should I get on a train for Kyoto now to punch this guy? But it would take too much time and money—blah blah blah.

After repeating similar exchanges several times—the manuscript was finally complete.

And then...

"I heard a rumor that you wrote a separate series with your friend."

Just where could this information have leaked from?

The ex-editor of *No Game No Life*, who had run away as far as his feet could carry him—er, I mean transferred—to Kodansha Light Novel Bunko, appeared.

"Come on, let's publish it." (with an outstanding smiiile)

"Uhh, you're saying that knowing that we don't have that kind of time, aren't y—"

"Come on, let's try our best." (with an enamored-looking smmmiiile)"

...

So yeah, this work had to jump through all kinds of hoops to be published.

Both Kamiya and Tsubaki had noticed that they hadn't really heard of co-authorship in light novels before. That was probably because when they themselves worked together, they would usually define each other's role clearly, like who would be in charge of the original concept versus the actual writing, and so on.

Then, as to why the afterword for this novel was done jointly...

"So, which one of you wrote this afterword in the end?" our editor asked.

"I mean, as for who wrote it—"

"Isn't that a trivial detail?" That's what the two of them—with very pleasant smiles and *quite* blank faces—had said.

"...Well, whatever. Well then, Mr. Kamiya will do the illustrations, and—what the, where did Mr. Kamiya go?"

"He logged off of Skype the instant he saw the word 'illustration.'"

And so, someone was abruptly added to the Skype call. Their name was Sino.

"I'm here because Mr. Kamiya told me he had 'an interesting proposition,' but..." they started innocently.

That's right, Sino hadn't known anything. However, Tsubaki was sure—

That right now, the editor was wearing an extremely sadistic smile—one that trumped even that of a certain chief—despite being unable to see it on screen.

"Nice to meet you, Sino. I've heard about you and your work from a lot of people. Indeed, I have a very, very wonderful proposition for you. Now then, shall we talk over there...?"

AFTERWORD (YUU KAMIYA)

This is Kamiya. I was able to beautifully escape from our editor's scheme to make me do the illustrations. Not only that, we were able to enlist the help of Sino, and because of that, I think that this work has become something better than if I were to have done the illustrations... *Clockwork Planet* was the result of the four of us (including the editor) contributing ideas—"a collaboration that belongs to all of us," if you will—and I'd be most blessed if you enjoyed it.

You might be wondering: Why is my version of Naoto's character design on the right of this page, then? ...Why, indeed. It's the proof that I almost failed to escape from our editor's scheme. Really, I couldn't thank Sino enough. What a lifesaver. Literally.

Writing and illustrating *No Game No Life*, and beyond that, even working as an assistant to my wife, who's doing the manga version of it right now—if I had to draw illustrations for this work as well, there's no doubt in my mind that we wouldn't have been able to publish this work.

Editor: "Ah, Mr. Kamiya. If *Clockwork Planet* is adapted into a manga, I'll be counting on you. ♪

Hmmmm!
I suppose I'll say just this in advance:

I refuse!

AFTERWORD (TSUBAKI HIMANA)

Hi everyone, nice to meet you. My name is Tsubaki Himana.

On this occasion, I had the pleasure of writing *Clockwork Planet* in the form of a joint work.

I know that I'm still wet behind the ears as a writer, but I'm extremely happy that, thanks to the help of many different people, I've become able to greet everyone like this.

"Won't you try writing this?"

There have been quite a few twists and turns since Kamiya said that to me and handed over this story's plot, but we were finally able to come to this point. "Do whatever you'd like." I took Kamiya's go-ahead and ran with it. Whether it was "I'm changing the characters," or "I'm changing the ending," or "I'm cutting out this important scene," I was always taking him for a ride. Yeah, I'm really sorry about that. If I had had my way, Halter would be gay and (rest omitted).

During one of our meetings, Kamiya said, "Ahh, I get it now. Naoto is my concept of a genius, and I take it that Marie is your concept of a genius. It's also interesting that they're complete opposites."

For some reason, those words left a deep impression on my mind.

In the end, the two of us even lost track of who thought of and who wrote what, but this work ended up becoming something that I couldn't have completed by myself—

correction, something that couldn't have been made into what it is now by either one of us alone.

Now then, I'd like to express my thanks to various people. To Yuu Kamiya, who gave me the opportunity to be involved in this project; Sino, who provided us with lovely illustrations; Ms. Ryo Hiiragi; Mr. Tomo Shoji, our editor; all the editorial staff of Kodansha Light Novel Bunko; and above all, all the readers who are holding this book in their hands, I express my deepest thanks.

2013/4 Tsubaki Himana

I LOVE
MARIE!

AFTERWORD [SINO]

This is Sino. I was lazing around in my room one day when I received the invitation to join this project, and that's how I became the illustrator for *Clockwork Planet*.

When I illustrate for novels, the thing I look forward to the most is coming up with the character designs. I had a great time doing the illustrations this time as well, so I'll be happy if you take a fancy to the characters in *Clockwork Planet*.

Both RyuZU and Marie came out adorable, but don't forget Naoto! He's cute, too!

Also, imagining designs for the new characters that will start appearing in future volumes, beginning with AnchoR, is so fun that I just can't stop myself. (Laugh)

As you can probably tell, I'm a bit of a blabbermouth, but still, I'd be happy if you pick up the next volume and the ones after that, too.

Mmm, I didn't get to draw many interesting scenes this time, did I… (Laugh)